W9-BUM-871

The
PRETTY
App

Katie Sise

Balzer + Bray
An Imprint of HarperCollins*Publishers*

Balzer + Bray is an imprint of HarperCollins Publishers.

The Pretty App
Copyright © 2015 by Bunny Eat Bunny Productions and Katie Sise
All rights reserved. Printed in the United States of America. No part of this book may be used or reproduced in any manner whatsoever without written permission except in the case of brief quotations embodied in critical articles and reviews. For information address HarperCollins Children's Books, a division of HarperCollins Publishers, 195 Broadway, New York, NY 10007.
www.epicreads.com

Library of Congress Cataloging-in-Publication Data
Sise, Katie.
    The Pretty App / Katie Sise. — First edition.
      pages cm
    Companion book to: The boyfriend app.
    ISBN 978-0-06-219529-6 (hardback)
    [1. Popularity—Fiction. 2. Beauty, Personal—Fiction. 3. High schools—Fiction.
4. Schools—Fiction. 5. Family problems—Fiction. 6. Contests—Fiction. 7. Application
software—Fiction. 8. Conduct of life—Fiction.] I. Title.
    PZ7.S62193Pre 2015   2014027575
    [Fic]—dc23   CIP
                                                                                    AC

Typography by Alison Klapthor
15 16 17 18 19   PC/RRDH   10 9 8 7 6 5 4 3 2 1

First Edition

To Brian, Luke, and William,
the best family a girl could ever ask for

Part 1

THE PRETTY APP

chapter one

"I'm Blake Dawkins," I said into the camera. "And I'll be your host today on *The Ex Factor*. Today's first guest is Xander Knight. Mr. Knight, please take a seat right here on this swing set."

Xander gave me a look over the top of the phone. "It's harder to film you when you make me move around," he whispered. A cold breeze had mussed his dark blond hair, and his vintage Chicago T-shirt was frayed at the collar. He wasn't exactly thrilled to be out here on the playground with me, but everything about Xander felt familiar and safe, and I was grateful to be spending the morning of my eighteenth birthday with him.

"Just sit," I said. "Please?"

The weight of his jock-boy frame made the swing set squeak like it did when we used to make out on the thing at the end of junior high. We've been broken up for months now, ever since my ex–best friend Audrey created the Boyfriend App and wreaked havoc on our entire school, including Xander and me. Not that there weren't a lot of other factors in our breakup—mainly that we'd fallen out of love—but something about that app set everything in motion.

Still. Being out here with Xander behind the school made me smile thinking back to those first days when we got together, when things felt new and full of goodness.

"Now, Xander," I said, using my best *I'm the host and I control the conversation* voice, "can you tell me what it was like to be dumped by the prettiest girl in your senior class? No, wait, by the prettiest girl in your high school? Possibly in the entire state of Indiana?"

"You know that's not really how it happened," Xander said, watching me through the phone's screen. "You didn't exactly dump me."

"Go along with it for the show," I said through a clenched smile. I just needed to get some footage to make sure I was getting better at this. I'd been practicing for as long as I could remember, but I was going to college in the fall, and if I wanted to audition for some TV stuff on campus, I needed to be perfect.

"It was terrible," Xander said, rolling his hazel eyes. "I cried for days."

That was more like it. "Did you try to get her back?" I asked him in my most sympathetic voice. Then I tilted my chin so the camera would catch my best angles. (The world is a visual place. It's crucial to remember that.) "Or did you just give up on the magic you had together?"

I was waiting for Xander to answer my *bring it home with a tough question* journalism tactic when a shrill bell sounded.

"Gotta go," Xander said, stuffing the phone into the pocket of his corduroys. "I'll email you the video later, okay?"

He didn't wait for me to answer, and he didn't look back as he raced across the JV lacrosse field toward school. He'd been doing this all week—it was like he couldn't wait to get to the cafeteria. Xander and I both had first period free, followed by midmorning break. Usually we walked into school together, but this week he'd been sprinting away from me as soon as the bell rang. I couldn't figure out what had gotten into him, but something was definitely up, and he wasn't telling me.

I glanced at my watch. Nine more minutes until Public was scheduled to announce their next big app. *The best app yet!* the ads all promised, followed by their new tagline, of course: *From the most innovative tech company on Planet Earth. Now, everything's Public.*

Public did a big marketing push like this once every few months, and it was all anyone was talking about online.

I stuffed my props into my mustard-colored satchel: a microphone for when I practiced live reporting, tissues to hand to my pretend guests when they got emotional, and cue cards so I'd be good at reading a teleprompter some-day (I'm not exactly the world's fastest reader, so I have to work on it). I checked my reflection in a compact mirror to make sure my makeup was still perfect—it was, thank God—and headed toward the brown-brick, horseshoe-shaped building that was Harrison High School. Normally

I'd try to strut my stuff a little—in case anyone was watching through the cafeteria's windows—but the lawn was too muddy, and I was scared to ruin the shoes my father got me. (The ones that made my mother say, "Remember when I still had my beauty and you used to buy me lovely things?" And she was only half-kidding.)

My dad liked to buy me presents that would make me look better. Prettier for the pictures we had to pose for now that he was running for office. He was so proud of how I looked. He never bought me books like *Hot Words for the SAT.* And even though I didn't miss pretending to care about what *garrulous* meant, I sort of wished he hadn't given up so easily.

The wind tossed my hair as I neared the side entrance to the cafeteria. A Milky Way wrapper skittered across the grass, coming to rest against the green shrubs that lined the exterior of Harrison. The shrubs had been carved into unrecognizable animal shapes by Save-the-Environment Club members. A bear? Muskrat? Someone had put a condom on a branch near one of the animals' would-be privates.

I took a breath, lifted my chin, and shoved open the door to the cafeteria.

It smelled like bagels.

Theresa "T. Rex" Rexford was talk-shouting in her low voice. "I'll flush myself down a toilet if she gets into Brown and I don't." Sara Oaks was trying to join the group listening to Theresa. Sara was the kind of girl who was always apologizing for everything, and always bursting into tears if someone even looked at her the wrong way. It made me want to keep my distance, but my two best friends, Joanna and Jolene Martin, wouldn't stop picking on her. Maybe other kids felt the way I did, because even though Sara was pretty, no one talked to her, and at least in our high school, being pretty usually guaranteed you a few friends.

A bunch of Harrison kids were checking their phones and making small talk, but no one said anything to me. I scanned the cafeteria for Joanna and Jolene, feeling more nervous by the second when I didn't see them. There were so many kids bumping into one another, so many bodies touching, making me feel anxious. It'd been like this for me with crowds—even small ones—ever since I was five and my dad lost me at the Indiana State Fair.

A cluster formed around Audrey's cousin Lindsay Fanning. Lindsay wore a black puffer vest over an off-white sweater that almost matched her platinum bob. She always looked like a girl from a magazine—not a model, but an editor or someone important leaving a fashion show.

"My sources say the unveiling is happening in New York City," Lindsay was saying to the group. Her green eyes matched Audrey's, and they glinted like she knew something no one else did.

"Happy birthday, Blake!" Joanna called from the sea of faces. Her honey-blond hair was pulled into a bun, with wisps strategically falling loose to frame her sky-high cheekbones.

Everyone looked up. Once their eyes were on me, I knew they would stay there, so I pushed back my shoulders and accepted my role. My lips were slightly pursed, and I narrowed my gaze just the littlest bit, the way models do.

Hundreds of eyeballs traveled up and down my figure. They all wanted things from me, whether they realized it or not. And not just other teenagers. Adults, too.

Teachers.

My friends' fathers.

Random strangers.

Beauty made people hungry. It made them want to take something without asking, and I felt like I had to give them what they needed because they'd steal it anyway. And I wanted to feel in control. So I told myself I was *letting* them stare at me. I was letting the girls imagine what it would be like to look like me. To be me. To wake up in my body and toss long, toned legs over the side of the bed. To pull a satin robe over a tight stomach and full breasts. To stare into the mirror and see a heart-shaped face with high cheekbones, flawless skin, and dark, dramatic eyes. I let them imagine what it was like to run polished nails through shiny, jet-black hair. To take off the robe and let it fall.

And while the girls were imagining what it would be like to wake up as me, the guys were imagining what it was like to wake up on top of me. That's a lot of people imagining stuff about me at once, and it made me feel see-through. Naked. Vulnerable. It's one thing to feel the eyes of a guy you like, but the wrong person's eyes on you can make you feel all sorts of bad. It was like that for me a lot, and I'm not saying I don't like being pretty, or that being pretty is hard, because that would be annoying and not true. Plus, it's kind of the only good thing about me. I'm just saying some things about it can be a mixed bag.

"I feel a little *nauseous*," I whispered to Joanna as she sidled next to me with two hulking Starbucks cups. She must not have heard my code word for *claustrophobic*, because she handed me a cup that smelled like mocha and dragged me into the fray.

My crowd-anxiety ratcheted up the deeper we pushed into the mass of students. The drama kids. The small-but-ever-present Goth contingent. Usually Xander was hanging with his lax buddies. Where *was* he?

"Happy birthday, Blake," Chantal Richardson chirped, and it made me happy even if she'd only said it because being class president meant you were supposed to say happy birthday to the people who elected you, even the mean girls.

Students moved en masse from the tables into the lunch line, elbowing one another for space, most of them talking about the new Public app. A siren sounded from far away. Someone laughed. Strains of Death Cab for Cutie filtered from a laptop. And somehow it still felt too quiet.

I turned and saw Xander standing beneath a ripped poster with stick figures giving each other the Heimlich maneuver. "He *wouldn't*," I muttered under my breath.

Xander's back was to me, but I'd recognize his body language anywhere—he was doing the repetitive head nod, the one where he acted like a bobblehead doll. It was his way of showing he was super-interested in what a girl was saying. It was what he used to do when we first met, and then later, when I was telling him a long, over-dramatic story when he really just wanted to make out. It was what he did when he liked someone.

He was talking to Mindy Morales.

Mindy was pretty, even if her wavy brown hair made her look like an unkempt lion. Gentleness emanated off her like a halo, like she could sense the exact type of compassion someone needed at a particular moment and give it to them. I don't know how she did it.

Worst of all, she was Audrey's new best friend.

Xander wasn't my boyfriend anymore, but we'd been together for three whole years, and it was my eighteenth birthday. He should've been sitting at my table so we could spend midmorning together. Excited to see me even if no one else was. Not talking with the enemy.

I bit my lower lip. I know it sounds weird that I didn't want to lose someone I'd already broken up with, someone I wasn't in love with anymore. But Xander, Audrey, and my older, pretty-much-estranged sister, Nic, were the only ones who knew what my family life was like, or the secrets I kept. I was scared of what it would feel like to have all three of them gone.

Joanna was pressed against my side, and I tried to concentrate on what she was saying, but then I saw Audrey. Dark pixie haircut, that emerald hoodie she wore way too often, skinny jeans that accentuated her cute figure. She was making her way toward us, looking for her friends. I tried to turn away, but I bumped into Joanna. Audrey was always the bigger person, and I knew she'd wish me happy birthday—I knew it. It made me hurt all over before it even happened.

"Happy birthday, Blake," she murmured. Her clear green eyes were bright, and her long, dark lashes didn't blink.

Like one stupid birthday wish could change the way she'd abandoned me when I needed her the most.

I turned my back. Everyone except Joanna moved away from me like my pain was contagious as I hurried toward the lunch line.

When Audrey's dad died in an accident at my dad's company the fall of our freshman year, I stood by her side. I did everything for her. She could barely remember which textbooks she was supposed to bring home each day after school, or which seniors we were supposed to avoid due to the unspoken Harrison social code, like the time she asked Bree Landers for directions to the girls' bathroom in the D wing. (Now Bree Landers works the concierge at Howard Johnson's. But back then it was like asking Gwyneth Paltrow for directions to the bathroom at the Oscars.)

I was the one picking up Audrey's pieces, and I was glad to do it; she was my best friend—she always had been. But then my father said this awful thing about her dad's accident and it blew up into a huge fight between us. It was like my family represented everything bad that had happened to her family. She defriended me on Public Party and pretty much stopped speaking to me for months.

It was a punch to the stomach. I lost Nic, then Audrey. The only one left was Xander, but a boyfriend isn't the same thing as a sister or a best friend. Joanna and Jolene were fine as far as friends go, but they could never be the kind of friend Audrey was. Sometimes it felt like no one could.

chapter two

Joanna cut the line and I followed, too out of sorts to think about anything except Audrey. We paid for matching tofu scrambles and cut through the students hovering around the new Public Corporation vending machines. The first one sold tech gadgets for cash at 10 percent off. The second one streamed music videos and concerts, and you could plug in your buyPhone to download songs. Built-in screens on top of the vending machines lit up with *BREAKING NEWS* banners. The image faded, replaced by a shot of Times Square in New York City. A skyscraper emblazoned with a Coca-Cola ad reached toward the heavens. Billboards advertising Broadway musicals curved around buildings.

Joanna and I ignored the screens and made our way through the cafeteria. I tried not to get upset when I saw Xander sitting near the Dumpster at a table with Mindy and Audrey's crew. Audrey and her boyfriend, Aidan, stared at Audrey's Infinitum laptop. Audrey wouldn't be caught dead with a Public computer—she only used products made by Infinitum, their biggest rival.

Aidan was a shy kind of cute—hands shoved in his pockets, tall and blue-eyed with a mop of black hair. Not my type, but perfect for Audrey. And he was nice to her. I kept an eye on them from a distance, and I could just tell.

Audrey's cousin Lindsay sat next to them with her computer-nerd boyfriend, Nigit. Nigit and I used to be friends growing up, but then our dads had a big blowout fight, and I think that's when he started hating me. And now I was having some kind of weird second-semester-senior-year melancholy that was making me wish more than ever that we could somehow erase every bad thing that had happened between us and start over. But I certainly couldn't be the one to initiate it: None of them would ever trust me.

I watched as Lindsay and Nigit craned to see Audrey's computer. The glow made Nigit's smooth brown skin look golden. Xander and Mindy stared at each other like they were the only ones in the cafeteria.

"Happy birthday, Blake," Woody Ames said from his seat at the end of our lunch table. Woody is the co-captain of the lacrosse team (and taker of my virginity), and he usually sat with us when he wasn't actively trying to sleep with someone new.

I smiled at him. "Thanks, Woody," I said. His brown hair matched his eyes and sweater. All that brown, plus his too-long canines, reminded me of a fox.

"We have something *amazing* planned for you tonight," Jolene said from her spot across from Woody. Her blue eyes matched Joanna's; so did her honey-blond highlights. Jolene was one year younger than us, but she and her sister could pass for twins.

"So how does eighteen look on me?" I asked, craving a compliment. I needed to stay afloat today.

"Gorgeous, as usual," Woody said with a smirk. Jolene nodded her agreement.

I slid into a seat next to Woody and watched him power on his laptop. I wanted to ask him about Xander and Mindy, but there was no point. He'd never tell me anything. "So who has a guess about what the app is?" I asked, pulling my tablet from my satchel. Tiny blue hearts from my sister's old sticker collection lined its white edge.

"Something life changing," Woody said sarcastically. He cared about apps about as much as I did.

"Do you *really* not know anything about it?" Jolene asked me, arching an eyebrow.

I didn't, but I gave them a half-smile like maybe I did. My dad had been in business with Public since grad school at MIT. He was one of Public's biggest investors right from the start—it was how he made his fortune—and he and Public CEO Alec Pierce were thick as thieves.

I pushed a smooth round button. An ivory glow warmed the screen as my tablet came to life. I tapped the Public Party Network icon.

Hello, Blake Andrea Dawkins. Ready to start the party? Enter Your Password.

I typed *nicoledawkins*. My sister and I always used each other's names for passwords. I wondered if I was still hers.

Welcome, Blake Andrea. Happy birthday from your friends at Public! You have three messages.

Only three?

I scrolled through the messages from Xander, Joanna, and Jolene. Then I checked my phone. Nic still hadn't called or even texted. Things hadn't been okay between us for a long time, but she still usually called to wish me a happy birthday.

"Are you seeing this?" Jolene asked, her pink fingernail tapping her tablet's screen. Joanna glanced over her sister's shoulder. Woody ate his salami sandwich and half-watched a pretty sophomore. I saw Jolene track the path of his stare and wished that just once she'd confide one of her secret crushes to me. When Audrey and I were best friends, there was nothing we kept from each other.

My tablet let out a series of *beeps*, and an alert flashed across the Public Party homepage. *BREAKING NEWS.* I clicked on the banner, and the screen showed Times Square again. A mob of girls screamed like banshees around a rectangular stage. Everyone else in the cafeteria must've been watching, too: Audio echoed across the lunchroom until the screaming sounded like it was coming from us.

I glanced back at the screen. The screaming girls' faces lifted to the sky, and they pointed and waved as their screams were drowned out by a snarling motor. The noise got louder and louder until no one in the cafeteria was talking anymore. We were all staring at our laptops and tablets blasting the video, while the lunch ladies looked at us like we'd gone insane.

On-screen, the legs of a helicopter came into view, followed by its hulking body. It trembled and teetered, then lowered slowly and touched down onto the stage. The Public logo blazed in orange letters on the tail. The door opened, and a guy swung his legs over the side of the chopper and jumped onto the stage. He was holding the sides of his helmet with small tan hands. Jolene and I caught each other's glance over our tablets. "WTF?" Jolene mouthed. I shrugged and looked back at my screen as the guy yanked off his helmet.

Pop star and Public spokesperson Danny Beaton's cherubic face emerged from beneath the helmet, and the crowd went nuts. The screaming wasn't audible anymore over the helicopter, but you could tell it was going on because the screaming girls' mouths were open and their neck muscles were strained. Except for the girl who had passed out. Someone was fanning her and trying to get her to drink from a plastic cup. Danny Beaton held his helmet beneath his arm and saluted the pilot. The pilot saluted back. Then the chopper lifted from the stage and took off into the sky. It looked a little wobbly again as it veered around a massive video screen.

A few kids looked over at me to see my reaction—like maybe I knew what was going on. I sat there smiling at my tablet, because I was supposed to be in favor of everything Public did. My dad liked to remind me that Public stock paid for my entire life, including my upcoming four years at Notre Dame. My grades aren't good enough to get any kind of scholarship—not even close. Audrey used to say that I was one of the smartest people she knew. But I just freeze up when it comes time to take tests—I can't help it. It's like every one of them is a trap, another reason for my father to seem disappointed and my mother to look smug, like she knew all along that I wasn't as great as my father used to think I was. The only tests I do well on are the oral ones. And how often do we have those? Like, never.

I only got in to Notre Dame because of my dad, and sometimes I think he's happy about that. It's like his power over me or something, his way of making sure I need him. I got into Notre Dame Early Action. (So did Audrey.) I didn't even apply to any other schools because I wanted to spare myself the humiliation of getting rejected.

Nic got into Notre Dame all by herself. She's pretty *and* smart, like Audrey. I shuddered to think how smart the kids would be at Notre Dame. But I would figure out my plan once I got there. I would survive college just like I did high school. I had to.

Goth Girl Greta Fleming yelled from a few tables over, "Public consumerism funds global warming!"

"Your face funds global warming!" Joanna shouted back. But everyone was too busy watching the Public show to pay them any attention. Danny Beaton strode across my tablet's screen, taking his place center stage. His hair-sprayed fauxhawk was crunched down from the helmet. The motoring sound had receded, and the screams were back. Peppy music trumpeted behind him as he tapped his thigh with a white microphone. A sexy lady dressed in a

17

low-cut suit paraded toward him holding a briefcase.

"The moment you've all been waiting for is here," Danny said into the microphone. He gave the woman a not-so-subtle once-over, and she blushed.

Danny Beaton was supposed to be the hottest thing for preteens and teenage girls. The sixteen-year-old pop star was cute, but he didn't do it for me, not since I was twelve and already taller than him.

Danny opened the briefcase and stared at the contents like he was seeing them for the first time. The camera cut to show the interior: plush velvet cradled a buyPhone with a glittery gold case. The glowing screen displayed a black app with simple pink lettering: *THE PRETTY APP.*

Gold and pink streamers fluttered in front of the camera, and the live audience went wild. I'd never seen something like this for an app release—not even by Public. Danny Beaton screamed over the audience. *"On behalf of Public Corporation, I'd like to announce the Pretty App!"*

I looked up from my screen at the rest of the cafeteria. Kids were either absorbed in the broadcast or reaching for their phones. I glanced quickly at Audrey. She wasn't smiling like everyone else. Her lips made a thin, straight line, and her green eyes were distant, almost like she was watching something else.

"Check this out," Joanna said, her fingers flying over her phone.

Xander caught my eye from his spot next to Mindy. I knew he was wondering if I'd known about this. I shook my head to tell him I hadn't.

18

Joanna tilted her phone so we could all see. Her screen flashed black with the same simple pink lettering.

Welcome to the Pretty App, the one and only app that finds America's prettiest teens and rewards them with fame, prizes, and a nationally recognized title.

An app that found America's prettiest teens? Like some kind of modeling-scout thing?

To begin, upload one cover photo and at least three gallery photos. Your photos must meet the following requirements:

1) A photo taken head-on of your full body

2) A photo taken of your full body in profile

3) A photo of your face

4) A photo of your face in profile

Crowd-source with the Pretty App's users for tips and secrets to become your prettiest self. Add the Pretty App's exclusive filters to make yourself look even better. Hashtag your city, state, and high school, and upload your photos. Know someone who's too shy to submit herself? Just snap the requisite photos of her and fill out the required details: Name, Age, Grade, High School*.

*The Pretty App is only for female students 16+ officially enrolled in high school in the United States of America. All others will be disqualified from participation.

I'm not sure what I expected, but it wasn't an app about prettiness. I cranked the volume on my tablet to hear Danny Beaton droning away. *"You—yes, you!—can be a part of the newest, hottest, most exciting app! The Public Pretty App is unlike any other."* Static hit Danny's microphone and drowned his words. *"A national beauty contest revealed in stages . . ."* Crackle. *"Stage One available today."*

Crackle. Crackle. The static stopped and the camera pulled back to show the number 1 painted in yellow on the front of Danny's portable stage. Music blared over the sound system, and Danny started singing.

> *"A queen pricks her finger on the thorn of a rose*
> *Three drops of blood on the morning snow fall*
> *Magic Mirror on the wall*
> *Who's the prettiest one of all?"*

My heart raced, because the answer had to be me: it was the one thing that made me special.

"This app is just a beauty contest," I heard Audrey say. "Aren't we beyond that?"

Danny fixed the camera with his trademark steamy stare. Then he said: *"Stage One: Download the Pretty App and upload your photos."* He ran a hand through his light brown hair. *"The Pretty App will upgrade itself to the next stage in two days."* The screen went dark as he uttered his final words.

"Be ready."

chapter three

I pulled into our circular driveway that afternoon and saw Nic's Volkswagen Beetle. No wonder she hadn't called: She'd come home to surprise me for my birthday, which was so much better.

Nic was a senior at Notre Dame. She was graduating in two months with a film, television, and theater degree. She wanted to write TV shows and screenplays in LA, though she didn't dare tell my parents that. Notre Dame was five minutes from our house, but Nic had lived in a dorm all four years and never came home except for Thanksgiving and Christmas. She told us it was because she got so much done while the other kids were back home with their families on break. I believed her—for a little while.

I turned off the ignition, my mind racing ahead to tonight. If Nic wanted to stay, I could suggest a few games at South Bend Bowl & Arcade, or a movie at U.P. Mall if she wasn't up for too much talking. It didn't really matter what we did; Nic was one of those people who could make anything fun, even a trip to CVS. I practically sprinted up the driveway. I went to stick my key in the lock, but the front door was cracked open. A chill ran over my skin. We always locked our doors.

I touched the wood, my fingers suddenly sweaty. I pushed the door, and light spilled into the foyer. My shadow stretched long and skinny across the marble tile.

"Nic?" I called, but there was no answer. Maybe she'd gone for a walk? I crept into the living room and saw a bunch of loose diary pages scattered across the floor. I knelt down and traced my fingertip over the writing scrawled in pencil.

Reasons:

We love each other

Mom and Dad will never understand, they don't feel what I do

The page was dated four years ago. I scanned my memory—the fall of my eighth grade year: Nic was a senior.

I snatched up the next page. Maybe there was some kind of clue here to whatever was going on with Nic. I scanned the paper, but it was just a bunch of numbers with South Bend area codes, plus a number written in red pen at the bottom with a 310 area code: Los Angeles.

Next to the paper was a journal that appeared to be an old scrapbook. Nic's handwritten block letters spelled *YOU AND ME* on the cover, and a lone movie ticket stub edged out from the side, dated years ago. Maybe it was something she'd made for Bobby Crawford, who she'd dated briefly during her junior year of high school. (I'd spied on their breakup from my bedroom window—Nic had dumped him on Halloween while wearing a witch's costume and straddling a broomstick.)

I put my hand on the scrapbook to trace the letters, but I couldn't bring myself to open it. I suddenly felt way too guilty for looking at her stuff, and I was about to stand up when a door slammed.

Nic appeared at the edge of the living room. I hadn't seen her in months.

In some ways looking at Nic was like looking into a mirror: Our clear complexions were identical shades of olive; our noses were the natural version of the tiny, perfect kind girls try for at the plastic surgeon's office; and our eyes matched, too—dark like coffee beans and curved like almonds. But Nic had dyed her hair a few shades lighter than mine, to a deep chestnut, and it was pulled into a low, messy ponytail. And she'd stopped wearing makeup, too. It made us look different, but in some ways, she was almost prettier without it.

"Hey, Blake," she said. She almost looked happy to see me. The tiny gold crucifix around her neck caught the light. A baggy gray sweater draped loosely around her waist. She used to wear snug-fitting stuff during high school, but not anymore.

"Nic," I said, "I'm so glad you—"

But I stopped midsentence when her hand went to her mouth. Her eyes widened when she saw my fingers on the scrapbook. "Why are you going through my stuff?" she asked.

"I wasn't," I said. "I mean, I was, but you left everything out in the living room, and I wasn't sure where you were, and I . . ."

Nic crouched to the floor and started to shuffle all the notebook pages into a pile. Then she took the scrapbook and cradled it in her arms like it was the most precious thing she owned. Her big brown eyes were wide as she stared at me.

Guilt welled in my chest. "I was just worried because the door was open and I didn't see you," I tried. I leaned forward and made the mistake of trying to help her. I gathered a few pieces of paper, but Nic grabbed my hand. "Leave it alone," she said. "Please, Blake."

I stood up just as a car crunched over the driveway. Nic scooped away the scrapbook and the papers, and then the door swung open. My mother marched into the living room wearing a navy tailored suit and holding a leather briefcase even though she hadn't worked in twenty years. It was just how she dressed, and she'd amped it up since my dad had started his campaign. Her silk blouse was tied at the neck, and her frosted blond hair was swept to one side. Audrey used to say it was like a tropical storm had blown into South Bend and coiffed her hairdo. It was so Audrey to use a word like *hairdo*.

My mom looked shocked to see Nic, but she quickly composed herself and turned to me. "Happy birthday, darling!" she trilled. "I wanted to surprise you, but you've beat me home."

Nic looked at my mother and then at me. The look on her face told me she'd had no idea it was my birthday.

"Hi, Mom." A hard lump lodged itself in my throat and made it hard to speak. I faked a smile.

"Everything all right in here?" my mom asked, looking from my sister to me.

Nic cleared her throat. "Fine," she said, gesturing to the papers she'd stuffed into her bag. "I was just about to give Blake her birthday card, but I can't find it in all of these papers."

Her eyes softened and pleaded with me not to say anything. But I never would. I stared at my sister, trying not to let everything I felt show on my face. Audrey and I had had a major falling out, but with Nic and me, I couldn't even put my finger on what had happened. There wasn't a single event I could point to, and it drove me crazy trying to figure it out. Nic just all of a sudden seemed like she couldn't stand being around any of us. She'd always had problems with my parents, but during her senior year of high school it magnified, and then I was suddenly on her list of people who couldn't be trusted, even though I was only in eighth grade.

Growing up, I thought Nic was the most amazing person who'd ever lived—she was funny, she was *so* smart, and she was special in that way some girls just are. Almost everything Nic said or did was something you wouldn't want to miss. Like when she was in fifth grade and convinced a teacher to hold a quiz until the next day because Mercury was in retrograde. Or in junior high, when she taped candy worms to my mother's bra and wore it outside her clothes while picketing the science lab with signs that read EARTH-WORMS HAVE FEELINGS, TOO. STOP DISSECTION NOW!

Nic turning her back on me during her senior year was the most painful blow I could've imagined. That whole year there was a tightness in my chest, like I couldn't ever suck down a real breath. A part of me was relieved when she left for Notre Dame, because it was too hard to see what I'd lost right in front of me.

That fall, when I started high school, I turned my focus to becoming Harrison High's It Girl. I figured if I could rule Harrison High School like Nic had done while she was there, then I was someone to be reckoned with, too, just like her. I was someone who mattered.

There were causalities along the way—kids I'd hurt. But I was hurting so badly, how else was I supposed to act? Kind, caring, and perfect like Audrey?

That's not me. And even if I wished I could be like her, I can't. You have to watch your back in my family.

My mom moved to the kitchen, and I decided to try again with Nic. "If you don't have rehearsal tonight, we could always do something before you go back to campus," I said.

Nic's dark eyes held mine, and I swear it was like she wanted to say something important to me. But then she looked away and I wondered if I was just imagining things. "I should get back," she said. "I have rewrites to do."

"Are they going well?" I asked, reaching for something we could talk about.

Nic nodded. She glanced over my shoulder into the kitchen and then back at me. "If you want to come to the show," she said quietly, "I can definitely get you tickets."

Everything inside of me lifted. "I'd really like that," I said as Nic smiled, and then my mom came back into the living room.

"Who wants a turkey dinner at Gustavo's tonight?" she asked, smiling like it was the best idea ever.

"I'm a vegetarian," Nic said.

"Do vegetarians not eat turkey?" my mother asked with a sigh, as she finger-combed her blond bangs. "They're birds. They don't have feelings like cows do. I don't even think they raise their own young."

"That's ridiculous," Nic said. "Of course they do."

The front door opened, and all three of us stood up straighter. I watched Nic suppress an eye roll when my dad called out, "I'm home!"

Yes, Dad. You are.

My dad's nightly *I'm home!* was one of the only vestiges of the *Aren't we all so normal?* behavior he displayed inside our house. Outside our house, in public, (and especially when we were at a campaign fund-raising event), he was the doting suburban father. He held our glances extra-long and smiled this strange smile when we talked, like he was just so proud of us he could hardly stand it.

But inside the house he was different. He wasn't the politician running for governor as a capital-C Conservative—*"Let's bring back traditional family values!"*—or the proud owner of R. Dawkins Tech. He was mercury rising, threatening the atmosphere with his silvery climb.

"Hi, Dad," I said, because he liked when we acknowledged him first. Nic once told me that was because his own father insisted on it when he was a young boy.

"How was your birthday, Blake?" he asked, kicking off his shoes next to a mirrored glass armoire stacked with interior design books that no one read.

"Great," I lied. "And I'm really glad Nic came home."

My dad turned to Nic, nodding. "And how's school going?" my dad asked her, setting his briefcase down on a mahogany side table next to framed photos of Nic and me fake-smiling on a skiing trip to Vail. He sat on the black velvet sofa with gold armrests—one of my mother's late-night internet shopping purchases. She was always upgrading.

"Fine," Nic said. "Not too much to report. Rehearsals are going well."

I saw my dad's jaw tighten. Nic got away with declaring a film, television, and theater major a few years ago because she promised my father she wanted to be a movie executive. He approved of that. But all of her performances and the plays she wrote were starting to give away what she really wanted. And lately, she was dropping more and more hints about wanting to be a screenwriter, like she wanted to prepare my parents for her move to LA post-graduation.

But then my dad smiled, which almost made me more nervous. "I think it's great that you're getting all of this fun out of your system before the real world comes calling in May," he said.

Nic smiled back fakely. "Plenty of people make their living in the real world as writers."

"And plenty starve," my dad said.

Please, stop. Not today.

My mother stood there silently. Sometimes that hurt more than anything—the way she never stuck up for us. I couldn't imagine what it would be like to have parents who were actually on your team. I used to fantasize about being Audrey's sister and living with her family in that tiny apartment, because then I'd know what it would feel like to be loved.

chapter four

So are we partying tonight or what?

I sent the text to Xander, Joanna, and Jolene that night in my bedroom after dinner when I was finally alone. I needed to get out of this house.

Joanna: You know it! Me and Jolene have been waiting 4 this night 4ever. Come here at 8!

Xander: See u there

Jolene: We r so psyched!

I let go of a breath. Things would work out fine now. Even though most kids at Harrison feared Joanna and Jolene, they all knew the sisters could throw a good party. They would show up tonight. They had to.

I opened my makeup bag. Just seeing the contents made me smile a little: the shimmery blush, the tawny bronzer, the black-as-midnight mascara. My newest tube of lipstick was silver and modern, like a tiny spaceship. Sometimes

I pretended I was putting on makeup to get ready for the camera. I once told my parents I wanted to be a television host, but they laughed and called it "insubstantial." The first notes to a sultry Emily Greene song came on, and I swiped a light pink gloss over my lips. Then I curled my eyelashes and brushed bronze powder over my face and collarbone. I dug into the back of my closet and found the tight black top I hadn't worn since the Danny Beaton concert last fall in Indianapolis. It made a low-cut *V* in the front, and I saved it for special occasions, like tonight.

I crept down the hallway past Nic's empty room. She'd taken off before dinner, and who could blame her?

My mother appeared at the top of the stairs. She touched a strand of pearls at her neck, looking me up and down. "What a darling sweater," she said. Fine lines danced on her cheeks when she spoke.

I smiled. I'd covered up the low-cut top with a fluffy pink cardigan that I planned to rip off the second I escaped the house. My parents freaked when I wore anything remotely sexy. My dad told me over and over that I couldn't be photographed wearing or doing anything risqué because it would ruin his super-conservative political platform.

My mom stepped closer. She seemed nervous, like she wasn't sure if that was okay. Sometimes it felt like there was a force field between the two of us: Love pulled us closer, but all the ways we'd hurt each other pushed us apart. It was like we wanted to be in each other's lives but didn't know how. "Be back before ten," my mom said.

"But it's my—"

Her face scrunched. "Don't test me, Blake," she said. "It's a school night." I smelled lavender in the Ralph Lauren perfume she'd recently gone back to wearing. It was the same perfume she'd worn when we were little, and it made me nostalgic for when things were easier. I moved past her and pounded down the stairs. Relief washed over me as I stepped into the cold night air.

In my car, I blasted the heat and blared music all the way to the Martins', trying to transform into *Blake Dawkins. Queen Bee. Glamazon. Prettiest Girl in Harrison. Bitch.*

I'd earned that last title. And there were only three months of school left; I couldn't change it, even if I wanted to. And why would I? I didn't want to know what the kids at Harrison would do to me if they weren't so afraid of me.

On the Martins' street, dozens of cars were parked in front of random lawns. Everyone knew the routine for drawing attention away from parties: park far away and walk.

I cut the ignition. Joanna and Jolene's house looked as rundown as ever. The wraparound porch held a splintery rocking chair and a metal watering can. Inside, the house was stuffed with dull brown furniture, tacky paintings, and religious statues.

I followed the perimeter of the porch. The sparrows lining the trees looked inky black in the darkness, and they made tiny squeaking noises as I crept over the lawn. The house's secret treasure was the basement—it was huge and had mirrored walls, like something out of a seventies movie. The best part was the private entrance down steep stone steps. I saw a glow emanating from the staircase and felt the first stabs of excitement.

Joanna and Jolene had been throwing parties since junior high. They posted the invites on a secret Public Party page so that everyone knew about the party without their parents being able to see the invite. They charged five dollars to enter, and more for food and drinks.

What really made the parties work was that Joanna and Jolene had the worst parents ever. And now it was just their mom, anyway, because their dad had run away to Phoenix with his new girlfriend, whose name was Daffodil or something equally disgusting. Mrs. Martin drank two glasses of red wine before bed and put in earplugs to sleep, so she had no idea what went on two floors below her bedroom. I don't think she cared, anyway.

"Is the party already awesome?" I whispered when Jolene peeked her head out the door. Dim yellow light illuminated the staircase as I started down the steep, narrow steps.

Jolene slithered onto the stone landing and shut the heavy door behind her. "We told everyone it was a surprise party," she hissed.

I smiled. That was better, because it would look like I didn't care about having a party, in case not a lot of people showed up. I wanted to thank Jolene, but I didn't want to make it seem like a big deal. I descended the final step and stood close to her. When I slipped a twenty into her pocket, she said, "You shouldn't pay, Blake. It's your party."

"Whatever," I said quickly, and hoped she wouldn't notice it was more than a five.

Jolene blushed a little, but then she shrugged it off. "Let's go," she said, pushing open the door. Warmth rushed toward us. The basement was packed, and I felt so happy looking out at all of the faces. Even if most of them didn't like me, at least they'd come.

"Surprise!"

Everyone screamed and clapped, and so did their mirror images reflected in the walls. They doubled the size of my party. A life-size Brett Favre poster stared at me like a guest about to throw a touchdown. I made out Kevin Jacobsen and Greg Sorin (co-captains of the potheads) standing with two theater girls next to a pole wrapped in pink tinsel. A guy named Marcus stuck his hand into a bright blue cooler. His boyfriend, Tim, yelled, "Happy eighteenth, Blake!" Even Goth Girl Greta Fleming clapped. For a few perfect seconds I could pretend everyone liked me. But then they went back to whatever they were doing so quickly that I barely had time to act surprised.

I looked closer. Most of them were snapping photos of each other. Not that it was unusual to see phones angled up taking pictures and video . . . but it seemed like *everyone* was doing it. Maybe they wanted to post proof on Public Party that they were invited to my birthday party? Or maybe that was wishful thinking. The end of senior year meant no one seemed to care as much about social status, and I wasn't really sure where that left me. With two friends and a school filled with kids who wouldn't think twice about me after high school was over?

I scanned my party. Debate team captain Sean DeFosse

held a professional-looking camera. He zoomed the lens on a girl who frequently wore crowns and liked to be called Princess Di. "Let's just do my face in this one," Di said, running pink lipstick over her mouth. "But make sure you get my tiara, too."

Carrie Sommers posed next to a green-painted pole. "Does standing next to this thing make me look more curvy?" she asked her cheerleading co-captain, Martha Lee.

"Lady lumps!" Martha yelled over the music. Then she took Carrie's photo.

Sara Oaks stood a little too close to Martha, like she hoped Martha would take her picture, too. Her light brown hair was braided in a fishtail that draped over her shoulder and looked like a dead possum, but I liked the way she'd paired chandelier earrings with a boyish white tank. Martha ignored her.

Joanna pushed through the crowd and wrapped her arms around me. "Rocking party, right?" she asked. She followed my stare to Carrie Sommers and laughed. "Public Pretty Pics are making everyone insane," she said. "Want me to take yours?"

I almost said *not here.* But what better place? All of Harrison was in this room. I scanned the faces. Audrey and her friends were absent. Probably hacking away at their computers or playing video games. But almost everyone else was here.

Xander was suddenly at my side holding a red plastic cup. "Drink?" he asked. I shook my head. I wasn't a big drinker; I was too scared I'd say or do something so dumb that I wouldn't be able to recover from it. "You look nice," Xander said. His blond hair was backlit by a blue glow from a lava lamp. I felt every inch he put between us.

"Do you want to hang out this weekend?" I asked him. "Maybe film some stuff?" It came out a little desperate, but Xander didn't seem to notice. He was staring sideways at the basement door. "Indoor lax tournament both days," he said, shaking his head. He finally looked away from the door and back at me. He must have read my expression because his face went guilty. "Wanna come to the tournament?" he added.

"I'd rather read *Anna Karenina* in Russian," I said, rolling my eyes. I pushed past Xander and grabbed Sean DeFosse by the elbow. "You. Me. Photo shoot. Now."

Sean collected himself and hustled after me. I moved through the crowd toward the back wall, where a yoga mat rested against a costume chest. The tip of a witch's hat protruded from the wood. I flung the chest open and dug my hands inside.

Rubber noses . . . fleshy wrinkled face masks . . . a purple velvet cloak . . .

My fingers found raspberry-colored Mardi Gras beads. I layered them around my neck and then found a soft pink feather boa to go on top of the beads. I glanced in the mirror to remind myself:

I am the prettiest person here. No one can take that away from me.

I climbed onto the costume chest just as "SexyBack"

blasted over the speakers. I'd do anything to shake this feeling—this loneliness. But it wasn't really working. My birthday hadn't exactly been anything special yet. Nic forgot it; my dad was awful at dinner; *Audrey isn't here.* I hated myself for thinking about her, but every time something important had happened during the past few years, I felt her absence like a piece of me was missing.

"Photograph me!" I shouted at Sean. I started to dance and felt kids turn and stare. I swayed my hips, stopping every so often to strike a provocative pose for Sean. His flash attacked me, and soon practically everyone was watching. I ran the pink boa behind my neck, feeling the feathers tickle my skin. I bent forward and blew Sean's camera a kiss. Then I got a little carried away and shimmied the boa over my chest. Everyone started clapping. I swung my hips so hard I almost pulled a muscle. I wrapped the boa around my neck and twirled so my backside was facing them. Everyone cheered as I shimmied my butt. I was about to take a bow when the basement door flung open.

Audrey.

She came?

Mindy Morales trailed behind her. I caught Xander craning his neck to see who was coming in. His mouth curled into a smile. Traitor.

The Justin Timberlake song petered out, and I was left standing all alone on the stupid costume chest with no music to dance to. I tried giving Jolene a dirty enough look to make her fix the music, but she was too wrapped up in whatever Woody was saying. Everyone turned back to their conversations and photo-taking. The silence was deafening.

Get them out of here. I suddenly didn't want Audrey here, seeing all of this. She always knew how I was feeling—sometimes before I did. I didn't want her to sense my sadness, my loneliness, my fear over losing Xander to her best friend.

I stalked across the room. Most of the kids weren't taking pictures anymore. They were staring in the direction of Audrey and her friends and then back at me. I made out Lindsay and Nigit holding hands and waving like they were the South Bend Snow Queen and King on a float. Aidan held Audrey's hand and said something in her ear. She looked kind of miserable, like my party was the last place she wanted to be. Obviously she only came because Mindy wanted to see Xander. I felt angrier by the second as I pushed through the crowd. My mind played options of what I should say when I got there:

You shouldn't be here. You don't belong. You ruined my life.

I was closer and closer, and then I was there, opening my mouth to say all of it.

But then words didn't come. Because *he* was standing there. This *guy*. This really tall, really, *really* hot guy.

My breathing came faster as I stared at him standing next to Aidan. He was even taller than Aidan—well over six feet—and his massive build made Aidan look scrawnier than ever. He had broad shoulders and big hands, and his forearms were muscular but not veiny. (I hate veiny forearms. So many girls overlook them, but I just can't.) His dirty-blond hair was thick with exactly the right amount of wave. He wore a hunter-green North Face vest over a long-sleeved thermal T-shirt pushed up to show off his forearms. His jeans were low-slung, and his blue Nikes were beat-up. There was a layer of blond stubble over his face.

My insides went funny when he turned to look at me. His eyes were dark and gray like a rainstorm, and they made his stare unlike anything I'd ever seen before. I felt my mouth drop but I couldn't help it. "Who are you?" I asked, my voice giving away how unsettled I was. I cleared my throat and tried to act normal.

His lips curved, but he didn't say anything.

Audrey eyed me. She knew me way too well.

I cocked a hip forward. "I have a right to know, because it's my birthday party."

The guy laughed. It was a low, deep rumble: a real laugh, like he thought I was funny. No one thought I was funny.

"I'm Leo," he said, extending his big hand. I didn't move. He laughed again and grabbed my hand with his. It was warm, and his grip was strong.

"I'm Blake," I said. "Blake Dawkins."

"Happy birthday, Blake Dawkins," he said.

Audrey shifted her weight. Aidan and Lindsay were watching us. Nigit was busy telling Mindy that Sepiroth would drive a hybrid car, and Mindy was telling Nigit that Sepiroth wasn't real. Was Leo friends with these people? Did they bring him?

"You came with the Trogs?" I asked without thinking. Trogs = troglodytes, the name most of us called Audrey and her geeky tech friends.

Leo laughed *again*. What was up with this guy? He showed me his buyPhone covered with the plastic case Lindsay had designed last semester: TROGS RULE OUR SCHOOL.

My heart sank. He was one of them.

Audrey tightened the light purple scarf she wore over her emerald hoodie. "Leo's a transfer from California," she said. Her pale cheeks were still flushed from the cold, and her eyes avoided mine. "He went to a really good tech school there. And now he's a junior at Harrison, so Ms. Bates wants us to show him around."

A really good tech school. So he was super smart. Just like them. Not like me.

I didn't know what to say.

"Do you find it upsetting that I'm a trog, Blake?" Leo asked. His gray eyes twinkled. He was messing with me. Embarrassing me. Why couldn't I just turn around and leave? I wanted to, but my legs wouldn't cooperate.

"I don't care what you are," I said. I cleared my throat again. Why couldn't I stop doing that? "I'm sure you'll all have a blast together in the scintillating computer lab."

Now he was grinning. One of those grins you can't fake, with straight white teeth and dimples in both cheeks. I looked down at my wrist, but I'd forgotten my watch. "I should go," I said. "You're only eighteen once, and I don't want to spend my night with Trogs and freaks."

Leo chuckled like he thought I was kidding. "It was nice meeting you, Blake Dawkins."

Sarcasm. Rude. I turned to walk away, but then I

smashed into Xander's annoyingly broad chest. Xander barely registered me. "You came," he said to Mindy.

"You invited these people?" I asked. Xander put his arm around my shoulders, and I smirked at Mindy. "Can you believe our Blake is eighteen?" Xander asked.

Lindsay nodded solemnly. Then she said in a high-pitched, fake-sweet voice, "Our Blake is a vision of who we all hope to be as we teeter on the edge of adulthood."

"Get over yourself, Fanning," I said.

The speakers came back to life with a Danny Beaton song.

"Bomp bomp bomp da bomp.
Ooooh Girl!
Ooooh Baby!"

"Should we get this party started?" Nigit asked, grooving his hips in his signature Michael Jackson move. He turned to Lindsay. "It's like the music gets into my body and takes over," he said, gyrating faster. "Like my arteries are filled with song, not blood."

I could feel Leo's eyes on me. I wanted them to stay there, and I hated myself for wanting it. Wanting *him*. A computer boy . . . Team Audrey member . . . *Trog.*

Nigit wriggled his fingers over his eyes in sideways peace signs. Audrey laughed.

"Steve Urkel called," I said. "He wants his suspenders back." I wanted to insult his dancing, but it was just so good.

"Whatever, Blakey," Nigit said, using the name he called me when we were little. It made my blood boil, but I didn't want to lose control in front of Leo. Then Nigit did a kick jump and landed on the basement floor in a split. I heard the fabric of his corduroys rip.

"Nice tighty-whities," I said, pointing at his crotch. I couldn't see his underwear, but it was a safe guess.

Nigit's smooth brown cheeks went pink.

Leo glanced between us, and then his slate-gray eyes landed on me. "I think I'm going to like Harrison High School," he said.

chapter five

Selfies take over the net! The photos are everywhere. And not just on Public Party Network. With filters better than a Vogue *cover shoot, THE PRETTY APP shows us American teens at their prettiest, and keeps our hearts pounding as we wait to hear the surprises Public has in store, like:* Fame, prizes, and a nationally recognized title!
Here are some of our faves showcased in the TeensBlogToo Photo Gallery. *Stay tuned for the reveal of Stage Two of THE PRETTY APP! We'll be live blogging when Danny Beaton takes the Times Square Stage tomorrow afternoon.*
Excerpted from www.TeensBlogToo.com by Xi Liang

By the next day, tons of kids had uploaded their photos. And everyone looked better than they did in real life. Filters like *Geometric* could shade a plump face so it was subtly more angular, and *Perfection* gave you clear, glowing skin. *Peroxide* whitened teeth, *Mascara* lengthened lashes, and *Flyaway* smoothed hair. Nothing obvious, just the kind of thing magazine retouchers do on a regular basis. It was kind of weird to think that models and movie stars got this kind of treatment all the time. No wonder they always looked amazing.

I X'd out of *TeensBlogToo*. Then I touched the sleek new Pretty App icon on my phone and clicked on *PUBLIC PRETTY COVER PICS*.

"That again?" Joanna asked, but she leaned closer to peer over my shoulder.

"You know you want to see them, too," I teased her, elbowing her gently. We were at U.P. Mall in the dressing room area of the Deb next to a disheveled rack of clothing. The college-age sales girls all acted too cool for us, and they kept flitting in and out and talking about whose turn it was to go on break. A techno remix of a Danny Beaton song thumped against my eardrums, and Joanna mouthed along with the words: "*Girlz, girlz, girlz, you got what it takes to make me go wild.*"

Jolene emerged wearing a cheap-looking lime-green sweater with cherries way too close to her nipples. "Um, no," I said as Joanna bopped her head in time with the Danny Beaton song. Jolene's face fell, so I added, "Because it's just not the right color this season." The wooden chair was making my butt go numb, and I wanted to go to Coach. But I was trying to be sensitive to Jolene's budget. "Why don't you try that one?" I asked, pointing to an aqua-colored three-quarter-sleeved T-shirt hanging outside her door.

Jolene smiled and disappeared with the top into her dressing room.

"Did you put your pictures up yet?" Joanna asked as I typed #HarrisonHighSchool #SouthBend #Indiana.

"Of course," I said. I'd selected a shot Sean took at last night's party for my cover photo. (One of the only photos that wasn't too sexy, just in case my parents saw it.) And then I added a bunch of pictures to my gallery, using *Candlelight*, which cast the perfect shadows across your forehead and cheekbones, and *Moonlight*, which darkened everything in the background of your photo and shone a silvery light only on your face and body. Other photo-sharing apps used filters to make the actual photographs look awesome, but the Pretty App used filters to make the *girl* in the photograph look awesome. It was so addictive. Who wouldn't want to click a button and look better?

Photos were searchable by name or high school, and nearly eight thousand high schools had entered. I wanted to see whether Audrey and her friends were participating. Almost everyone else had gone Pretty App crazy. Why not them?

FANNING, LINDSAY. I tapped the screen and a full-body photo of Lindsay in a kimono-style ikat-print dress came to life. Then the slideshow flashed a close-up of her face with bright red lips and lashes heavy with mascara. Stylish, as usual. And she hadn't used any of the filters as far as I could tell.

"What do you think Stage Two of the app's going to be?" Joanna asked, staring over my shoulder at Lindsay.

"We'll find out tomorrow," I said, typing *MORALES, MINDY*. Click. I frowned at digital Mindy and how perfectly her mane of caramel-colored curls framed her delicate features. She'd used *Moonlight*, too, and the full-body profile showed how big her boobs were. Xander loved big boobs. He was cliché like that.

"The blogs are saying it's going to be even bigger than last year's app contest," Joanna said.

I raised my eyebrows at her. "I'll believe it when I see it," I said, trying to play it cool. But what if she was right? You had to be able to build an app to enter last semester's Public contest, which meant I had a better shot at winning the Kentucky Derby. But if this year's contest involved prettiness, then I had a chance.

I searched McCARTHY, AUDREY. For her cover photo, Audrey had posted a white piece of paper with light blue watercolor letters spelling: *I am so much more than a pretty face.*

I blew out a breath. No arguing with her there.

Chantal Richardson, Sara Oaks, twin-girl basketball players from Harrison, and a bunch of kids from other high schools commented on Audrey's picture with things like:

I'm with you!

Boycotting the Pretty App!

Get real, Public!

Jolene's door flew open, and she posed for us wearing tiny black corduroy shorts and the aqua T-shirt. She looked gorgeous. "Get the top," I told her. "I have shorts like that you can have. I don't wear them anymore."

Jolene's face lit up. "Seriously?"

"Seriously," I said. "Now put your socks back on before you catch something from the carpet."

Jolene paid for her top, and we left the Deb right as the manager was telling one of the salesgirls that she couldn't hit on customers. Piano music filtered through the mall, and the smell of hot pretzels hit me like a wave. The air was so chilled I had my army-green jacket zipped to my throat. I was about to complain about the temperature when pain shot through my right foot.

"Ow!" I cried out. A little boy wearing Superman pajama bottoms collected his scooter from where it'd caught on the toe of my metallic kitten heel. He laughed and then zoomed away from us while his mother sucked on an Orange Julius and screeched, "Scotty!"

"Maybe you shouldn't let your spawn ride a scooter *in the mall*," I said to the mom, who huffed and puffed like walking was an Olympic sport.

She ignored me. And then I heard laughter.

The hair on my neck prickled as I recognized the laugh. I turned and my breath caught. It was *him*. Standing near the color-coded mall map with Audrey, Lindsay, Aidan, and Nigit.

Leo.

I took a step toward him and grimaced, sure my toe was broken. "Leo," I said through a tight jaw. "How nice to see you again."

He was drinking an iced coffee, and I'd never seen a guy who could make drinking an iced coffee look sexy until that moment. "Hey, Blake," he said, smiling. His low voice hit me somewhere in the stomach. "You okay?"

Audrey looked nervous. She toyed with the pocket of her jeans and inched closer to Aidan, who considered me like he always did: with disdain. Nigit and Lindsay were holding hands and staring at me, too. Where was Mindy? My mind flashed to her rolling around in bed with her big boobs bouncing all over Xander.

"Thanks for your concern, but I'm fine," I lied. My toe felt like it was being stung by a jellyfish.

I could feel Joanna and Jolene tighten beside me.

"Want to come to Sephora with us?" Leo asked, still grinning. "Lindsay here was just telling me how your ideal nail polish should match your blood."

Lindsay looked at me through leopard-print glasses. "It's true," she said, nodding. "People get confused when picking out the ideal red polish for their skin tone. But if you just prick your finger a little bit, your ideal polish color is the one that matches your fresh blood."

Audrey turned to Lindsay and said, "You can't be serious," but she was smiling. She adored her cousin.

"That's so *Twilight*," Nigit said, pretending to bite Lindsay's neck.

What was wrong with these people? And why were they sort of charming even when they were being so freaking weird?

"You're disgusting," Joanna said.

"We'll pass," Jolene said.

"No," I announced, easing my weight off my run-over toe. "We won't." I didn't like the way Leo was suddenly shifting the dynamic of our friend groups. The Trogs didn't invite us to do things. Ever. And we didn't invite them. "We'll go," I said. I wasn't about to let some hot guy waltz in and shift the balance of power. "Won't we?" I asked Jolene and Joanna.

Jolene sniffed.

"Why not?" Joanna said. "I'm always happy to draw blood."

I smiled at Leo like we'd won.

Audrey rolled her eyes. Lindsay slung a yellow-taxi-colored tote over her shoulder and said, "Let's go then. Beauty awaits us."

Audrey took Aidan's hand, and I felt weirdly alone. I didn't know how to hang out with Audrey anymore. Lindsay and Nigit shuffled by and I suddenly felt paralyzed. I wasn't sure how to fall into the group. Should I try to lead the way or stay back? Leo was standing there wearing his hunter-green vest again, and I realized we sort of matched, which made me happy in a super-dorky way, which I didn't exactly feel comfortable experiencing.

I cleared my throat. "That vest makes you look like a drug dealer," I said to Leo, and then I started following Audrey and Aidan. Leo's laugh echoed in the cavernous mall, and I tried not to smile as I turned back to look at him. He caught my eye and held my glance just like he'd done at the party last night.

No, no, no, I told myself as I turned away from him. He was a Trog, which meant he probably liked straight-A-student kind of girls. Or girls who wore leather necklaces and thumb rings and wanted to save the rain forests. Or girls who stood outside school in androgynous white polo shirts holding clipboards and registering new voters.

Not aspiring television hosts who were only good at being pretty.

Ick. What was wrong with me? Why was I doubting my Blake-ness? Leo might be one of them, but that didn't mean he was immune to beautiful girls.

I flicked my jet-black hair over my shoulder and put some extra oomph in my walk. Nothing cheesy, just a little swing in my hips. Thank God I was wearing my Citizens jeans, the ones that hugged my butt like Saran Wrap.

I swore I heard Leo let out a low whistle, but maybe I just imagined it.

We all piled on to the escalator behind Aidan and Audrey. I squashed next to Jolene and watched the top of Audrey's dark pixie cut lean against Aidan's shoulder. Her geek-girl romance looked even cuter from this angle, and I felt a pang of jealousy. Audrey and I used to come to U.P. Mall together all the time after school. We'd dare each other to do stuff, like when Audrey dared me to stand up in the middle of *Inglourious Basterds* and scream, *"I have restless legs syndrome!"*

"So what's up, Blakey?" Nigit asked from two steps behind me on the escalator. I swiveled to see him push back his Coke-bottle glasses with a white-gloved hand.

"Why do you want to hang out with us?"

I wasn't sure how to answer him, so I settled on the truth. "The end of senior year has me feeling nostalgic," I said. Nigit actually nodded and looked like he understood what I meant, which surprised me. I pointed to his glove. "Why do you wear that thing?" I asked.

"Michael Jackson is my fashion icon," he said. "I'm thinking yours might be Keira Knightley."

I felt my mouth drop a little. The last thing I'd expected was one of these weirdos to flatter me.

"You're spot-on," Lindsay said, clapping her hands. "Blake's natural style is a mix of Keira's edginess and Jessica Biel's reserved glamour."

Nigit puffed his chest.

"I thought Blake was going for a Cruella de Vil thing, from what I've heard," Leo said from behind us.

I turned and took in his smug smile. "And exactly what have you heard, Leo?" I asked, thinking of the four thousand terrible things he could've already heard about me from anyone at Harrison.

Leo ran a hand over his jaw, looking pensive. "Well, a few kids told me you were up for some sort of Kindness Queen nomination."

I felt my cheeks get hot. And then the escalator dumped us on the ground floor. Jolene didn't move fast enough, and my feet knocked into hers. I stumbled, and Audrey reached out her hand to grab my arm, saving me from a face-plant.

Nigit laughed, and embarrassment flooded me. What was I doing with these people? They hated me: They were

51

making fun of me right to my face. Anger swelled in my chest, the way it always did right before I said or did something I shouldn't.

I turned to face Leo. "Look, you loser Trog. Let's get one thing straight. You do *not* want to get on my bad side. Why don't you ask all those Harrison kids how *that* goes."

Leo held up his hand. "Whoa, tiger," he said. "I was just joking around."

"Well you're not very funny, are you?" I grabbed Jolene and Joanna and tugged them in the opposite direction from Sephora. The Trogs stood by the escalator, watching us leave.

"They're not worth our time," Jolene said as we hurried past Piercing Pagoda.

"I know that," I said. I felt on the verge of tears and tried to swallow them back. I hated feeling embarrassed. I hated feeling out of control.

"Don't let them get to you," Joanna said. "No one cares what they think anyway."

Joanna and Jolene hooked their arms through mine. At least they were trying; at least we had that.

We maneuvered through Macy's toward the exit, and no matter how upset I was, gliding past the makeup counters calmed me the littlest bit. I stared at the lipsticks—their beautiful corals, reds, crimsons, and mauves—and the blushes, all rosy pinks and creamy oranges. I smelled the woodsy and floral perfumes. I slowed and reached my finger out to touch the prickly bristles of a Bobbi Brown brow brush. I could've stayed in the makeup section forever, imagining a future filled with beautiful things—but then I saw Nic at the far end of the floor, near the shoes. I started to make my way toward her, but I stopped when I saw her raise her hands and gesture like she was arguing with someone.

"Wait here," I whispered to Joanna and Jolene.

I rounded the Clinique counter to get a better look at Nic. She was arguing with someone standing behind a towering platform-sandal display. Her lips were pursed and her face was contorted like it did when she was about to cry. My first instinct was to go to her, so I edged closer, around a table of shagreen clutches. As I neared her, I made out Samantha Cavelli, a girl who had graduated from Harrison the year after Nic and now went to Notre Dame, too. Why would Nic be arguing with Samantha Cavelli? I didn't even realize they were friends.

Then Nic started to cry. Samantha glanced around, suddenly looking helpless. I moved toward my sister, but then Samantha put her arm around Nic and it felt like I wasn't needed. That hit me hard, and I backed away and hurried toward Joanna and Jolene.

"Let's get out of here," I said, barely able to look at them. It was too embarrassing to admit how far my relationship with Nic had fallen, but I knew Joanna and Jolene sensed it. It was like I couldn't hold on to anyone important. Not Nic. Not Xander. Not Audrey. I didn't want Joanna and Jolene leaving me, too.

chapter six

The next afternoon we were all sitting in an upperclass-
man seminar called College Prep, which was supposedly
meant to motivate the juniors and prepare the seniors. But
it was mostly about *study habits* and not about stuff we really
needed to know, like *how to date two guys at once without
looking like a ho*. The class was taught by Taylor Marley,
also known as Hot Gym Coach, which was ironic because
HGC struck me as the kind of playboy who drank beer and
caught STDs in college.

We had to meet in the auditorium because so many kids
were taking College Prep that a regular classroom couldn't
hold us. Dusty maroon-colored velvet curtains draped
along the stage like a breeding ground for moths. The scalloped white pillars on the side of the stage were the only
thing about Harrison that reminded me of a fancy private
school. (I'd always wanted to go to private school so I could

act like Serena van der Woodsen, but my dad always said public school was a better option for Nic and me in case he ever decided to run for public office.) I checked my phone for a reply from Nic. Last night after I saw her at the mall, I'd texted:

We could still hang out this week if you want. Maybe a movie?

I figured if I could get her alone, maybe I could ask her about what was going on with Samantha Cavelli. But she hadn't responded yet.

"Today we're going to talk about selecting your course load," HGC said. He blinked under the glare of the auditorium lights, and his brown eyes looked a little bloodshot, like he'd been out partying. "This can be a very stressful decision," HGC went on, in the same *stay calm, but this is really important* tone our seventh-grade health teacher used to break the news about erections.

HGC was the lacrosse coach, and he was dressed in his uniform like the rest of the team because they had a home game today. His whistle was visible beneath his maroon-and-gold jersey, and so were his nipples, which made me feel like maybe he should wear an undershirt.

College Prep was the first class Audrey and I'd had together in years, because she was in all the smart-people classes. She sat two rows in front of me on a blue velvet seat. Nigit, Aidan, Mindy, and Lindsay sat close to Audrey. Jolene, Xander, and Joanna were next to me. I tried not to notice Xander's furtive looks in Mindy's direction.

Hot Gym Coach looked a little wobbly as he wheeled

an ancient-looking television and VCR to the front of the class, making me even more sure that he was hungover. "Today we're going to watch a video that addresses the importance of selecting a class schedule that is both manageable and leads you toward your chosen major."

Nice. A video. We didn't usually get to watch them in this class.

HGC looked like he was about to throw up as he fumbled with the remote. He put a hand to his head. Sweat beaded on the back of his neck.

"Uh, Xander," he said. "You're good with these things, right?"

Xander jumped from his seat. He strode to the front of the auditorium, his muscular shoulders flexing beneath his uniform.

Clank went one of the back doors. I turned to see Leo waltz in with a messenger bag slung over his shoulder. "What's up Harrison High?" he said loudly, and because nothing interesting ever happens at this stupid school, a bunch of kids started clapping.

"I hope you have a hall pass, Mr. Bauer," HGC said.

"I hope you have Advil, Mr. Coach," Leo said as he moved down the aisle. He clapped HGC on the back and said, "You don't look so good, Gym Boy."

HGC's face went red at his slightly receding hairline, and at first I thought he was going to kick Leo out of class, or worse. But then he turned a greenish color and stumbled past Leo and Xander and flew through the exit.

Everyone was quiet, and then Leo started laughing.

"I guess that concludes today's episode of College Prep," Leo said, and everyone started laughing right along with him like he was Louis C.K. and this was his stand-up routine. Leo's grin was huge, and the dimples I'd seen at Joanna and Jolene's party were back. He was wearing another one of those long-sleeved thermal shirts; this one was chocolate brown and looked perfect with his wavy blond hair. And the way he stood up there in front of the class with everyone eating out of the palm of his hand made him sexier than ever. We almost never got new faces at Harrison, unless you counted the foreign exchange students. We certainly never got new faces that looked like Leo's. A bunch of the girls were giggling and whispering to one another. Leo picked up Coach's microphone from the stage.

"I propose we watch a different video," Leo said into the mic, running a hand over his blond scruff. "Anyone in favor?"

Everyone cheered, except for Goth Girl Greta Fleming, who'd fallen asleep with her head tipped up toward the ceiling and her black lace veil skimming the floor behind her. Leo ducked down toward his messenger bag and yanked out his laptop.

"Go, Leo!" Nigit yelled out. He and Aidan Bailey were grinning like fanboys. I could sort of see why they worshipped Leo. He was like the hot, confident version of a regular Trog—a Trog 2.0. For a fleeting second it struck me as odd that Leo was hanging out only with their group. Why hadn't he branched out socially, or started hitting on half the girls in school who clearly drooled over him?

"Thanks, man," Leo said with a chuckle as he powered on his computer.

"This better be what I think it is," Jolene said into my ear.

I was thinking the same thing. Danny Beaton was supposed to announce Stage Two of the Pretty App at two p.m. It was 1:59, and we'd all been complaining about having to miss it because of useless College Prep.

Carrie Sommers stood up. "I'd like to take this time to tell you all that the Cheer Squad will be performing an original dance to 'Oops! . . . I Did It Again' at today's lacrosse game. You can see a preview on my Public Party page, but let me just say that if you like Britney mixed with Bollywood, you are going to l-o-v-e *love* this dance." And then she pumped her arms with her elbows splayed and her fists near her perky C-cups.

Everyone looked bored except Leo, who said, "I'll be sure to check that out, Carrie." His voice was kind, like he meant it, and Carrie smiled hugely before she sat down.

Leo went back to typing away at his keyboard and then propped it above the television. Danny Beaton lyrics blared from his laptop. The screen showed the Times Square stage, where Danny was strumming a ukulele. Dalmatians sat next to firefighters on the side of the stage, and at first I thought it was some kind of tribute to servicemen, but then the firefighters started taking off their clothes and I realized they were strippers. Is it me, or is the pop music industry constantly trying to out-ridiculous itself?

Danny Beaton shouted into his microphone. *"What's up, America?! Are y'all ready for Stage Two of the Pretty App?"*

The Times Square crowd was even bigger than last time. The spectators—nearly all girls again—whooped and hollered and waved their phones in the air.

Danny did a sideways kick jump and landed in a split, then popped back up again like his body was made of string cheese. I rolled my eyes at Joanna. *"Eight hundred thousand of you have uploaded your prettiest photos,"* Danny said, sounding like he was trying to be Ryan Seacrest from *American Idol.* *"And now it's time to unveil Stage Two of the app that's sweeping America."*

Right then another one of those sexy glamazon models strutted her stuff across the stage. She wore a firefighter uniform tailored to fit her sleek frame like sausage casing. The neckline plunged between her boobs.

Danny said, *"Wowza,"* as the model handed him a suitcase that glittered like a chandelier. He opened the case and retrieved a tiny chrome bullet that looked like some kind of tech gadget. He inspected it like it was a rare gem and then inserted it into his phone. The screen glowed, and Danny gazed at it with fake wonderment. And then, of course, he started singing.

"Whoa whoa whoa. Uh-huh. Yeah.
It's time to find her.
It's time to find the one.
You know who she is.
She's the girl every guy wants.

She's the girl every girl wants to be.
She's the prettiest girl.
She's the prettiest girl in the world.
Find her."

Danny gave the camera one of his soap-opera looks. *"Download the Pretty App Stage Two,"* he said, holding America's stare. *"It's time to find the prettiest one of all."*

My heart pounded. I suddenly had the awful feeling that I had something to lose. What if I wasn't allowed to compete because of my dad's involvement with Public? Though, he wasn't an employee, just one of their many investors. (A big one, but still.)

I whipped out my phone like everyone else. Leo looked pensively hot as he stared at all of the Harrison kids tapping their screens. It was like he was memorizing the frenzy. I opened the Pretty App, and new instructions danced across the screen in pink lettering.

Welcome to Stage Two of the Pretty App.

You've uploaded your prettiest photos, and now it's time to vote on Pretty Potential to find the Prettiest Girl in your high school. Simply rank every female student in your high school for looks alone on a scale of 1–10. The girl with the highest average will become the Public Pretty and be entered into a nationwide contest to win a spot on a new reality show featuring the one and only Danny Beaton.

★The Pretty App is only for female students 16+ officially enrolled in high school in the United States of America. All others will be disqualified from participation.

My mind raced. A reality show? A beauty contest at Harrison? I had to at least win that part—I had to.

Murmurs rippled across the auditorium. I looked up to see Audrey whispering something to Aidan. Chantal Richardson stood up and said, "We don't need to do this. We don't need to rank each other. This is *not* a good idea." A few kids clapped, but most were staring at their phones and talking among themselves, seeming not to care about what she'd said.

Leo looked over the rows of students, and then took out his phone and started texting. Nigit said, to no one in particular, "Can dudes vote, too? Because my vote goes to Lindsay Fanning, the love of my mortal life." Leo looked at Nigit and said, "No, bro, the app's for chicks."

Joanna leaned so close I could smell her watermelon gum. "You have to win this thing," she said.

I nodded, feeling my skin go hot and prickly. She was right. And something about hearing her say the words out loud made me think I could.

chapter seven

I couldn't stop obsessing over my Pretty ranking. Who even knew how much longer I had to look like this? God gave me a gift with a shelf life. There were only a dozen or so more years until my looks would start to fade. A slow, drawn-out torture.

But I couldn't focus on that now. I could only focus on winning this thing.

That afternoon, Joanna, Jolene, and I were in my bedroom eating organic kettle chips. The air smelled like grease and salt.

"What do we need to do to get rid of these things?" Joanna asked, holding her chip in the air and pretending to feed one of the crazy-strange *Phantom of the Opera* masks my mom had hung on my wall. "Yum, yum, yum," she said.

I hated those masks. Their deranged grins stared back at

me every time I sat at my desk and attempted homework. But my mom loved them. And when she told me the story about how *Phantom of the Opera* was the first musical she ever took me to, I couldn't bring myself to complain about them. I actually thought keeping the masks might make her come into my room more often, but she never really did. I don't think she felt comfortable in small spaces with Nic and me anymore.

Jolene laughed at Joanna feeding the masks, but I felt too fidgety to join in. "Let's check our rankings," I said, climbing from the bed and moving to my desk. I turned on my laptop and opened Public Party.

Public was featuring the contest front and center on our pages next to the Pretty App icon. *Click here to rank the Pretty Potential of your high school!* I entered Jolene's name and her cover photo sprang to the screen. Her light eyes were shining, and the beauty mark on her chin looked so perfect it could've been drawn on by a makeup artist.

JOLENE MARTIN. PRETTY RATING: 8.8

"Eight point eight!" I said, both excited for her and relieved she wasn't beating me.

Jolene managed a small smile. "What's yours?" she asked.

I entered my name. The photo of me pursing my lips for Sean DeFosse's camera popped onto the screen.

BLAKE ANDREA DAWKINS. PRETTY RATING: 9.4

I couldn't help but smile. My score had gone up two-tenths since I'd checked it an hour ago.

"I have an idea," Joanna said. She set the bag of chips on my bed and moved across the floor. "Let's make a campaign page for you on Public Party. We can load a bunch of your best photos."

What a good idea.

"I don't know," I said, wanting her to work for it a little more so she'd tell the kids at school she had to convince me to do it. I didn't want any of them knowing how much I wanted this. Because what if that made them want to take it away?

"Come on, Blake," Jolene said, standing beside me at the computer. "Let *us* do it."

"Okay," I said, smiling as she clicked on my photo gallery. "If you guys think it's a good idea."

"It's a *great* idea," Joanna said as Jolene grinned.

We scrolled through my archived Public Party photos. I'd used the Pretty App filters on some of them, and they already looked the best. There was the one of me in my bikini in Turks and Caicos, where I'm feeding a bottlenose dolphin and my hair is doing a Victoria's Secret catalog scrunched-up saltwater thing. Then there was the one from last fall's Danny Beaton concert. It was a close-up of my face, and I'm wearing this Bobbi Brown glitter eye shadow that makes my eyes look extra dramatic. I'd used a Pretty App filter called *Mermaid* to make it look like I was underwater. Sounds cheesy, but it actually made the photo look kind of cool. And then there was the picture of me volunteering at the South Bend Soup Kitchen, which my dad made me do for a family photo op. That one could win points: My dad taught me by example that anything bad you do can be forgotten with a little good press.

"This one's cute, too," Jolene said, pointing to the one of Nic and me on horseback from a few years ago, when we used to ride together.

"I don't think we should put up one of Nic," I said, shaking my head. Nic was weird about social media. She was the only college kid I knew who didn't post anything and everything about her life on her Public Party page.

"It's kind of outdated, anyway," Joanna said, clicking on another one with me and Xander after one of his lacrosse games.

"We *have* to use this," Jolene said.

She was right. It was perfect. Xander's head was tilted toward me, and we stared at each other in profile. We looked so happy, even though we'd just had a huge fight and were on the verge of breaking up. That was the funny thing about Public Party pages: You could make your life look so beautiful and perfect, even if it wasn't.

"I bet Xander would win if they were doing this contest for guys," Joanna said.

"Or Woody," Jolene said. And then, maybe to cover up her Woody-tracks, she said, "But that was all before Leo showed up."

I stared hard at Jolene and Joanna as they exchanged a glance. They had so many secrets between them: secret thoughts and secret looks.

"What?" Joanna said. "He's so hot."

"He's a Trog," I said.

Jolene shrugged. "Hot is hot."

Joanna assembled all the pictures and used a pretty purple font to title the page: *Beautiful Blake.*

"That's it?" I asked. "You're not going to say anything about the Pretty App contest?"

Joanna shook her head. "It's classier this way," she said. Then she blushed a little, almost like she could feel me thinking something mean about how she wasn't the arbiter of classy. But I wasn't thinking that. I was thinking she was right.

"You know what we should do?" Joanna asked, once my page was up and running. "We should make an Ugly Page for someone at Harrison."

Jolene laughed as Joanna clicked around on Harrison students' ratings. There were girls who'd submitted their photos (or maybe someone else had submitted them as a joke?) with scores of 1's and 2's. I felt a wave of relief that I'd never know what that felt like.

"Oh my gosh," Jolene said. "We should do Sara Oaks."

Joanna clapped her hands over her mouth. "Yes," she said through her fingers.

"But Sara's not ugly," I said.

"Does it really matter?" Joanna said. "She's a loser."

Maybe she was. But she also seemed a little fragile. At least the other losers at school had a few friends: Sara was floating out there with no one. "Yeah, but we don't want her to come totally unhinged."

Joanna laughed like I was making a joke. Then she scrolled and found all kinds of unflattering pictures of Sara on Public Party. It was like no one taught her how to untag herself, or maybe she liked being tagged by people because it made her feel like she had friends. There was one of her sitting all alone at lunch with her face squished like she was trying to fart or something. Someone had captioned the photo: **Tater tots not agreeing with you, Sara Oaks?** And then there was one of her in the swimming pool during gym class. She wore oversize goggles, and the top of her suit flopped open and you could see the nipple of one of her barely there boobs.

"Maybe we shouldn't do this," I said. The nipple picture was giving me a sick feeling. Joanna and Jolene looked at me like I'd suggested we wear matching denim vests to prom.

"OK, fine," I said. "Do what you want on your own time. But don't use the nipple picture. It's basically porn."

Jolene rolled her eyes. She and Joanna started packing up their things, and we didn't say much as they got ready to leave. I'd be lying if I said I didn't think they were going home to make that page. And the thing is, if you don't stop someone from doing something you know is wrong, then you're almost as responsible as they are.

Maybe that was my first mistake. It definitely wasn't my last.

chapter eight

ARE YOU SICK OF BLAKE DAWKINS AND HER CONVENTIONAL
BEAUTY? (*NOT TO MENTION HER SNOTTINESS?*) ME TOO. SO
WHY NOT VOTE FOR ME, GRETA FLEMING, AS HARRISON'S
10.0 BEAUTY. GRETA FLEMING: A NEW KIND OF PRETTY.

That was the sign Goth Girl held up near the entrance
to the cafeteria the next afternoon.

"Don't say anything," I hissed to Joanna and Jolene. I
wanted to rip the cardboard from Goth Girl's hands, but I
couldn't do it with everyone watching, and that wasn't the
way to win high Pretty scores. Public was announcing the
winners today, and I was trying to lie low until voting was
over and my top spot was secure.

Next to Goth Girl stood Nina Carlyle, who glared at
me. Her boyfriend, Max Laudano, held a Twizzler between
two fingers like a cigarette. Nina had almost made it to the

Olympics for luge, which is basically just sledding, and when I'd pointed that out she'd acted like I'd insulted her very reason for living. Which maybe I had. That started an insult war between us, and let's just say the girl still had it out for me.

Nina smirked as Joanna, Jolene, and I got closer, and then she tipped over Max's black cello case so that it fell near my feet. The noise scared me, even though I saw it coming, and I flinched.

"My cello!" Max cried. He knelt down and put his head next to the case, like how they teach you to check for breath sounds in CPR.

Joanna rolled her eyes. I grabbed her and Jolene and steered them past Nina and Max. "Let's eat in the courtyard," I whispered.

"But don't you want to be in the cafeteria in case they announce you as the Prettiest?" Jolene asked.

"*When* they announce you as the Prettiest," Joanna said smugly.

We got in the lunch line. The vegetarian option looked like throw-up and smelled like wet earth. It made me think of Nic.

"Not really," I said, steering us toward the roast turkey. I'd been feeling weird ever since I'd seen Sara Oaks that morning. She'd caught my eye and then bolted in the other direction. She looked like she'd been crying, which meant she had probably seen the Ugly Page Joanna and Jolene had undoubtedly made. I found myself wanting to tell her I didn't make that stupid page, but she was gone before I had the chance.

Joanna, Jolene, and I each got turkey and potatoes and made our way through the cafeteria. I hated when we were running late, like today, because it meant the cafeteria got packed before we could make it to our seats.

"You'll be fine once you sit down," Joanna said softly, which meant I looked about as good as I felt.

Jolene pushed open the door to the courtyard and cool fresh air kissed my face. I gulped it down until it burned my lungs, and I felt normal again. "Much better," I said, starting along the stone trail that led from the cafeteria's door to an oversize oak tree.

My heart sank when I saw them sitting at the base of the oak with their brown-bag lunches and vitamin D–deprived skin.

The Trogs.

I stopped. Stared at them.

Audrey's almost-black pixie hair was spiking in twenty different directions, all of them wrong. Her thin fingers held an apple out to Aidan like she was Eve or something. Lindsay wore a metallic silver top with a futuristic collar that made her look like a robot but in an awesome way. Nigit, Aidan, and Mindy were hunched over a tablet that sat on a flat stone between them.

It took me a second to register that Leo wasn't with them.

"Do you want to eat in the cafeteria instead?" Jolene asked.

I didn't want to retreat from the Trogs like we'd done at the mall, but I didn't want to sit there eating so close to them. I just wanted to relax—why was I always so on edge at this stupid school?

Nigit looked up from the tablet. "Congratulations, Blakey," he said. He looked back down at the shining white screen, but I couldn't see what he was looking at. My heart leapt with the possibility that he was talking about the Pretty App Contest.

"For what?" Joanna asked, and I knew she was thinking the same thing. She crept along the stones to get closer to Nigit's tablet.

My phone buzzed and I tried to balance my tray on my hip. If I could just check the app—

"Congratulations!" boomed a deep voice behind me.

I turned and my tray slid down my arm. I caught it seconds before my turkey took flight. Leo stood there holding a tray with the vegetarian dirt-food piled high next to a burger. He saw me looking at it and said, "Sometimes I think the wheat berries cancel out the soda and the lard."

I laughed—I couldn't help it—and forgot about the Pretty App for a split second.

"Are you here to celebrate with us?" Leo asked, nodding toward the Trogs. He looked into my face and studied me like he could read my thoughts. "You don't know?" he asked, smiling. "That's cute." Then he moved past us and settled himself on the lawn next to Mindy. He cracked a can of Coke and started slugging away like he'd forgotten I was there.

"You won the contest, Blake," Audrey said. She even sort of smiled.

"The Pretty App contest?" I blurted.

Aidan looked up. He generally ignored my existence, but this time he said, "Yeah. The Pretty Contest. Now maybe you can take down that page you made about Sara Oaks." He took a bite of Audrey's apple. "Or we can," he went on, "but that would take us longer because we'd have to hack your accounts and figure out your passwords, which we could later use against you."

"Is that a threat?" Joanna growled.

I won the contest?

"Yeah," Aidan said. "I guess it is."

Leo started laughing. "People, calm yourselves." He took the bun off his burger and loaded the vegetarian crap on it. Then he put it back on and took a huge bite, smiling in my direction as he chewed. "Let's break bread together and toast Blake's victory," he said.

I couldn't help it. I started smiling at the Trogs. I'd won something! I never usually won anything. It's not like I entered beauty pageants as a child. Everyone knows that only leads to substance abuse.

"Okay," I said, giddy. "Let's celebrate."

"Have you lost your mind?" Jolene asked, not bothering to whisper.

I shrugged. I wasn't really sure what had gotten into me. I moved across the stone trail and sat next to Audrey. Joanna followed a beat behind me. She stood with her tray balanced over Nigit's head, and for a second I was worried she'd drop it on him, but she finally sat, and then so did Jolene.

"Nice day for March in South Bend, right?" Leo said, smiling at me.

Joanna was wearing a short skirt, and she tugged at it, clearly annoyed, as she tried to arrange herself on the grass.

"Gorgeous," I said. *Just like you.* I broke our stare and pulled my phone from my pocket. I needed to see it for myself; I needed to know the Trogs weren't pulling one over on me.

I clicked the Pretty App and there it was.

Results are in! Public Pretties announced here!

Seeing my name spelled out on the screen gave me an odd little thrill.

Mindy looked over my shoulder. "You deedn't believe us?" she asked, her speech disorder only slightly improved since she started talking again last semester.

"Should I have?" I meant it as a genuine question, but Mindy looked uncomfortable, and she didn't say anything. She busied herself wiping a fleck of dirt from her ankle boots.

"So what're you going to do to celebrate?" Leo asked, devouring his burger like he hadn't eaten in days. It annoyed me how sexy I found his caveman-like food manhandling.

"I'm not going to celebrate," I said quickly. I picked at a blade of grass near my feet. "It doesn't really mean anything."

"Sure it does," Leo said. "It means you're the prettiest girl in your high school as voted by your peers."

"But she already knew that," Audrey said, holding something so fancy and French-looking that I was sure her mother had cooked it. "So what does it change?"

Leo thought for a minute. He swallowed another bite of his burger and said, "It could change everything. If she's selected to compete on the reality show, she could gain fame and fortune." He winked at me and my stomach went fluttery.

"Or notoriety," Lindsay said. "Like that girl you two liked from *The Bachelor*."

I bit my bottom lip and tried to avoid Audrey's eye, but she laughed first, and then I couldn't help myself, I started laughing even harder than she was.

"Remember?" she asked, barely able to catch her breath as the rest of them stared at us.

Audrey and I used to watch every episode of *The Bachelor* and *The Bachelorette* together. During the winter of eighth grade, less than a year before everything had gone wrong between us, Audrey was sure this one girl who was kind of cheesy was going to win, but I was positive it would be the other girl, so we made a bet that whoever was wrong had to wear an outfit inspired by the cheesy girl to school. I lost, and Audrey made me wear super-short cutoff sweatpants with a glittery heart on the butt, a half-shirt she made by cutting the bottom off a white Hanes tank top, a fake belly button ring, and sequined stilettos. And the rule was that I couldn't tell anyone at school that I'd lost a bet. Audrey and I couldn't stop laughing that entire day. Every time we saw each other we'd just lose it. My ribs hurt by the time we got back to her apartment and I tore off the clothes.

Tears pricked Audrey's eyes now, just like they always did when she really got laughing. I knew the Trogs were her best friends, but I never saw her laughing with them like she used to with me. She was still giggling when Nigit raised his water bottle and said, "To Blakey."

The other Trogs raised their drinks, too, even Aidan. Joanna rolled her eyes, but Jolene halfheartedly raised her seltzer.

"We knew she'd win," Joanna said snottily, not bothering to join in with the rest of us clinking our water bottles and sodas. "She's the most popular girl in school."

"She's not," Nigit said as he tapped his Coke to my Evian. "I mean, no offense, Blake, but everyone pretty much hates you."

It felt like a slap. Silence descended on all of us like a hot, itchy blanket. No one said anything for what felt like hours. Not even Leo.

Lindsay turned to look at Nigit. "Sweetie," she said. "We've talked about the difference between your inside voice and your outside voice." She smiled at me like maybe I'd laugh, but I couldn't—not even a fake one.

Somewhere behind my eyes went hot, and it took every ounce of effort I had not to cry. I wanted to say something, but I knew if I started talking my voice would give away how upset I was.

Joanna opened her mouth to do it for me, but Audrey spoke first.

"Not everyone hates you," she said softly. She uncurled her legs and leaned closer. "I don't."

I met her eyes with mine. It was the first time I'd felt comfortable holding her gaze in a long time.

"Me neither," Lindsay said, shaking her platinum-blond head. "I think you add some spice to Harrison, though you *have* acted in a questionably moral manner in the past. Also, I think your fashion choices are daring and forward, but cohesive."

"I hate you a little," Aidan said, but he was smiling, and his timing was perfect, and everyone—including Joanna, Jolene, and me—laughed.

"Should we sing 'Kumbaya' right now?" Leo asked, and Mindy playfully elbowed him, and for a split second I thought about her liking him. The jealousy that spiked through me caught me so off guard it made me stop laughing, and I was pretty sure Audrey noticed my reaction before I could compose myself.

I looked down at my plate and cut a piece of turkey. I busied myself eating for a few moments, until Leo asked, "So seriously, what are you going to do to celebrate?" The corners of his eyes crinkled, and I had to pry my glance away from his perfect face.

"This *is* sort of celebrating," I said, gesturing around at all of us sitting on the grass.

Leo laughed. "Oh, come on. This can't cut it for a girl like you," he said.

I took a sip of my water. "*A girl like me?*" I said, my words lilting up at the end. "What does that mean?"

Leo's gray eyes were intense, but then he smiled, lightening up his face. "I'll show you what I mean," he said.

I felt my eyebrows arch. "Oh, really? How?" I asked. There was a challenge in my voice.

Audrey cleared her throat, and I was acutely aware of everyone's gaze on me.

Leo laughed that low, gravelly laugh of his. I felt my face get hot, and I knew Leo saw it, too. His voice was even when he said, "I'll pick you up tomorrow at eight"—he paused for just a beat—"a.m."

chapter nine

"Eight *in the morning*?" Joanna asked for the thousandth time as we made our way across the parking lot after school. The sound of ignitions roaring to life mixed with the smell of exhaust. Harrison kids moved through the lot in groups of twos and threes, chattering about things other than the Pretty App contest. No one had really made a big deal about me winning besides the Trogs. It was a letdown, but I didn't want to admit it, not even to Joanna and Jolene. It would've been nice to feel like I'd accomplished something, just for a few days.

"Who goes on a date on a Saturday morning?" Jolene said, unwrapping a caramel and popping it into her mouth.

I kept my voice down as we walked past a cluster of freshmen. "At least it'll be easy to convince my parents to let me go somewhere with someone they've never met," I said. "I can make up something school-related."

"I don't trust him," Jolene said, shaking her head. "I don't trust any of them."

"They're just Trogs," Joanna said, glaring at Jolene like she'd complimented them by calling them untrustworthy.

"And they were nice today," I said.

"But they're way smarter than we are," Jolene said. "What if they're up to something?"

"Like what?" I asked as we moved around the potheads throwing a Frisbee and laughing at nothing like they were a commercial for reasons to stay drug-free. "We're the ones who cause the drama around here," I said. "Not them."

The truth was, I didn't know Leo all that well. But I liked the way I felt when I was with him. And maybe it was reckless, but something told me to trust him.

"Blake?" Chantal Richardson said cautiously as we got closer. She stood on a yellow stripe of paint, cradling a stack of neon-green paper like a newborn. "Congrats on your victory," she said. It made me smile, which seemed to relax her a little. "Can I interest you all in some information about the school vote on Monday?" she asked. She held out a flyer with VOTE FOR EQUALITY printed across the top. "I think it's high time we offer a separate bathroom for transgender students."

"Sure," I said, taking a flyer. "We'll vote for it." There was only one transgender kid in our school, but these were the times when I wanted to help out with student government stuff—like, when it actually mattered, not when they were doing boring crap like making crepe paper flowers for a dance. But I didn't really do that kind of thing, and

Harrison wasn't the kind of place where you could just safely start being someone else. I shoved the flyer into my lavender Mulberry bag and kept walking.

"So how'd you do on that take-home test?" I asked Jolene, not wanting to talk about the date with Leo anymore. I was nervous enough without them asking me a million questions.

"B plus," she said. "Finally."

"Maybe that's something we should celebrate, too," I said. "Ice cream?"

Joanna and Jolene debated between two ice-cream shops, and we were almost at Joanna's beat-up station wagon when I got a text from Nic. My stomach felt sick when I recognized the screen shot of the Public Party Page Joanna and Jolene had made about Sara Oaks.

Are you freaking serious with this?

Nic texted below the picture.

I froze.

I know this was you and the Martins because no one else would do something like this. You guys don't get how pathetic this is. And dangerous. Don't you read the news? Don't you know what this makes kids do?

My heart pounded as I read her words. I wanted to tell her I hadn't been the one to make the page. But I hadn't stopped it, either, and she'd know that. I was trying to figure out how to reply when she texted:

Who do you think you are?

chapter ten

The last time I was up before seven on a Saturday morning was during eighth grade, when Audrey's dad won tickets to a Notre Dame football game. ND was playing Boston College that day, and Audrey's dad wanted to walk the campus at sunrise for good luck. We were eating steak sandwiches by eight a.m., and drinking root beer in the student center at nine. It was one of the best days of my life, just being with Audrey and her dad, watching them share Notre Dame together: the campus, the football, the mass after the game. And now that she was going to Notre Dame next year for school, too, I wondered what it would be like going to the same college as her, something we used to dream about when we were younger. I wondered if there was any way to get us back to where we used to be, or even just a little closer.

I checked Public Party, like I always did when I woke

up. The site was announcing deliberation at Public head-quarters to choose the twelve Public Pretty App Reality Show contestants from among the thousands of high school Pretty App winners. They were calling the show *The Pretty App Live*, and Pia Alvarez was the host.

Pia Alvarez got her start on a reality singing contest years ago, and ever since she's been hosting television shows and covering news on *Entertainment Tonight*. I got a fluttery feeling just thinking about meeting her and being able to see her host live.

I tapped my mouse pad and imagined what it would be like to be a TV host. I'd meet so many new people. And it wouldn't be like school, where I was bad at the whole point of it, which was getting good grades. If you're really book smart, you don't get what it feels like to have to go to school every single day and suck at it. It's exhausting. I couldn't even imagine what it would feel like to wake up and spend the day doing something I was actually good at.

I clicked on the button marked *DETAILS* and a video came to life. Photographs of former Miss America winners flashed with the caption: *A CONTEST UNLIKE ANY OTHER.* Then the video cut to Victoria's Secret–style models stomping down the runway wearing underwear. The video freeze-framed on one of the models with glittery silver wings blowing a kiss to the audience. A caption slapped over her midsection read: *BORED BY BEAUTY? NOT ANYMORE.*

The screen flashed new photos of gorgeous teenage girls that I guessed were the Public Pretty high school winners.

I got nervous, like maybe they'd show my picture, but of course they didn't. Danny Beaton's disembodied face appeared, hovering over the photos. His fauxhawk was extra-gelled, and he smiled as his face floated like a goldfish over the screen. *"Twelve among thousands will be handpicked as the most beautiful girls in America,"* he said. *"They will compete for the title of Prettiest, but the winner will become more than just a pretty face."* Some kind of drumroll sounded, and Danny Beaton played air drums and made a rock-and-roll face that looked like he'd practiced it in a mirror.

When the drumroll ended, he said, *"She'll become the United Nations' Citizen Ambassador of Health and Beauty, and she'll secure a modeling contract with top makeup brand Adore."* Danny shook his head with a smirk like he had a secret. *"The Public Pretty winner will be a spokesperson for an entire generation. So ask yourselves: Are you ready for* The Pretty App Live*?"* He stared into the camera with his doe-like brown eyes blinking. *"Tune in this Friday for the live premiere of* The Pretty App Live. *Check your local listings for showtimes."*

The screen went black and I sat there in a daze. It wasn't like I had a real chance; there were thousands of high schools in the contest. But now I wanted it even more than before I'd seen the ad. *More than a pretty face? Citizen Ambassador? Modeling contract with one of the best makeup brands in the world? Spokesperson?* That would mean a bunch of television appearances. It could be my big break into the world of TV. It could be my big break out of my parents' house.

My dad dropped something in the kitchen that sounded

like glass, yanking me from my daydream. I heard him call for my mom and I froze—bracing for them to argue—but there were only the sounds of her voice comforting him in placating, high-pitched tones like she was talking to an infant. I'd told them both last night that I was heading to Starbucks with a classmate to study this morning. They seemed fine with it, even a little proud, but I was worried they'd see Leo and get the idea that it was a date and change their minds.

I slipped into jeans and a long-sleeved, tissue-thin gray T-shirt. I didn't want to look like I was trying too hard, but I still spent extra time on my makeup, experimenting with a smudgy new Tarte liner and applying two coats of mascara. You have to be aggressive with mascara; it looks the best if you attack your lashes at a horizontal angle, the way violinists act when they get really into a solo.

Just before eight, I tiptoed downstairs and stared through the light blue pane of glass that bordered the front door. If I ran out right when Leo pulled in, I could avoid a conversation with my parents.

I checked my watch for the thousandth time. I heard my dad curse again in the kitchen, and my nerves went haywire. My dad was obviously in some kind of foul mood, and it was already 8:01, and what if Leo wasn't coming at all? I started to open the door, figuring I'd just wait outside on the porch, when a mustard-yellow vintage Mustang curved around the bend of our street. I watched in disbelief as it pulled into our driveway.

Leo opened the door and stepped out of the car carrying

a bouquet of wildflowers. He wore olive-colored chinos and a crisp blue oxford shirt.

I tried to breathe as he walked toward me cradling the flowers in one arm, and I was so taken aback that I forgot about needing to get going before my parents saw him. Leo was halfway up the driveway before I could think straight. "No, no, no," I said. I moved across the lawn, waving my arms in the universally understood gesture for *STOP*, but he didn't. He kept moving toward me with his massive white grin, his dimples like pinpricks of sunshine, his free arm waving like he had no cares in the world.

"Leo, we should go, we should really—"

"Nonsense," Leo said as he strode toward me. Unlike the untailored, lopsided way that most guys wore button-downs, Leo's fit him perfectly. It nipped in at all the right places, and you could see how built he was beneath the fabric. The sun was glinting on his thick blond hair, and the whole thing was like an Abercrombie and Fitch ad. I went weak in the knees, which I'd always thought was a made-up expression, but which turned out to be a perfect description for how he was making me feel.

"I have to meet your parents," Leo said, still smiling that wide sunshine grin. "It would be rude not to."

I opened my mouth to protest, but then his arm went around my waist. We'd never been that close. His arm felt heavy and strong and warm and perfect. He pulled me a little closer and kissed my cheek. Was this really happening?

"You look surprised," Leo said as he pulled away.

"I—I am," I said, staring him up and down and trying

to get myself together. He usually wore his Levi's in school, and I'd never seen him dressed up like this. "I thought we were just going to get brunch or something," I said.

"We are," Leo said, guiding me gently toward our front porch. He rang the doorbell and said, "In Chicago."

"What? Leo—no, no, no, you don't understand." My heart was racing. Chicago was almost two hours away. "My parents will never go for that, they're not—"

The door swung open. It was both of my parents.

"Hello, Mr. and Mrs. Dawkins," Leo said smoothly, like he didn't have an ounce of nervousness in his entire being. "I'm Leo Bauer." He stretched out his hand.

I looked at Leo and then at my parents. My mother was fake-smiling, but my dad had the oddest expression on his face. His eyes went wide with the kind of look you'd give someone you were surprised to run into. He was probably just startled by Leo and his fancy car. I was, too.

"These are for you," Leo said, passing the wildflowers into my mother's hands. Then he looked at my father as my mom gushed over the bouquet. "I was thinking I'd take Blake to Chicago today for an afternoon together," he said.

My heart pounded against my ribs. My mother's mouth dropped an inch, but my father's face went still, just like it always did before he lashed out. I wanted to jump in and say Leo was only joking, but the look on my father's face was so severe it stopped me from saying anything. I just stood there, waiting for the moment when everything crashed.

"That sounds wonderful," my father said in a monotone.

What?

"Blake could use some city culture," my dad went on, running a hand self-consciously through his hair. I was so shocked he was letting me go that I barely registered his insult.

"I imagine Blake will fit right in with city life," Leo said, and even though he was smiling, it was like he was also standing up to my dad's insult. It made me want to kiss him.

My mother glanced from Leo to my dad, holding her flowers and beaming like Miss America. I think a part of her always wanted to be more laid-back—to let me do the things she never got to as a teenager, like go on a date to Chicago with a hot boy. She'd married my father so young; her entire life had been ruled by him. And now he scared her just like he did the rest of us, and I got the feeling from stories her old high school friends told me that she wasn't who she used to be. "It sounds lovely," she said. I felt a wave of sadness watching her mauve lipstick crack when she smiled.

"Indeed," my father said, putting his hand on the door like he was going to shut it in our faces. "And we don't want to keep you." He looked at Leo. "Blake's weekend curfew is midnight and we expect her home by then."

"I plan to have her back by eleven," Leo said, like he made the rules. He slipped his arm through mine, and as composed as my father had been up until that moment, I saw him bristle at Leo's touch. I carefully extracted myself from the embrace, and Leo didn't push it.

I waved to my parents as we walked toward the car. Leo opened my door, and I thought about Audrey and how we used to make fun of the ridiculous, over-the-top dates the couples took together on *The Bachelor*. I had the fleeting desire to text her and tell her that being the girl on the over-the-top date didn't feel so ridiculous. Now that it was actually happening, it felt kind of amazing.

I slid onto the tan leather seat. There were two steaming cups of coffee in between us, and when Leo climbed in on the opposite side, he said, "I figured you were a milk-and-sugar kind of girl."

I smiled. "Skim?" I asked.

"Obviously," he said.

I thanked him as he backed down our driveway and zoomed down the street. I considered my jeans and flats and then turned to Leo, who was smiling so deviously that for a second I worried he'd say this was all a trick—just a joke that I'd fallen for. But instead, he said, "You look nice," which felt oddly date-like, and even though I knew that was the definition of what we were doing, it didn't really feel like it yet. Or maybe I just didn't want to let myself hope that it was something romantic. I couldn't get a read on this guy: What if this was just more of his typical showmanship? This could all be about doing something cool, not about doing something cool with me.

"I should've changed," I said, gesturing to my T-shirt and then to his oxford and chinos.

"I think you look great," Leo said, turning on the radio.

A DJ announced a Mariah Carey song as the first one in a Top Ten Songs of the Nineties countdown.

"How did you do that with my parents?" I asked. The DJ started singing along with Mariah, missing her high notes by an octave. "That was like a magic show."

Leo adjusted the radio until a DEVI song came on. "Parents aren't that complicated," he said, as moody guitar chords filled the car.

"I'm pretty sure mine are."

He shrugged. "I find that if you just treat adults like you're all on the same playing field, it goes well."

I drummed my fingers on my thigh. "You're pretty confident," I said.

Leo laughed. "Not always," he said, glancing at the manicured lawns racing by. "So do you like Chicago?" he asked.

"I love it," I said.

"Good," Leo said, smiling. He rolled down the car's windows. "I hoped so." The wind attacked us as we picked up speed, and my hair flew behind me like Beyoncé's does in concert. "Have you been to California?" Leo asked, his fingers tapping along with the hard bass of the song.

"No," I said, shaking my head. "But I want to go to LA. Just to see it."

"You'd like it there," he said. He turned to me and grinned. "I can see you in LA."

He sounded genuine, and it made me so happy to hear him say that. "I want to be a TV host," I blurted.

Leo cocked an eyebrow, and for a second I thought he'd

have a reaction like my dad. I'd only ever told my parents, Nic, and Audrey about wanting to do TV. Audrey and Nic both said it was a natural fit.

"Like, your own show?" Leo asked.

"Maybe," I said, feeling less nervous now that he hadn't laughed, or acted weird. "Or just reporting news for stations like MTV or the other ones that do entertainment news. I don't know yet. I haven't really been able to try it. Except for in my bedroom mirror and when I can convince Xander to film me."

"Xander films you in your bedroom?" Leo asked, and I could hear the effort it took to keep his voice neutral.

I tried to hide my smile. "Trust me," I said. "There's nothing sexy about it. I practically have to beg him to do it."

Leo's shoulders relaxed a little. "Maybe I could help you sometime," he said. "I used to do commercials in LA when I was a kid."

"Really?" I asked.

"Really," he said.

"Like for what kind of stuff?" I asked, imagining a little version of Leo singing about toys.

"Soup, cereal, brownie mix," Leo said. "Mostly food. I was a skinny kid. I think I made people want to go out and eat."

I laughed. "Okay then," I said, warmed by how seriously he was taking the whole thing. "Maybe you could help me sometime."

Leo glanced over at me, his hand tapping the wheel

again. "I'd like that," he said. "And you could always take an on-camera class, too."

I looked away from him. It was embarrassing to blame my parents, but it was the truth. "My parents would never let me," I said.

"So don't tell them about it," he said. And then he smiled, like he had an idea. "Maybe you just need to be picked as one of the contestants for *The Pretty App Live*." It surprised me the way the name rolled off his tongue. "Then you could see behind the scenes how TV shows really run," he said.

"Pia Alvarez is going to be hosting that show," I said. "She got her start on a reality show, too, and—"

"I know about Pia Alvarez's career," Leo said. And then he looked sort of embarrassed that he'd said it. "I'm a dork like that," he said, laughing, but he was the least dorky person I knew. He was Justin Timberlake compared to the other guys at Harrison.

"Would you want to be on it?" Leo asked as he coasted the car onto the interstate toward Chicago.

"On the reality show?"

Leo nodded. "I think you'd be good," he said, angling between cars. "You'd cause lots of drama, just like you do at Harrison."

I laughed. "Of course I'd want to be on it," I said. "Who wouldn't?" And then I thought of Audrey. She definitely wouldn't, and I suddenly felt vain for wanting to be on a reality show about prettiness. "I mean, I'm not saying it's the most important thing in the world, or anything like that."

"It's okay to be honest about what you want," Leo said. "If you want to be on a show, you want to be on a show. You don't need to be the cool girl around me."

"I wasn't trying to," I said, but my words sounded untrue.

Leo opened the console between us and pulled out a green pack of gum. He offered me a piece, and when I took one, my fingertips brushed his. He glanced over and smiled, and then he popped a piece into his mouth. "Good," he said, chewing the gum and filling the car with the smell of mint, "because I already like you." His gray eyes sparked with something I couldn't read, and my heart went wild with what he'd said and the way he was looking at me. A smile played on his lips right before he said: "And not just because you're pretty."

chapter eleven

wanted to believe him.

I wanted to believe him so badly that by the time the Chicago skyline came into view, by the time we'd zig-zagged past other drivers for miles and miles, by the time Leo pulled in front of Bubby's Café and Pancake House—I did. I believed him. Totally and completely.

Leo opened my door and offered his hand to help me out of the Mustang. I stood on the sidewalk and took in the blue-and-white tiles framing the door and the diner-style glass windows. Fifties-era red lettering spelled BUBBY'S across the entrance. A chalkboard announced *All-You-Can-Eat Pancakes!* in blue chalk, and a life-size Marilyn Monroe statue stood above a sidewalk grate and blew us a kiss.

I'd been to Chicago so many times, but I'd never seen this place. My dad always took us to boring, stuffy restaurants with starched white napkins and crystal water glasses. And any other ordinary guy who was trying to impress me on a first date would've taken me somewhere predictable, like the Parker House Hotel or some other fancy place. And even though that's what I'd been expecting, as I looked through the glass windows to the diner's red cushioned booths, I felt oddly relieved at Leo's casual choice. I watched him plink quarters into the parking meter, and I felt like I was seeing him differently.

Leo looked up and laughed a little when he saw me staring at him. "I told you your jeans were okay," he said, nodding toward the diner. He smiled, hooking his elbow through mine and guiding me toward the entrance. I felt shivers on my skin where he touched me, and I tried to relax, tried to remind myself that this wasn't a big deal. He was just a guy, and I'd been out with lots of guys before.

Inside the diner, we crossed a black rubber mat and moved toward a freckled hostess with a nametag that read CANDY. The fluorescent lighting made her red hair look like it had caught on fire. She batted her lashes at Leo when he gave our names.

The diner smelled like maple syrup, and it was packed. We backed up next to a row of gumball machines.

"So do all girls love you?" I asked Leo when we were out of earshot of the hostess.

"I don't know," Leo said, playing dumb. "Do they?"

I felt myself blush, so I pretended to be interested in the gumball and plastic-toy machines. "The hostess does," I said teasingly. We both looked back up at the hostess typing away on a keyboard, her fake purple nails clacking against the keys. "She's probably emailing her friends about you right now."

"Or she's finding us a table," Leo said.

"Or uploading a photo of you to her Public Party Crushes Page."

"Let's hack her account and find out," Leo said, grinning.

I knew he was joking, but I shuddered at the reminder that he knew how to do all the same hacking stuff that Audrey did. "Please don't ever break in to my computer," I said, running my fingers over the gumball machine's cold metal dial marked 25 CENTS. A skinny waitress flitted by, and I lowered my voice. "I know all about backdoor access capability from Audrey."

Leo laughed. "Really?" he asked. "Audrey still does that kind of stuff?"

I sniffed. "I wouldn't know."

"Maybe you should be more careful around that girl," he said, his eyes on me.

I shot Leo a questioning look. "What's that supposed to mean?" I knew Audrey way better than he did, and there was nothing to be careful about with Audrey. She could protect you and your secrets better than anyone else in the world. "And I thought you two were friends," I said.

The sun poured through the glass windows onto Leo's shoulders. He suddenly looked uncomfortable standing there with his back pressed against the gumball machine. "We are," he said. "It just seems like it got contentious between the two of you for a while there."

"Yeah, well. Things got complicated between our families when Audrey's dad died," I said, even though it was so much more than that. But I barely knew how to put it into words. I was still reeling from what had happened between Nic and me back then, and when Audrey's dad died it was like she lost patience for the mean stuff I'd started doing. But wasn't that part of high school? Weren't mean girls supposed to rule with an iron fist?

If they think you're weak, you already are, my dad used to say to Nic and me.

I thought of Nic's text about Sara's Ugly Page. And then I thought about Sara crying at school yesterday, and I started to feel queasy.

"I'm talking about the Boyfriend App stuff," Leo said as Fats Domino's "Ain't That a Shame" came on over the juke box.

I raised an eyebrow. Was he really going to bring that up?

Piano chords danced through the restaurant. The old-timey sound made me picture waitresses in the fifties carting around trays of pancakes on roller skates like they did in the framed photographs on the wall.

"I read Public's press releases, Blake," Leo said. "You accused her of stealing the idea for the Boyfriend App from you."

"There were other things at play," I said, bristling.

If Leo wanted to know what I meant, he didn't let on. He just stood there, staring at me, and then the hostess was back, smiling at Leo like a commercial for dental work.

"Right this way," she said, leading us to a booth.

We slid onto the cushioned seats, and Leo changed the topic to a singer named Dave Wanamaker who was coming to play South Bend. "If you've never seen him, you have to," Leo said. He tore the paper off his straw and popped it into his ice water. "There's this one song called 'Loveletter' that will blow you away. His lyrics are amazing, and his band sounds different from anything else out there."

I watched how bright his eyes got as he talked about the music and how his fingers tapped a rhythm on the table like he was drumming along to one of the songs in his head.

"Sounds like you like music almost as much as computers," I said, squeezing a lemon slice into my water and licking my fingertips.

Leo nodded. "Definitely," he said. "Music can take you to another place. You can be in one kind of mood, and then you turn on a certain song and you feel totally different." He ran his thumb over the spiral that bound the thick menu. "What gets you like that?"

I took a sip of my water. "I don't know," I said truthfully. "I guess, in my house, there's only one mood, and it's usually the one my dad's in. The rest of us just kind of stay out of his way."

I'd said it quickly and without much thought. But as the truth of what I'd said sunk in, I felt indescribably sad.

Leo considered me carefully. "That doesn't seem very fair."

"It doesn't, does it? But now that he wants to get into

politics, we're all on an even tighter rein. I overheard him tell my mom that he needs to rehab mine and Nic's images if we're going to be a proper political family. He wants us to be his golden daughters or something."

Leo shook his head. "Have you thought about what it will be like this fall, when you're free of him?"

I wished it would be that easy. "I don't think I'll ever be free of him," I said. "At least, not in college." And then I said aloud a feeling I'd had for a long time, one that I'd never given words to. "Notre Dame is an amazing school, but I'll still be under my father's eye there. He lives five minutes away from campus, and he knows everyone. He'll be monitoring what I do there, especially if he gets elected." Anxiety shot through my body, and I felt my throat tighten with every breath. "I wouldn't even have gotten accepted without his legacy there. It's like there's no escaping him, no matter what I do."

"What if you just didn't go to college?" Leo asked. He pinched his straw and jabbed at his ice cubes.

I laughed. I couldn't help it. It was so outrageous that I couldn't even imagine what my parents would do if I suggested it. "Yeah, right," I said. "What about you?" I asked. "Where do you want to go for college?"

Leo shrugged. "Nowhere as of now," he said. "I might take a few more years off from school."

"A few more years off?" I repeated, unsure of what he meant. "Have you already—"

"I just mean I need some time to think about what I

want," Leo said quickly.

"Ready to order?" A waitress approached our table with a notepad, and I realized we'd never even opened our menus.

"What sounds good to you?" he asked me.

"Pancakes with bananas and whipped cream," I said. It was what I always ordered at the pancake house in South Bend. A sure bet.

"We'll have two coffees with skim milk and two orders of pancakes with bananas and whipped cream," Leo told the waitress.

I smiled, feeling my anxiety melt a little. "We were fine when I was younger," I told Leo when the waitress left. I pushed the long sleeves of my gray top over my elbows. My thin gold bangles jangled together with a soft clinking sound. "My dad and I, I mean." I was surprised by how much I wanted to talk about things with someone I barely knew, but in some ways, that made it easier. Leo hadn't known me for years, like the rest of the kids at school. And something about him made me feel like he wasn't going to hold anything against me.

Leo folded his hands on the table and waited for me to go on.

"It's almost like it would've been easier for him if I could've just stayed that way forever," I said. "Young and pretty and quiet and perfect. That's all he's ever really wanted for me: to be a pretty little obedient girl. But I couldn't always be that. It was like when I became a teenager, I suddenly became flawed and capable of embarrassing him, and now he can hardly stand to be in the same room as me."

"It doesn't have anything to do with you," Leo said.

I tilted my chin, unsure of how that could be possible.

"It's his own shit," Leo said, running a hand over his jaw. "He's the one putting that crap into your relationship, not you. You'll always love each other, but he's f-ing up the relationship with his baggage. He may or may not learn that, but it's not your responsibility to fix him."

He sounded like a teenage Trog version of Deepak Chopra, but he also sounded right. "How do you know stuff like that?" I asked him.

A smile spread over his smooth skin. "I'm from California, remember?" he said. "We take personal growth workshops before we're in pre-K."

I laughed. He was catching me unaware, and that hadn't happened in a while. Everything in my relationship with Xander had followed a routine course. There was the lunchroom together, passing notes between classes, dates, make-outs. After a while, it all got a little boring. Something told me being with Leo would never, ever get boring.

"What are you thinking about?" Leo asked.

I felt myself redden, so I changed the topic back to California and we talked a little about Leo's favorite places in LA for a while, until a waitress came and set down our pancakes.

Leo cut a slice of pancake even bigger than the one I

did. He dipped it in whipped cream and held it up close to mine. "Cheers," he said, knocking them together. "To our day in Chicago."

"To our day in Chicago," I said as we locked eyes.

Leo let out a laugh. "And to people who surprise you," he said, smiling that wide smile, his gray eyes bright.

chapter twelve

"So what about your parents?" I asked Leo when we were back in the car, speeding past the Art Institute.

"Divorced," he said.

The sun glinted on the car, and I reached for my sunglasses. "And that's why you moved?"

A funny look crossed Leo's face—something between embarrassment and impatience—but it was hard to tell if it was because of what I'd asked, or because of the drivers careening into our lane and making it hard for Leo to exit. My hair whipped across my face as Leo took a tight turn and cut off a silver BMW. The driver flipped us the bird and yelled something that sounded like: *"Kids!"*

We cruised into a garage across from Millennium Park. Leo got our ticket, and we didn't say anything else until we were out of the garage and crossing the street.

"I know it's a little cornball, but I wanted to do touristy

things with you," Leo said as we walked into the entrance of the Lurie Garden.

"It's not corny," I said. "This is one of my favorite places." My eyes swept across the urban oasis, the acres of garden flowers and greenery smack in the middle of downtown Chicago. I looked at Leo and saw that he was smiling.

Our feet padded along the wooden planks lining the walkway past a cluster of dark purple tulips. I breathed in the thick smell of grass and flowers. Two girls who looked like art students sat on the walkway with their sketchpads, each one making her own rendition of the tulips.

"My parents split when I was little," Leo finally said. He opened his dark leather wallet and put the parking ticket inside. "My dad was a hippie."

"Your dad was a hippie?" I asked, as we moved across a boardwalk that took us over stepped pools and five feet of exposed water.

"Yeah. Not a sixties hippie. A wannabe hippie. It was weird," Leo said, laughing. He stuck his hands deep into the pockets of his chinos. "Now he sells insurance."

I wanted to take Leo's arm and lead him down to the step closest to the water. I just wanted to sit next to him, stare into the glistening pool, and listen to him talk. But I was too nervous to touch him. This all felt so perfect, and I worried I could somehow ruin it. I'd never felt so unsure of myself, or like every little detail mattered, and it scared me to think that someone I barely knew could make me feel this way.

We walked quietly past white daffodils and bright green

wild ginger. I liked how we didn't need to fill the silence between us, and I liked how when we did speak to each other, what we said had substance. It made me think of how often I just chattered away at Harrison with Xander and my friends: how often I talked without really connecting to anyone. Something about Leo's interest in me still felt a little off, but I couldn't put my finger on it. Maybe I was just being paranoid, or maybe I wasn't used to someone like him. He felt different.

"So you live with your mom?" I asked. I stopped next to a patch of violet aster flowers and traced the thin, triangular petals.

Leo nodded, not meeting my glance. His hand grazed the flowers carefully, like they might break with his touch.

"And what about her—what does she do?"

"She doesn't work anymore," Leo said when we started walking again.

"So then why did you move to South Bend?" I felt nosy asking, but I really wanted to know. "And don't you miss your friends?"

Leo shrugged. "It was just time for a change, I guess," he said.

That was his mom's reason for moving from California to South Bend? I wanted to press him, but I didn't. Families were complicated: Maybe there was something he wasn't ready to tell me yet.

The early spring sun was bright as we walked along the Seam, the corridor between the light and dark sections. They were called plates, and they were like two different worlds of the garden. The Dark Plate was filled with lush vegetation set free to grow wild and unrestrained. It made for a dramatic contrast with the Light Plate, which was filled with bright, controlled landscaping. Last year I tried to write a paper on the Garden, focusing on the plates and the West Hedge, a topiary that told the Greek story of the nymph who escaped from Apollo by becoming a laurel tree. But I couldn't get into words the way the garden made me feel, the way it took me into its care and ushered me through the four seasons of change like we had a relationship all our own. I got a C on that paper. It made me never want to write about anything meaningful to me again.

"Does it bother you that I'm not smart?" I asked Leo.

It came out quickly, and I couldn't look at Leo after I'd said it. Still, I felt him turn to me. He stopped walking, but I couldn't. I walked ahead on the Seam and left him standing there.

"Blake?" he called. I heard his feet clap the wood as he closed the distance between us. Then, more urgently, he said, "*Blake.*"

He grabbed my hand and I whirled to face him. I stared into his steel-gray eyes, searching for my answer there, but I couldn't find it. I hardly recognized his face so still and hard.

"There are a lot of different kinds of *smart*," he said, his hand warm around mine.

I was suddenly very okay with how close we were and how it felt to have him touching me.

"You're still in high school," he said. He cleared his

throat. "*We're* still in high school." His grip tightened. I didn't want him to let me go. "So you only know about *high school smart*," he said, "which is how you do on tests, which is totally different from all of the other kinds of smarts there are out in the real world."

I nodded slowly. A part of me knew he was right—I could feel it, especially here, in the garden, in Chicago, far away from Harrison and my father and my world in South Bend.

Leo lowered his voice. "You just need to think about what you want to be, *who* you want to be." His hand dropped mine and he stepped closer, gently taking my arms in his grip. "Don't take this the wrong way, okay?" he said. "But I don't really get the impression that you even like who you are. At least, not the person you are at school."

I swallowed the lump in my throat. My eyes started blinking fast, and I knew I was a breath away from tears. "But this is who I am," I said, my voice rasping over the words. "I've been this way for so long." And I could go on being this way for so much longer if that's what I wanted. I could go to Notre Dame in the fall and be the beautiful, bitchy ice queen for four more years.

Leo shook his head. "Then why are you so different today, here with me, when we're all alone?"

He'd put his finger on something I couldn't name. Today with Leo, far away from school, I was the way I used to be with Audrey when we were alone in her room, or the way I used to be with Nic when we were younger. I was unguarded. I was softer. I was kind, even. And I felt *free.* I wasn't worried about what anyone thought about me, and I wasn't hanging on so tightly to my place at school.

"I used to be different," I said, my voice still rough. "I used to be normal. And kind."

"Normal's overrated," Leo said. "But kind isn't." He nudged a pebble on the Seam with his shiny brown shoe. And then he pulled me so close I could smell his sweet and salty boy smell. "Change back," he said softly.

I suddenly felt exhausted. I wasn't even sure how we'd gotten to this place, to this conversation. I wanted to lean my head against Leo's chest and close my eyes. But instead I pulled back and looked into his face. "Why do you care?" I asked.

Leo smiled, but he didn't answer, so I pressed him. "I mean it," I said. "You barely know me."

He loosened his grip on my body, which was the last thing I wanted. "I guess there's something about you," he said. He gave me a small shrug, and then kicked at the stone again. "You kind of remind me of how I used to be. I used to care so much about being the best programmer that I would've done anything to outshine everyone I programmed with—even stuff I shouldn't have. I did do some of that stuff, and I got into trouble." He ran a hand through his light hair. "There were these people who got me out of it, and I'm trying to be better."

A shadow passed over us as the sun ducked behind dove-white clouds. I didn't completely understand what he was trying to tell me.

Leo gave me a long look, almost like he wasn't sure how far he wanted to take this with me. But then he let out a breath and started talking. "I was in *a lot* of trouble," he said. "I was only fifteen—still a kid, really—but doing stuff I wasn't supposed to be doing. They found out, and they didn't report me."

I nodded. I didn't ask him what he'd done—I didn't need to know. If he wanted to tell me, he would.

"Maybe we can be each other's clean slate," I said. If Leo could change, why couldn't I?

Leo grinned. "Clean slate," he said, nodding. "I like that." But then the grin disappeared. He lowered his voice as a group of elementary school kids wearing neon-yellow T-shirts paraded past us along the Seam. "There are things I should still tell you," he said. "I mean, maybe not now. But at some point. If we keep hanging out."

If we keep hanging out. I loved the sound of it. I wanted to memorize the way he said it, the way it felt to hear the words pour out of him.

Leo held my hand all the way through Millennium Park until we were face-to-face with the Bean.

"Whoa," Leo said. He took in the enormous silver sculpture and nodded appreciatively, checking out the buildings and people reflected on the surface. "All the surfaces must be convex," he said.

He looked over at me and I giggled. "What?" he asked.

"That was cute and dorky," I said.

"Oh, I'm a dork all right," he said, laughing. He grabbed my waist and pulled me close. "And I plan to dorkify the coolest girl in school," he said. He leaned in to whisper, "That would be you."

His lips brushed my cheek and I shivered.

Tourists sidled next to us, raising their cameras to snap photos and calling to each other in languages I didn't recognize.

"Let's go under," I said. I took Leo's hand and guided him beneath the cavernous stomach of the sculpture, where it was a lot less crowded. Even in the small space, with him, I didn't feel anxious. I looked up and saw Leo and me reflected in the Bean's glossy surface, our reflections warped. The sculpture made me short and round. The angles in my face were all but lost, and I looked like some kind of blob. I wanted to look away, but I couldn't—I couldn't stop staring at the alternate version of myself. I saw Leo reflected, too, and the way he stared back at me in the mirror, smiling at our foreign alter egos. We were barely recognizable. If I'd been born this way, my life would've been entirely different, which made it all seem like a total crapshoot. Something so random as genes could make or break your social experience and how other people treated you. Did it have to be this way? Did it stop being this way after high school? After college? Ever?

Our heads were still tilted up, both of us staring into the sculpture, when Leo traced the distorted outline of my face. He was touching my real skin, but we were both watching his hands move over my warped skin in the mirrored reflection. I watched as he inched forward, bent down, and covered my lips with his. And then my eyes closed, and I suddenly didn't care which version of me Leo was kissing. My heart went wild as his mouth opened, warm on mine as he pressed his body against me.

"Leo," I said softly when he pulled away a few manic heartbeats later. I opened my eyes and let my gaze settle on his full mouth. I touched the blond stubble on his jaw and looked into his eyes, seeing shades of blue-gray come to life as he stared back at me.

Schoolchildren paraded beneath the sculpture and chattered away, pointing at their reflections and taking photos, but Leo and I never once broke our stare, not until the kids marched out the other side and left us alone, not until Leo smiled one of his small smiles, different from the others I'd seen, and leaned forward and kissed me again and again and again, until everything around me quieted and the only thing I could feel was us.

chapter thirteen

At the hole-in-the-wall, incredibly adorable restaurant that Leo picked for dinner, we rehashed every detail of our day. I tried to let everything sink in, but a part of me still couldn't believe this was happening. I couldn't stop thinking about our kiss. I couldn't stop thinking about the way Leo's mouth had opened against mine, the way his breathing got just a little heavier as we moved to fit into each other's curves. And even though I hadn't thought about school yet that entire day, I suddenly wondered what it was going to be like at Harrison on Monday. Were we going to pretend like nothing had happened this weekend? Or were we going to act like we were seeing each other? *Were* we seeing each other?

Leo seemed almost as nervous as me: It was like the confident Leo I'd gotten used to was gone. We were quiet for a few moments, spreading butter onto warm pieces of bread. When Leo looked up at me, I thought he was going to say something serious. But then he asked, "So does your uncle the principal wear a toupee?"

I giggled. "That's actually his real hair."

"Really?" Leo asked, shaking his head. "That's some seriously funky hair."

We laughed, and then Leo glanced down at the hand-printed menu. There were only twelve tables in the entire restaurant. Two waiters wearing flannel shirts moved silently, filling water glasses and announcing the specials with lilting French accents. A twentysomething girl with dark flowing hair DJ'd at a booth in the corner, and the air smelled sweet, like dessert.

"Do you speak French?" Leo asked as we read over the list of food. There were no translations on the menu.

I shook my head. "If you ask Mrs. Betts, I barely speak English."

"I have her, too," Leo said, laughing, "and she doesn't like me, either. And what's up with the amount of reading she assigns? Does she do that for the seniors, too? I couldn't even do it if I was trying."

"I thought Trogs always tried in school," I said.

Leo shrugged. "Maybe in some subjects," he said. He busied himself in the bread basket, and I looked down at my menu.

"I'm gonna guess that *soupe* means soup," I said, pointing to the page.

"And *champagne* means champagne," Leo said, smiling as he looked over the wine and beer list. "I'm not going to drink," he said, tapping the keys in his pocket like that was the only reason, like it wouldn't be a big deal to show a fake ID if he got carded. It made me wonder what his life was like back in California. Did he go out to eat all the time and drink wine whenever he felt like it? "But do you want something?" he asked.

I shook my head. I wanted to remember everything about tonight. "Just a Coke."

"You're as wild as everyone's told me," Leo said.

I pointed my bread at him. "No more of that. No more listening to what other people say about me. Clean slate, remember?"

"Fair enough," Leo said, and then the waiter came and took our order.

When he left, I leaned back in my seat and stared out the window at the cars zooming past and the people strolling the street.

"Maybe you'll get picked for the reality show, and then you'll get your chance to go to LA," Leo said, taking a sip of his water.

I smiled. "There are thousands of girls to choose from. Though I appreciate your vote of confidence."

"You never know," Leo said. He traced the jagged edge of his knife against his index finger. "You said before that you'd want it." He looked up at me. "But are you sure you mean that? You know how reality TV is, how they cut and edit to make people look a certain way. It's not exactly flattering most of the time." He held my glance like he was trying to tell me something important.

He was probably right. But we were playing make-believe anyway, and it wasn't like he could grant my wish, so instead of agreeing with him, I said, "Yeah, but like *you* said, I'd get to see what Hollywood is really like. So yeah, I'd do it." I met Leo's gaze. "I'd want it."

He glanced away from me. "If that's what you really want," he said.

That night, on the drive home under an inky, cloudless sky full of stars, I wondered if everything that had happened today was too good to be true. I'd never felt like this before—not even about Xander in the beginning. I felt like I had something special, something all my own, something that could take me away from my regular life and the pain I sometimes felt living it. I felt like I had someone who could help me change and who could take away the fear of what that change meant. And maybe it was just one day, and maybe I was getting my hopes up way too far, but if I just wanted it enough, maybe it could be true.

Leo and I were quiet for most of the ride back to South Bend. There were so many things I wanted to ask him, so many things I wanted to know about him, but I reminded myself that we had time. I didn't need everything answered tonight.

In front of my house, Leo turned off the ignition. He walked me to the front door, and everything felt different standing there with him. I didn't have the scared feeling I usually felt when I was standing outside of our house, wondering what was waiting for me inside.

Leo leaned forward and his lips brushed mine gently, but then he pulled back. I'd had guys try to kiss me—*really* kiss me—on the front step before. But it was like Leo knew I'd be too nervous to kiss so close to my house. Instead, he gestured toward my bag. "Can I put my number in your phone?" he asked, looking sheepish and flushed even in the darkness.

I nodded, too happy to say anything as I handed it over. Leo typed in his number, and then the phone buzzed. "Nic's your sister, right?" he asked as he passed it back.

Can you come to campus? I need you.

I stared at the text, rereading it to make sure I was seeing it right. I hadn't heard from Nic since yesterday afternoon, when she chewed me out over text about Sara Oaks.

Nerves filled me as my fingers tapped the screen.

I'll be there.

"Everything okay?" Leo asked.

I put my phone into my pocket. "I don't know," I said.

Leo nodded and took my hand. The last thing I wanted was to cut our date short, but there wasn't another option. Nic hadn't needed me in a very long time. I couldn't imagine what it was about.

"I need to go," I said to Leo.

"Do you want me to come with you?"

I shook my head. "I should go by myself. My sister needs me." Pride crept into the words as I said them. There used to be a time when all we needed was each other, and I remembered how good it felt. "And I still have a few hours before my curfew," I told Leo. "I'll text my dad where I'm

115

going so he doesn't think I'm out late with you."

"I'm not afraid of your dad," Leo said.

"Oh," I said. Really? "That must be nice."

Leo smiled at first, but then his face got serious. "You're the one who scares me," he said.

"What's that supposed to mean?" I asked, my voice gentle.

Leo's eyes went down to the stone porch, and when he looked back at me, I read real concern playing on his face, something I'd never seen there before. "Leo," I said softly.

He took a long breath, and then he said, "I'm worried you'll get to know more about me, and maybe you won't like what you find out."

"Do you know the things I've done?" I asked. "Do you know how I got my reputation?" I tried to smile to make him feel better, but nothing felt very funny.

"But this is different," Leo said. "I—"

I kissed him. I didn't need to know—not right then, not that night, and not after the most perfect day of my entire life. What I needed was Leo, no matter what stupid computer things he'd done a couple of years ago.

Our lips were warm pressed together as the night air swirled around us. Leo's mouth was hungry on mine, and I felt the unmistakable tug of my feelings for him making me want to be even closer, making me forget every reason I had to hold back. His hands went into my hair, and I felt lost in the kiss, like there was nothing else that mattered.

"Blake," Leo said against my lips. He pulled away but left his hands in my hair. "I didn't expect today to be so . . ."

My palms were pressed against his chest, and I watched as he looked away, nervous. "Perfect," I said softly. "Me neither." The wind howled through the trees, catching the leaves and making them dance. "And I want to stay with you," I said, letting my arms fall to my side, trying to find the willpower to pull away. "But I have to go to Nic."

Leo nodded, and I could tell he understood.

"You'll call if you need me?" he asked.

"I promise," I said. And then I squeezed his hand and made my way to my car. I watched in the rearview mirror as Leo backed down the driveway. Moonlight caught his hair as he sped down the street, and I had the distinct feeling that everything—including me—had changed.

chapter fourteen

" I 'm here to see my sister, Nicole Dawkins," I told the stern-faced woman in a Notre Dame guard's uniform twenty minutes later. "She lives in Lewis Hall?" I said, hating the way my voice went question-y when I got nervous around adults. I rolled down my car window a few more inches and smiled. The white-haired woman sat behind a pane of glass at one of the entrances to Notre Dame. She had the same pinched look Joanna once had when she got a UTI, so I pretty much figured there was no way she was letting me on campus. I gave it one last try, gesturing to the plastic bag next to me. "She's not feeling well, so I'm bringing her favorite soup?" I'd stopped to pick up butternut squash soup and ginger candy. The combination used to pull Nic out of any funk.

The woman frowned, but she wrote me a parking pass and opened the gate. "Go on ahead," she said.

I drove slowly along the winding road toward Nic's dorm. A cluster of students jogged along the sidewalk in spandex and reflective Windbreakers. Night was my favorite time to visit Notre Dame. Kids were up and walking the campus, holding textbooks or listening to music. It made me feel like there was a whole different life at college, like there were too many good reasons not to sleep.

The lake to my right was as black as midnight, and the sky was filled with stars. I loved this campus. No matter how much I associated Notre Dame with my dad, I also associated it with the memories I'd made here the countless times I'd come with Audrey and her dad. I couldn't believe I was going to be here in the fall. It felt surreal.

I passed the brick health center and took a left into the cul-de-sac in front of Nic's dorm, a yellow-and-brown building built in the 1960s. I parked, careful to balance the hot soup and the small, violet-colored notebook I always kept in the glove compartment. The notebook held a screenplay called *Our Dog Greta* that Nic had written for me to act in when we were ten and six. I'd kept it close to me since then, flipping through it every once in a while. I thought seeing it might cheer her up.

Inside Lewis Hall, I crossed the blue-gray carpet and tapped the elevator button, nervous as I rode to the third floor. The doors clanked open to bulletin boards tacked with flyers for upcoming dances and fund-raisers, and support group meetings for students with eating disorders. I stepped closer to study a poster that read STEALING BEAUTY: AN ORIGINAL PLAY BY NICOLE DAWKINS. I got goose bumps looking over the graphics: a girl danced alone in front of a mirror, and the look on her face was sad and faraway. Sometimes I felt like going to Nic's plays was the only way I'd gained real entry into her life during the past four years. I was memorizing the performance dates when a girl with wet hair opened the door to the bathroom and nearly crashed into me. "Oh my God, you scared me!" she said, giggling. She wore a fluffy yellow towel and smelled like a banana.

"Sorry," I mumbled, moving to the side so she could pass with her shower caddy jam-packed with lotions and shower gels.

I walked slowly down the narrow hallway. Purple, green, and blue marker messages were scrawled on the dry-erase boards hanging on the dorm doors. *Breakfast tmrow at 7?* . . . *Ur mom called* . . . *Irish Connection tonight at 11.* One cracked me up: *Shmegan*, it read. *When you're back from doing this:* (the girl had drawn a boy and girl making out) *call me! Love, Dish.*

Maybe things didn't have to be the same here. Maybe I could make a whole new life for myself at Notre Dame. I could be someone different from the person I was at Harrison, different from the person I was in my dad's house. Just thinking about it felt good, like drinking cold water when you're sweating at a football tailgate in August.

I stopped in front of room 319. NICOLE DAWKINS, the tag of paper announced. I knocked and took a few deep breaths before the door swung open.

My hand flew to cover my mouth when I saw her; I

couldn't help it. Nic's eyes were bloodshot, the skin beneath them puffy like marshmallows. Tears streaked her face, and her dark hair was stringy like she hadn't showered in days. "Oh, Nic," I said. I was inside her room with my arms around her before I could think twice. It'd been so long since we'd hugged—but the weight of her tiny body felt so familiar to me, the way her shoulders curved just right for me to rest my cheek on them.

"What happened?" I asked. "Are you all right?"

Nic pulled back and shook her head. "There's this video," she said. "And now it's up on a blog. And I need you to get Audrey here *now* to help us get it down." Her words were fast, almost frantic. "I'll explain everything to you—I promise. But please, Blake, please. I know you're not friends with her anymore. But we need her."

I started to protest—little sounds escaping me in whispers—but what else could I do? How could I say no to Nic?

"Okay," I said, fingers trembling as I pulled out my phone. A video of *what*? What had she done?

I scrolled through my phone—I'd never been able to bring myself to delete Audrey's number. I pressed it against my ear and listened to her line ring and ring. I was about to give up when I heard her soft voice on the other end. "Blake?" she said, and I wondered if that meant she hadn't deleted my number, either.

I cleared my throat. "I need your help," I said quickly. "Please." I didn't want her to think this was some kind of trick, so I passed the phone to Nic. Audrey had idolized

Nic when we were younger, and she was hurt, too, when we were thirteen and Nic changed.

My sister spoke in a hushed voice that verged on begging. Audrey had the biggest heart of anyone I'd ever known, except maybe her own dad. I knew she'd come.

Nic thanked Audrey, her voice choked with tears, and hung up. She gestured to her unmade bed, and I sat. I placed the soup on a nightstand and put the journal on the corner of Nic's bed. Her light blue comforter was covered in tiny purple stars, and fluffy white pillows lined the wall next to Elmer, the lime-green Uglydoll with which she'd never been able to part. A poster of Leonardo DiCaprio in *The Great Gatsby* hung next to a framed *Scarface* script signed by Al Pacino.

Nic stared at her wooden desk chair and then at the bed, like she was deciding where to sit. When she finally chose the bed, she took Elmer into her lap and fidgeted with the torn blue pants he wore. The doll was as familiar to me as my own hands. She'd had him since I was five.

I pulled the comforter over my legs, suddenly nervous. I wasn't sure what she was about to tell me, and I wanted to say the right things. I wanted her to know I was here for her no matter what she'd done.

Nic's tears came again as she moved her hands over the Uglydoll. "This is hard to say," she said. "And I've wanted to talk to you about it for so long."

"It's okay, Nic," I said, "whatever it is, it's okay."

Nic sniffed and let go of a long breath. "Do you remember Samantha Cavelli? She went to Harrison three years ahead of you, and now she goes here?"

I nodded. I wasn't sure whether or not to mention that I'd seen them together arguing in the mall. I wanted to, but I figured it was better to just let Nic talk.

Nic's eyes went back to the Uglydoll. She ran her fingers over the thing's worn lime-green fur, tracing a path along his arm and neck. She took a breath. "Samantha is my girlfriend," she said in a soft voice.

"Okay," I said, nodding, letting it sink in and waiting for her to tell me more. I was surprised, but in a way it made sense; my sister had always really valued her relationships with girls in a different way from guys. She'd dated a few guys in high school, but it was like she'd connected to girls more or something. So I wasn't super shocked, and in that moment, I was just waiting for her to get to whatever bad thing she'd done that someone had gotten on video.

Nic looked up. She tilted her chin. "*Okay?*" she repeated.

"Yes," I said, again not getting it, and Nic started laughing a shy kind of laugh I'd never heard from her before.

"I just told you I'm gay, Blake."

"Yeah, I know that's what *girlfriend* means," I said, suddenly smiling, too. "But what's the bad news?"

An incredulous look passed over Nic's face. "You don't—you're totally fine with it?"

"Fine with you being gay? Of course I'm fine with you being gay," I said. "Is that what you were worried about telling me?"

Nic practically jumped across the bed. She threw her arms around me and held me tighter than she ever had. She

123

pulled away, her hands still holding my shoulders. She was grinning, and even with her tear-streaked face, she looked like she was going to be okay. "Thank you, Blake," she said. "Thank you, thank you."

"I didn't even do anything," I said, but just then there was a knock on the door. Audrey must have been right by campus. Nic and I looked at each other. "I'll get it," I said. I grabbed a box of tissues from Nic's desk and handed them to her. I crossed the room and opened the door to see Audrey standing there with her hands in the pockets of her skinny jeans and a worried look on her pale, makeup-free face. She wore a black hoodie and scuffed-up pink-and-black-checkered Vans. Her green eyes searched mine, but I didn't know what to say. "Thanks for coming," I finally said. I wasn't really sure how to talk to her, and something told me she felt the same way. How could two people go from being best friends to this?

Audrey stepped inside, closing the door behind us and clicking the lock. Nic stood and clasped her hands together like she was about to make a speech. She looked petrified. "Thanks, Audrey," she said quickly. "Um. It's over here. I mean, the video," she said, gesturing to the computer.

Audrey and I followed her across the navy rug, and the three of us stood awkwardly in front of the laptop. "I'll sit," Nic said, her nervousness palpable as she yanked out the chair. She sucked in a breath, and then typed in a web address, pulling up a blog. It looked pretty amateur, with neon colors at the top spelling out *Notre Dame Night Life* and a picture of the famous golden dome on the left side.

In the center were blog posts. On the right were video clips lined up with captions beneath them like *Keg Stand Championship.*

"No one even knows who runs this thing," Nic said. "There's an email address where you can send in videos from parties, and if they're funny—or scandalous—they usually get posted." Nic scrolled down to a freeze-framed video showing her and Samantha sitting on the wooden swing outside Nic's dorm. "I don't even know who took it, but someone posted this," Nic said, her voice breaking. "And I tried writing to the email address a thousand times tonight, asking whoever runs the site to take it down, but they won't."

She looked up at me. "A lot of kids at school already know about Samantha and me. But if Dad's people see this video, he's going to be dead politically. I want him to know that we're together, but not this way. Not till after the election." Her dark eyes were wide with fear, and I felt my heart clench with everything I knew my parents would do to her.

Nic turned back to the computer and pressed the triangular play button. The video showed Samantha taking Nic's hand on the swing. Nic put her head on Samantha's shoulder, and then Nic lifted her chin, and they kissed each other. The video stopped a few seconds later, midkiss.

It's not like it was anything too passionate, but it was intimate, and anyone who watched the video—including my parents—would know they were together.

Nic put her head in her hands and started crying, sobs shaking her tiny shoulders.

Audrey ran her hand over my sister's back. Her hip brushed mine as she moved closer to Nic, and for the first time in a while I didn't stiffen at her nearness. "Nic," Audrey said gently. When my sister didn't look up, Audrey knelt down so they were eye level. "Let Blake take care of you," she said. Then she gestured to Nic's seat. "And let me take care of this."

Nic stood, nodding. "Thank you," she said, wiping her face with the back of her hands.

I guided Nic to the bed. We both sat facing Audrey, and I put my arm around my sister's shoulders. Audrey's fingers flew across the keys.

We were silent, watching her. I'd seen her program so many times, and I could tell by her body language that something was wrong. She was hunched over the computer, eyes narrowed. Her fists had balled above the keyboard.

"I can't do this," she said matter-of-factly. She whirled around and faced us. "The video optimization program is written in C code. I can crash this server with a denial-of-service attack, but that won't stop the blogger from reposting the video once it's back up."

Nic stared back and forth between Audrey and me. "So what do we do?" she asked, her voice rising with panic.

"We should call Leo," Audrey said, her eyes on me. "It'll be a breeze for him. Trust me."

"Who's Leo?" Nic asked.

I felt my cheeks go pink as Nic turned to stare at me. "*Blake?*" she said as she read everything written on my face.

"Leo is this new guy at school," I started. She'd just been so honest with me. How could I not tell her every-thing? "And I . . . really, *really* like him."

Audrey's eyebrows shot up. Maybe she knew I had a crush, but I don't think she realized I felt like that. "What happened today?" Audrey asked, her body arching forward in the chair.

"You saw him today?" Nic asked. "Like on a date?

I nodded. "In Chicago," I said, my voice nervous.

"He took you to *Chicago* for the date?" Audrey asked, her eyes wide.

I told them yes, and my stomach went wild and flut-tery just thinking about it. And sitting there talking with Audrey and Nic like this felt like we'd been transported five years back in time. I felt a little wary, but mostly safe.

"It was perfect," I said. They were both staring at me, waiting for me to go on, but I didn't really know what to say, how to describe it. I didn't have Nic's way with words. "I just . . . I feel like he gets me."

Nic was smiling, despite everything, but Audrey almost looked worried. "Maybe you should be the one to call him, then," Nic said. Then she elbowed me gently. "If you're, like, his lover or something," she teased.

I laughed, but Audrey didn't. I scrolled through my con-tacts. I smiled when I saw how Leo had entered his name in my phone: *Leo Trog Bauer*. His line rang a few times before he finally picked up. "Hello?" he said gruffly, in an unfriendly voice that caught me off guard. But then I real-ized he wouldn't recognize my number—I hadn't called his phone yet. "Leo? It's me," I said. And then, nervous, I added, "Blake."

"Hey," he said quickly, his voice changing to the one I recognized. "Everything okay with your sister?"

"Not exactly," I said. "Someone posted this video of her, and she needs it taken down as soon as possible. Audrey's here."

"Audrey's there?" Leo asked, like that was the important part.

"Yeah," I said, wondering what the big deal was. Maybe he was shocked that we were coexisting in the same room. "She says she can't figure out how to get the video down, but that you might."

"Text me the address," Leo said. "I'm on my way."

chapter fifteen

"I tried to tell Mom and Dad during senior year," Nic said a few minutes later. Audrey and I were sitting next to her in the bed. "But they have no idea Samantha and I are still together."

"Senior year in *high school*?" I asked. "You knew then?"

Nic nodded, and I tried not to let on how hurt I was that she'd kept this from me for so long. "You were only thirteen, Blake," Nic said, and I knew she'd already sensed how I felt. "I wasn't ready to tell you, and I wasn't sure you'd understand yet. And then after Mom and Dad's reaction, I was sure I could never tell anyone again."

"What did they do?" Audrey asked, tucking her skinny legs beneath her butt. If anyone knew what my parents were capable of besides Nic and me, it was Audrey.

"Oh, God," Nic said, shaking her head. She looked pained. "They said it wasn't right, that it wasn't *natural*, and that I was never to see Samantha again. I tried to explain how much I loved her and how it wasn't anything to be ashamed of, how they didn't understand what we had, our bond."

As Nic spoke, my mind flashed back to the list I'd found on the notebook pages:

Reasons

We love each other

Mom and Dad will never understand, they don't feel what I do

It was all about Samantha, and the reasons they should be able to be together. I'd been so focused on everything between Nic and me that I never imagined the list could be about another girl. I thought back to that year—how angry and hurt Nic had seemed, how she'd suddenly just turned away from all of us, like we were her enemies. I was only thirteen, and maybe I couldn't have helped her, but I wished she'd given me the chance. Instead, she'd been hurting all by herself, and so had I.

"I wish you'd told me," I said. I didn't want to make it about me, but I had to say something.

"I know, Blake," Nic said gently. "But it was all so bad—and it's *still* so bad with Mom and Dad—that I just needed space from our family."

"Can't we at least try?" I asked. "We could survive them with each other."

Nic was quiet, and then Audrey cleared her throat. "Everything that happened to me would've been so much easier if I'd had a sister," she said. She said it like it was the truest thing in the world, like it was something we should've realized a long time ago, something we never should have let slip away.

Nic took a breath. She looked from Audrey to me, and then her gaze held mine. "We can try," she said. "But you need to quit some of the stuff you pull at Harrison. I get that you hurt people because you feel like crap about your own life, but you still need to stop."

What was it with today? "You sound like Leo," I said, a little embarrassed that she was saying this kind of stuff in front of Audrey.

"I'm serious," Nic said. "Now I know what it's like to be the one getting bullied. I went from being the queen bee at Harrison to the gay girl. Kids are better to each other in college, but there's still some of it," she said.

Guilt and sadness poured through me. The thought of anyone making fun of my sister made my stomach turn. Tears started again, spilling over my lashes.

"Okay, okay," I said. "I promise."

Audrey squeezed my hand. And then she elbowed me gently. "I think you're becoming a softie or something," she said.

"*Never*," I said with extra attitude, and even Nic laughed.

I wasn't sure what was happening to me, and it's not like I really believed in signs from the universe, but it did seem like someone or something was nudging me forward.

"Does Samantha know about the video?" I asked. "Is she worried?"

Nic nodded. "We knew someone took a video or a picture or something that night, but we didn't recognize the kid, and then he ran away. Sam's been terrified for days. Her parents aren't psycho narcissists like ours, but no one's ever come out in her family, so she doesn't know what it will be like, and plus she's the only daughter, and her mom makes her watch things like *Say Yes to the Dress*. And Sam's embarrassed about the video, too, and that's the worst part. This isn't how we wanted to tell the world. We haven't stopped fighting."

"I saw you in the mall," I blurted. "With Samantha. I don't want you to think I was spying. And I left right away when I realized you were having an argument with her. I didn't know anything about your relationship."

There, I'd said it. *Honesty*: Something new for me.

Audrey looked at Nic and then me, and I waited for my sister to get pissed, but she didn't. She just nodded, and said, "I don't want to lose her. I've been in love with her for five years, and she's everything to me. That's why I came home on your birthday. I didn't expect you or mom to come home early, and I was getting together the scrapbook I'd made and the letters I'd written that I keep in those jewelry lockboxes Dad gave us. I wanted to show her how long I've felt this way. But this isn't easy. You can't imagine how hard it is to be gay, even now. We want to hold hands when we walk around campus, but there are still some people who say awful things when we pass."

This time, the knock on the door made me jump. I was unbearably nervous for Nic to meet Leo after what I'd just told her. I practically leapt off the bed. I opened the door to see Leo standing there with his hands jammed into his pockets, just like Audrey had stood. Maybe it was a Trog thing.

Leo looked taller than ever in Nic's doorway. He'd changed from the clothes he'd worn to Chicago into a gray T-shirt, Levi's, and dark red Converse. His hair was rumpled, and I wondered if I'd woken him when I'd called. He looked so cute, and I was surprised at how relieved I felt that he was there. Maybe he could fix this. I wrapped my arms around his neck, and he kissed my cheek, returning my hug. "You okay?" he asked.

I pulled away, telling him that I was. Leo stepped inside the room and I locked the door behind him. "This is my sister, Nic," I said, and Nic gave Leo a small, sad smile. "It's nice to meet you," she said. "And thank you."

"Don't thank me yet," Leo said, his tone more serious than I was expecting.

Audrey stared up at Leo with a strange look on her face—not exactly the kind of look you'd give one of your friends. She almost looked wary, or unhappy that he'd actually shown up. "C'mon," she said, sliding off the bed. He followed her to the computer. They talked in hushed tones, and then a smirk played on Leo's lips. "It won't be a problem," he said. He looked at Audrey like he was daring her to challenge him.

Audrey put her palms up. "Do your thing," she said.

Leo sat at the computer. He didn't press play on Nic's video, and somehow, in that moment, it felt like one of the kindest things I'd ever seen anyone do. His long fingers were splayed as he attacked the keys, and his movements were faster and choppier than Audrey's had been. More confident. I shuddered as he typed *MD5SUM GIRLSKISSING.AVI*. I didn't know much about programming, but I figured that was the title the creep who ran the website had given to the video of my sister. A progress bar ran along the bottom of the screen:

72%

87%

99%

After a few more moments that felt like an eternity, Leo whirled around in Nic's chair with a devious grin on his face. "I'm all done," he said. "No more video. Ever."

"How?" Nic asked. Her voice was filled with relief, but you could tell there was a part of her that worried it was too easy.

"I generated what's called a checksum," Leo said quickly, "which is just a digital signature of a file. And then I wrote a script on the server that looks for that checksum, and I set it to run automatically every 30 seconds. Every time the checksum is detected, the file will be automatically deleted. Buh-bye, video." He grinned, looking utterly satisfied with his work. Even Audrey was smiling. Watching them made me realize how much they loved code, and in that moment I understood it more than ever before: I saw the thrill of it. "You Trogs are more badass than I've given you credit for," I said, and Leo laughed.

Nic climbed from the bed, shaking her head. "Thank you," she said, wiping tears from her eyes. She threw her arms around Leo's neck and thanked him again and again, her words getting lost in his T-shirt.

Leo locked eyes with me as Nic hugged him. "Happy to help," he said gently. My insides felt funny as he stared at me.

Nic pulled away. She turned and looked at me for a few beats. Then she moved across the rug with her arms out. When her arms folded over my shoulders it was like being home. Not home as in our house, but home as in the way people described feeling like they were exactly where they belonged. I didn't want to leave her. What if the next time we saw each other things went back to the way they'd been the past few years?

"Thank you," Nic said. "For everything."

I held her tighter to me. "We're on the same team," I said. "Please remember that. I need you, too."

Nic nodded against my shoulder. "I'm sorry I ever forgot," she said. Then she pulled away and looked into my eyes. "You'll remember your promise, too?"

"I'll be better," I said. It was time: I'd do it *now*, before it was too late. "But not too much better." We both smiled.

I glanced at Audrey and Leo. "Thank you," I said.

Audrey looked nervous for the first time since she'd gotten here. "Can you take me home?" she asked. "Aidan drove me. I can always call him for a ride, but I just figured—"

"Of course," I said. I wanted to link my arm through hers, but I didn't want to push it. Instead, I held the door for her to pass through, and Leo followed.

"Just call Audrey and me if you need anything else," Leo said. "We're like Ghostbusters for computers."

It was a silly thing to say, but it seemed to be exactly what Nic needed. She laughed and said, "Nice to meet you, Leo."

I waved to Nic as Leo shut the door. The three of us stood in the hallway. "I can't believe you did it," I said. "You're both so hard-core."

"It was all Leo," Audrey said quickly, examining the back of her hands. "You ready, Blake?"

"Sure," I said, reaching into my bag for my keys. Audrey was acting oddly eager to get out of there, and it seemed pretty clear that something had gone down between her and Leo. I could ask Audrey in the car, when we were alone, but the chances that she'd confide in me were slim, even after tonight.

We made our way silently down the hall and waited for the elevator. When the door opened, Samantha Cavelli walked out, carrying a bouquet of daisies. Her blue eyes were focused on the flowers, and she didn't look up at us. But Audrey and I exchanged a smile when we saw her head toward my sister's room.

chapter sixteen

A brand-new black Land Rover waited at the curb outside Nic's dorm. I was somehow both surprised and
not surprised when it turned out to be Leo's. He either
had a thing for nice cars and owned more than one, or he
had rented the Mustang especially for today. Both options
made him more of an enigma. South Bend wasn't the kind
of town where teenagers drove around eighty-thousand-
dollar cars, or rented vintage Mustangs to take someone on
a date. Maybe it was a California thing?

I could feel Leo watching me notice the car. I thought
about saying something, but suddenly his mouth was
against mine. The kiss was fast and chaste, but I was still
taken aback that he'd done it in front of Audrey. When he
pulled away he said, "Good night, Blake," and then walked
off like it was no big deal.

I could barely catch my breath as I watched him climb

into his car. The ignition roared to life and he sped away.

"I don't feel like going home yet," Audrey said suddenly. I whirled around to face her. If she was surprised by the kiss, she didn't let on.

"Oh, okay," I said, unsure of what she wanted me to do.

"Want to go to the Grotto?" she asked.

I considered her standing there with her skinny hip jutted out. She seemed so much more at ease with me. Maybe it was because we were at Notre Dame, where we had only good memories together.

I checked my watch. I still had half an hour until I had to be home, but I texted my parents anyway, just to be safe. "Back way?" I asked Audrey.

"If you can do the hill in those shoes," she said, smiling as we started walking.

"So that's why you always wear sneakers?" I asked, my voice teasing. "So you can handle any terrain?"

"Whatever, Cinderella," she said, and I tried not to laugh, but I couldn't help it. I was wearing pointy, silvery flats that *did* kind of look like glass slippers.

We hadn't been alone like this since last semester. But it didn't feel strained like it did back then. It felt like it used to.

We walked quietly past Nic's dorm and over the grass. There were winding stone stairs that led to the Grotto, but when we were little, we'd made a pact never to take the stairs, only to race down the hill, no matter how old we got. We'd always say how when we were roommates at Notre Dame we'd have to explain to all of our new college friends why we had to take the hill. Then Audrey would say how we'd be old grannies together and we'd still have to take the hill, even with our fake hips.

Maybe we weren't going to be roommates, but at least we were going to school together here in the fall. At least we'd made that part come true.

"I can't believe this is going to be our home in a few months," Audrey said as we crossed the grass. I could see the top of the hill and the thick trees separating us from the Grotto.

"I was just thinking about it," I said. "Don't forget what we promised about the hill."

"How could I?" Audrey asked.

We stood at the top of the hill and looked out at the dark lake in the distance.

"Ready?" Audrey asked.

"Go!" I shouted, and we took off, our legs moving faster and faster as we picked up speed down the incline. I nearly wiped out on a patch of wet grass, and we were both laughing when we hit the bottom. Audrey put her hands on her knees to steady herself. "I'm glad we're both going here," she said, catching her breath. "It's what we always wanted."

"It's what your dad would've wanted, too," I said, hoping I wasn't overstepping.

Audrey glanced at the night sky. "That's for sure," she said. I watched her tilt her head all the way back to look at the stars, and then I did the same. We stood that way for a long time, our breath slowing. A bright half-moon lit up a piece of the sky above us. My eyes glazed as I stared at the stars sprinkled around it, and I got that same feeling again: *I could be someone new here.* I could be someone who wasn't so concerned with what everyone else thought, someone who didn't keep others at arm's distance, who wasn't feared by everyone around her. I could be someone I liked, someone I believed in. Notre Dame could be a fresh start for me. It could be a whole new life.

Audrey touched my shoulder and looked at me like she could read my mind. "Now let's get our prayer on," she said, making me laugh.

We moved over the dirt and through a patch of trees until we arrived at the Grotto. It was my favorite place on campus. Hundreds of glittering white candles filled a hollowed-out cave-like stone formation. Kneelers lined the front of an iron gate where students gathered to pray. Even at night there were usually plenty of Notre Dame kids who came to the Grotto to pray or sit quietly. But tonight was quieter. Audrey and I practically had the place to ourselves.

"It relaxes me just seeing it," Audrey said.

"Me too," I agreed. "Maybe we'll both get placed in Lewis and then we'll be near the Grotto."

Audrey looked at me. It was the closest I'd come to mentioning our dream of rooming together in a very long time. "Yeah," she said. "Maybe."

Audrey went to the iron gate and knelt down. I followed, settling just a few inches from her. The glow from the candles pushed back the darkness. I stared up at the statue of the Virgin Mary and then at the thick trees surrounding the hill into which the Grotto was carved. We knelt like that for a while, and I tried to pray, but I kept getting distracted. So much had happened today. There was Leo, of course. And Nic revealing her big secret. And then this new thing with Audrey, whatever it was.

"I want you to be careful with him," Audrey said suddenly, her sharp words breaking through the still night air.

I turned to her, but she was facing forward, her hands clasped in prayer. When she finally looked at me I saw how nervous she was.

"Careful?" I asked, having no idea what she was talking about.

"With Leo," she said. "I want you to be careful."

"Why?"

She shook her head just slightly. "Something's not adding up," she said. "He won't talk about his life back home. He didn't move here with either of his parents. He's living alone in a huge apartment, and his programming skills are so far past mine it's like he's a professional."

"So he's better than you," I said. "So what? That *is* possible, Audrey, for someone to be better than you at hacking." I didn't want to fight with her, but she was over-reacting. And if that's all she had to go on, then it wasn't really fair to Leo. "Maybe something happened to his parents. Or maybe they disowned him for the trouble he got in when he—" I stopped short. I'd opened my big mouth, and I had no idea whether or not Leo had ever told Audrey and the Trogs about his past, or whether it was a secret he'd only told me.

"Trouble?" Audrey repeated.

"Never mind," I said quickly, hoping I hadn't said too much. "The point is, just because someone doesn't have a perfect family life and is better than you at coding doesn't mean there's something wrong with him."

"I know that," Audrey said, her voice rising in pitch. "I just don't want you to get hurt."

My grip tightened on the black iron gate. "I can handle myself."

"Fine," Audrey mumbled. She looked down at her hands again. "Maybe you're right."

"We should go," I said.

I finally had something good in my life; I finally had a guy who made me feel like girls felt in the movies, or in the books I read. I wasn't going to let Audrey cast a shadow on it because of her jealousy about Leo being a better programmer.

Audrey let out a long breath. "It's your call, Blake," she said, pushing to a stand. "Just like always."

chapter seventeen

From: Blake.Dawkins@Public.com
To: Sara.Oaks@InfinitumMail.com

Dear Sara,
I just wanted you to know that I had Joanna and Jolene take
down the page they made about you on Public Party. I'm really
sorry I didn't stop it in the first place.
Blake
P.S. Maybe think about untagging yourself from unflattering
photos? It's just not the best idea to leave up the ones where
your bathing suit is basically falling off. No offense. I'm just
trying to be helpful.

On Monday morning, I met Joanna and Jolene in the parking lot outside of school. I'd spent practically all of Sunday
staring at my phone and waiting for Leo to call, which I

hadn't done with a guy in years. But he never called; he never even texted. And it's not like we'd made a plan to talk, but it just made me even more nervous for today. I wasn't sure what it was going to be like at school, or how we were going to act when we saw each other.

"You look amazing in those," I said to Jolene when she and Joanna got closer. She was wearing the black corduroy shorts I gave her, with thick, gray patterned tights, and they looked even better than the pair she'd wanted to buy at the Deb.

Jolene mumbled a quick thank-you, and when I got closer, I saw mascara smudged beneath her lashes. Her light blue eyes were bloodshot, and Joanna looked upset, too. If they were normal sisters, I'd have figured they'd had a fight on the way to school, but I'd barely seen them argue in the years I'd known them. It took some gentle prying, but Jolene finally confessed her crush on Woody.

"And then I asked him if he'd ever want to go to junior prom with me," she said as we stood in the parking lot, the early morning sun making it feel like spring. "And he just sort of smirked and said, 'We'll see.' I mean, it's not even his prom. But it's like he can't take himself off the market in case some other junior girl asks him."

Joanna squeezed her sister's hand. "I was the one who convinced her to ask him," she said guiltily.

We started walking toward school, and I listed all the reasons Jolene could do better than Woody. (Number one: He actually made really weird grunting noises like an English bulldog the time we hooked up.) I wanted to go through the main entrance because I was dying to see Leo, but I didn't want everyone to see Jolene like this. So I guided them around the D wing toward a back door, where it was usually quiet. But when we rounded the corner, there were a group of theater kids sitting on benches, listening to music and drinking from Styrofoam Dunkin' Donuts cups. A bell buzzed inside Harrison, and all at once they jumped up with their bags and music and water bottles. The commotion swallowed us, making me itchy with nerves.

"Move," Jolene hissed at a freshman with glasses and a beehive-esque hairdo.

Nic's words echoed through my mind: *I get that you hurt people because you feel like crap about your own life.* And even though it sounded straight out of an afterschool special or *Barney & Friends*, I couldn't really deny the connection.

"She didn't mean that," I said to the freshman, forcing a smile even though claustrophobia was taking over me.

"What was *that?*" Joanna asked when we got past the group.

The metal bar was cold in my hands as I pushed open the back door. "I'm turning over a new leaf," I said, holding the door for her. "There's a new study—from Finland or Iceland, or somewhere cold like that—saying random acts of kindness have health benefits."

Joanna's blond eyebrows arched. The door clanked shut behind us, and we made our way silently to our separate homerooms. I kept my eyes peeled for Leo and thought about the things I could say if we bumped into each other. *Hey, how was the rest of your weekend?* Or maybe that was too casual.

145

Maybe something like, *Hey, thanks again for everything you did for my sister.* Or maybe something about our date? *Saturday was amazing. I haven't stopped thinking about you.*

I slowed in front of the computer lab and saw Audrey and Aidan talking to their teacher, Ms. Bates, but Leo wasn't with them. Audrey turned and saw me, and I quickly looked away, a little embarrassed. We'd driven home from the Grotto on Saturday night barely saying anything to each other, and when I'd dropped her off, she'd said, "Take care of yourself, Blake."

Something about the way she said it left me feeling like I'd lost whatever small spark of friendship had flickered between us that night.

I didn't see Leo in the hallway between classes, and he wasn't at lunch that afternoon. I tried texting him: You okay? Harrison=Dull City without you, but he didn't write back. I got desperate enough to ask Xander and Woody if they'd seen him, but they hadn't. And when Xander mumbled something like, "So now you care about Trogs?" I couldn't even be bothered with a comeback. Why hadn't Leo answered my text? What if something was wrong?

I was scanning the auditorium for him at the start of College Prep when Hot Gym Coach waltzed in with his nipples on high alert under his lacrosse jersey. "Good afternoon, soon-to-be high school graduates," HGC said. "Today we're going to talk about balancing your social life with your academics."

"Snooze fest," Kevin Jacobsen said behind me, reeking

so strongly of pot I worried I was getting high for the first time off his cliché flannel shirt.

Class went on forever, and I was so busy thinking about everything that had happened over the weekend that I didn't notice a bunch of kids were staring at me. But then Joanna elbowed my rib. "What the hell is going on?" she asked.

I glanced up to see Goth Girl peering at me through her black lace veil. Chantal Richardson had turned in my direction, too. Carrie Sommers opened her mouth into a huge *O*, and then put three fingers up on either side of it to make a *WOW*, one of her favorite cheerleading moves. Nina Carlyle was ESPing death wishes in my direction with her dagger-eyes stare, but that was normal.

"I have no idea," I said to Joanna, and then Theresa "T. Rex" Rexford boomed out in her deep voice, "Woot woot!" and Lindsay's friend Princess Di held up her phone and said, "Holy crap, Blake!" Nigit said, "Holy Sepiroth," and soon everyone was talking and staring in our direction.

"Would someone like to share what's going on?" Hot Gym Coach asked, standing erect like an armed guard at a monument.

Nigit shot up from his chair. He loved having the right answer. "I'd like to share, Coach, sir," he said, like he wasn't sure how to talk to an athlete. "Blake Dawkins was selected as one of twelve most beautiful girls in America. If she chooses to accept her candidacy, she may appear on a reality show sponsored by Public Corp., and she may gain fame and fortune."

My throat felt like it was closing.

Nigit turned to face the class like he expected them to clap. Then, to HGC, he said, "Thank you, sir, for the opportunity to answer you."

All eyes were on me. It suddenly felt like time had stopped with everyone's face frozen in awe, and I felt my anxiety skyrocket. I sank down an inch or so in my seat. Could this possibly be real?

Joanna shoved her phone in my face. I grabbed it and saw the evidence right there in front of me: my name on a list with eleven others. A banner above our names read: *THE PRETTY APP LIVE: THE NATION'S FINALISTS.* My hands started shaking. How had this happened? Was I seriously chosen out of all of those thousands of girls? Maybe Public looked at my application more closely because they knew my dad? Or maybe it was because Audrey, Nigit, and Aidan were last semester's finalists. Maybe the contest people recognized Harrison High School on my profile?

My insides felt like they were on fire. This could be the start of my new life—it could be the way Leo and I talked about it: I could go to LA and see what it was like there, and watch TV-making behind the scenes. And who knew what could happen to me because of this show? Everything could change.

Xander jumped up from his seat in the front row near Hot Gym Coach. He pumped his fist in the air and yelled, "That's my girl!"

I definitely wasn't his girl, but something about it still

felt good, like he was proud of me. I couldn't remember the last time I'd done anything to make anyone proud. And If I could do this one thing—if I could go to LA and win the contest—maybe I'd make a whole bunch of people proud. Nic. My parents. The other kids at Harrison. Maybe they'd remember me as someone different than I really was here. Maybe they'd forget my mistakes. Maybe *I'd* forget my mistakes.

Nigit jumped up, not quite as athletically as Xander, but just as excited. "Go, Blakey!" he shouted. A few more kids stood up and started cheering. Nina Carlyle yanked Max Laudano back down as he tried to stand, but obviously I couldn't please everyone. Even the kids who weren't standing or cheering were all staring at me in awe, looking almost happy about it.

Joanna and Jolene were freaking out on either side of me, clapping and squealing. "Stand up, Blake," Joanna hissed.

"Take a bow or something," Jolene said, trying to nudge me out of my chair.

"This is probably the best day of your life," Joanna said.

"Besides your wedding," Jolene said, and I couldn't tell if she was serious.

"Stand *up*," Joanna hissed again.

But I couldn't. My nerves were going so wild I worried I'd fall out of my chair. Was this really happening? Was I really going to LA to be on a TV show? Were my parents even going to let me do this?

My parents. I had to convince my parents—especially

my dad. Politicians' daughters do *not* go on reality shows. My mind whirled as I tried to take it all in. And then Hot Gym Coach raised his voice to say, "Congratulations, Blake," over the chatter of the students. He checked the fat black rubber watch on his wrist. "Class is dismissed five minutes early," he said. "You should all congratulate Blake on a job well done."

"It's not like she did anything," Nina Carlyle pointed out from her seat on the far end of the row.

"Uh," Hot Gym Coach said, stalling, like he didn't know how to answer her. Maybe because she was right: I didn't *do* anything. But so what? Was it really that different from how God gave some people smart brains? I didn't get one of those. I got *this*.

I sat there, glued to my chair, wishing Nina hadn't said it and wishing someone would jump to my defense, but most of the kids just nodded like they agreed with her. I busied myself checking my phone as they all packed their bags. There was an email from *Tag.Adams@Public.com*, and I opened it to see a welcome letter with five documents attached. Maybe contracts for me to sign?

I skimmed the letter, which was mostly a congratulatory note that announced filming would start in four days in Los Angeles and that I was allowed to bring one guest to accompany me. The last paragraph said I had to scan and return the attached contracts with my signature within twelve hours or my spot would be forfeited.

I clicked on one of the attachments and glanced over some of the clauses:

Any immoral behavior bringing negative attention to PUB-LIC CORPORATION as so deemed by PUBLIC CORPORATION will not be tolerated. Engaging in such behavior will cause any contestant to forfeit the right to compete and may result in PUBLIC CORPORATION seeking damages (punitive and otherwise).

CONTESTANTS in The Pretty App Live may not leave the grounds at any time unless escorted by staff during the production of the live shows. Failure to comply will result in immediate dismissal from the contest. Please be advised that film crews and hidden cameras may record any and all action on the Pretty App Live campus at any time at the sole discretion of PUBLIC CORPORA-TION (save in restrooms and shower areas). PUBLIC CORPORATION holds the sole rights to this footage and may use it for broadcast, promotional, and marketing materials at any time in perpetuity.

It all felt so unreal. I scanned the auditorium and watched other kids sling backpacks over their shoulders. Were they going to come talk to me? They were definitely talking *about* me. I heard my name echoed through the auditorium.

"I can't believe this!" Joanna was saying as Jolene unwrapped a chocolate-chip granola bar.

"You could be famous, Blake," Jolene said, taking a bite. The smell of chocolate filled the air between us.

"You're going to meet Danny Beaton," Joanna said. "Maybe you'll even start dating him or something."

I didn't want to date Danny Beaton, but I smiled anyway, like I was enjoying all of this. I didn't want to date anyone other than Leo. Where was he?

The same group of theater kids we'd seen behind school that morning walked up the red-carpeted aisle toward the exit. They were staring at me, but they didn't stop to say anything. And then one of the girls used her overenunciated theater voice to say, *"What a sweep of vanity comes this way!"* It sounded like Shakespeare, and she was most definitely poking fun at the Pretty App contest, and at me. The others pretended not to think it was funny until they passed us and started giggling. Whatever. They could have their stupid plays. I had *television*.

Goth Girl shuttled along after the theater kids, not stopping, either. Same went for the potheads, and same for Nina Carlyle and Max Laudano. They were definitely all talking about it among themselves, but it was like no one wanted to share it with me.

I tried to pay attention as Joanna and Jolene went on about how crazy it all was. I sat there trying to act like my two best friends were enough, like I didn't need anyone else.

The Trogs made their way up the aisle, and I held my breath. Maybe our courtyard lunch last week was enough to change things. Maybe they'd stop. I messed around in my lavender handbag, pretending to look for my keys or my makeup or some imaginary thing I'd lost. When I could feel them there, waiting outside of our row, I looked up. Audrey, Aidan, Nigit, Lindsay, and Mindy were grinning.

I shoved my phone into my bag and stood. I couldn't help but smile back.

Nigit held up his hand and waited until I high-fived him, and then Mindy did it, too. "Way to go, reality star," Aidan said, his dark blue eyes bright.

"If you need any help picking out your outfits for the competition, just let me know," Lindsay said. "I can be on fashion emergency call twenty-four/seven until you leave." She was smiling so warmly I knew she was serious.

"Thanks," I said, "I'd like that."

The rest of the auditorium had mostly cleared out. Sara Oaks had given me an appreciative wave—I wasn't sure if it was because of the contest or the email I'd sent her. Even Joanna and Jolene were smiling more than usual, like they were fine with us standing there and talking to Audrey & Co. Audrey was the only one who looked a little nervous. "This is really incredible, Blake," she said. "Maybe we can get together before you go and talk."

I was grateful for the chance to spend time with her, especially after I thought I'd ruined it last night, but what did she want to talk about? Why couldn't she just be happy for me?

Woody and Xander were at my side before I could answer her.

"Congratulations," they echoed each other. Xander put his hand on my waist and gave me a squeeze. I saw Mindy notice, and I had the urge to tell the two of them to just get over it and start dating, but they'd figure it out soon enough. After everything that went down this weekend, I had a feeling I'd actually be fine with it when it happened. Maybe even happy for them.

Xander's light hair was overdue for a trim, and it was puffy on top. I touched it and said to Audrey, "It feels like Rodentia," and she burst out laughing.

"What's Rodentia?" Xander asked.

"Audrey's fatboy hamster who overexerted himself on his wheel and died," I told him as Audrey tried to stop giggling, her serious mood suddenly dissolved. It felt so good to make her laugh. "Was he hot like me?" Xander asked.

"Super sexy hamster," I said.

Xander grinned and pulled me against his side. "I'm really proud of you," he said. "This is a huge deal."

"Thanks," I said. It felt good to be near him like that again. Even if I didn't want him to be my boyfriend, I still wanted us to be close. We had so much history, and he liked me all those years for who I was, even when I was far from perfect. I smiled at him, and Joanna started asking about when I had to leave for LA. I was about to say I still needed to convince my parents to let me go when Leo burst through the side door to the auditorium.

His dirty-blond hair was sticking straight up like he'd just run a hand through it. His gray eyes were on me, and there was a fury there I hadn't seen before. I wasn't sure if it was because Xander and I had our arms around each other, or if something was really wrong.

"Leo?" I said as he came closer, and I wondered if he could hear every question I had for him echoed in that one word: *Where have you been? Are you okay? Are we okay? Is there even a* we *or am I the only one who feels it?*

I'd never seen him like this. His faded jeans and dark green T-shirt were wrinkled like they'd been pulled off the floor. He moved in my direction with an urgency that scared me.

"Blake," he said. He glanced at the others like he'd just noticed their presence. And then his eyes went to Xander's hand on my waist. He stepped dangerously close, his body language signaling for Xander to back off. But Xander didn't. He just stayed there at my side, his hand dropping easily to my hip. "What's up, Leo?" he asked.

I hadn't told Xander about my date this weekend with Leo because there was no reason to. But if Xander hadn't already sensed something, he would've today, when I'd asked him if he'd seen Leo around.

Still. Xander and I weren't together, and I didn't like feeling like a pawn in some weird guy showdown. I inched away from his grip.

Leo ignored Xander. "Can we talk?" he asked me.

"Yeah, sure," I said, backing away from Xander. I mumbled good-bye to the Trogs and zipped up my sweater. "Out back?" I asked, pointing to the exit door that led to the woods behind school. Leo nodded. I could feel the Trogs staring at us as Leo took my hand. We hurried over the carpet and out the door. My heart pounded as the cold air bit my skin. We crossed the grass, squinting as our eyes adjusted to the sunlight. The woods were a few yards away, and there was a spot along one of the trails with a fallen log that was perfect for sitting.

Leo followed my lead over the stones that marked the entrance to the trail. We covered the dirt without speaking, and Leo's footsteps were hard behind mine. I moved between the trees until we found the fallen oak. I brushed my hand over the gnarled bark. Leo sat first, almost like the weight of his worry was forcing him down. I sat close to him and took his hand. Whatever was wrong felt like something huge. His gray eyes were unfocused as he stared at a divot in the dirt near our feet. "Blake," he said, not looking at me. "I need to go back to California for a little while."

No. *No.* He couldn't leave me—not now.

"Good," I said quickly, without thinking. "Me too. For the show. You could come with me. The email Public sent said I could bring someone. Please, Leo," I said, hating the shake in my voice.

Leo lifted his chin. His eyes met mine for the first time since we'd sat. "I can't," he said softly. "I have to get back right away. It's for work."

"I don't get it," I said, my words choked. "You're in high school. How can you be called away for work? That doesn't make sense."

"I promise I can explain things to you," Leo said quickly. "Soon. But not right now. Please, you just have to trust me, Blake. No matter what happens, no matter how things seem, everything I feel for you is real." He took both of my hands and held them tight in his. "Promise you'll believe me."

Audrey had been right: Leo was hiding something. She

was trying to protect me, and I'd basically accused her of being jealous of him. "I don't understand what you're telling me," I said, trying to fight off tears.

"I have to do this one last thing for work. And then I'm done with them."

"Who's *them*?" I asked. What *was* this, *The Bourne Identity*?

"The people I was telling you about," Leo said.

I imagined some start-up company in California taking advantage of a high school kid who messed up a few years ago, and it made me pissed. "Maybe my dad could help you fight back," I said, "so you don't have to work for them anymore. He might get elected to office soon, and he knows a lot of people. Maybe he could do something."

Leo's entire body went rigid. "No, Blake, absolutely not," he said, drawing back like I'd slapped him. "You can't tell your dad about this conversation. Not ever."

"Okay, jeez, calm down," I said. "I won't."

"You're not recording any of this with your phone, right?" Leo asked.

"Excuse me?"

"Sorry," he said quickly, running a hand through his thick hair. "I guess I'm a little paranoid."

"A little?" I asked, trying to lighten a mood that suddenly felt way too dark. But Leo didn't laugh. He didn't even smile. "Let me help you," I said. "If you just tell me what's going on."

Leo shook his head, and his features folded together. "I have to go, Blake," he said. "Just remember what I told you." He lifted my chin and stared into my eyes. *"Everything I feel for you is real,"* he said again, and then he put his hands behind my neck and pulled me to him. His kiss wasn't soft, the way it was in Chicago. His mouth was urgent, his lips pressing mine like he never wanted to let me go.

But then he did. His breathing was heavy when he pulled away. His gray eyes bore into mine like he was asking me something I didn't know how to answer.

And then he left me sitting in the dark cover of the woods, all alone.

chapter eighteen

I drove home that afternoon shaken and on the verge of tears. My mind alternated between the contest and Leo as I sped along Route 31 with Notre Dame's golden dome shining in the distance. Leo was leaving me, and I wasn't sure when—or if—he was coming back. I had no idea what went on in his other life, the one he lived before me, the one to which he was returning. He was so secretive about everything. Why couldn't he trust me enough to confide in me?

And then there was the contest, and more than ever before, I wanted to escape to California. I didn't have the excitement of Leo here, and even though things had changed for the better between Nic and me, and maybe even between Audrey and me, I still craved an escape from my parents and from Harrison, where I may as well have been a pariah. I'd alienated everyone with what I'd done to them over the past four years. No one was going to forgive me anytime soon, and it was all my fault.

LA could be a whole new start.

If my dad let me go. I rehearsed how I was going to ask him as I cruised past American Pancake House and the hotels that scattered the road with vacancy signs. Our town was so much quieter during Notre Dame's spring semester, when football season was over. There were no GO IRISH! signs posted on lawns, no tailgaters wearing Notre Dame jerseys and smelling like beer and hot dogs, no marching bands blaring trumpets and pounding drums.

In just a few months, I'd be a part of it.

Maybe I could tell my parents that competing on the show would be good for my résumé after I graduated Notre Dame. Maybe it would set me apart or something. And it could be character-building, too, which my dad used to say was the reason he was making me get braces, even though I overheard him tell my mother he couldn't look at my crooked teeth one more day. Character-building is just the kind of thing politicians like to talk about. Especially conservative ones.

Maybe I could make the reality show sound good if I just presented it in the right way. For a few delirious moments, I even imagined my mother saying she wanted to go with me. I saw us putting on makeup together, and her telling me she'd always wanted to be close like this but that she was under so much pressure at home. And then I imagined her telling me how terrible she felt that she'd sacrificed my feelings all along to make my father happy.

But I knew it wouldn't happen like that, even as I dreamed it. My mom barely seemed comfortable spending time alone with me. It was like I made her nervous or something, like she was more jittery when I was around. And it felt like it was getting worse now that we were about to be in the public eye. Maybe having Nic and me around set her nerves on edge because in some protective, maternal way she worried about what my father would say to us, or what this impending campaign might do to us. Whatever the root of her anxiety, there was no way she'd want to do a whole week of mother-daughter bonding. Plus, a reality show seemed beneath her as a potential political wife. I just needed to hope they wouldn't think it was beneath *me* as a potential political daughter.

I had to convince them to let me go. And if I couldn't, maybe I could resort to extreme measures and take off. I was eighteen; I didn't need a legal guardian to agree to anything. The thought made me jittery in a good way: my first few days of officially being an adult and I was already thinking about running away to Hollywood.

I pulled my Jeep into the driveway and saw my dad's BMW parked next to my mom's SUV. My heart thudded against my chest as I angled behind their cars and turned off the ignition. Why was my dad home already? It was three o'clock. This couldn't be good.

I walked slowly up the driveway, wishing I could stop time to practice my speech more before facing them. I unlocked the door and heard my mother using her singsong phone voice, which was an octave higher than her regular voice.

"I *know*," I heard her say. "We just can't believe it. Well, of course, Robert can. He's always thought she was the most beautiful girl in the world. And now there's proof, I guess." Her voice turned a little sour at the end, but she lifted it again to say, "I've got to be going. I have so many congratulatory calls to return."

I stood in the foyer, frozen. She was definitely talking about the show and she sounded happy. I dropped my keys into a white porcelain bowl on the cherrywood table. "Hello?" I called out.

Footsteps pounded the stairs. My father appeared wearing a dark suit. "Blake!" he boomed. He descended the bottom steps and stood so close to me that for a second I was sure he was going to hug me. I froze. He hadn't hugged me in years. His arms lifted, but then he dropped them down against his sides like they were deadweight. He leaned back on the heels of his shiny black shoes while I prayed for the awkwardness to pass.

"Sweetie!" my mother said as her nude pumps clicked down the hall. She wore a taupe blazer over slim-cut navy pants. The three layers of pearls made her look like a first lady. (Not Michelle. More like Hillary.)

"We're thrilled, Blake," my father said, extending his hand.

I shook it and felt how warm his skin was. Could they really be talking about the contest?

My mother was grinning the smile Nic called the

Political Wife Smile, the one she used for photo ops, and my father was doing something similar.

I hadn't done anything else to make them happy. It had to be the contest. "I'm so excited, too," I said. "And really grateful." *Because I can't wait to get away from you.* "Because it will be a great opportunity."

"It certainly will," my father said. "If you win, you'll be a Citizen Ambassador. The United Nations honor will go a long way with voters. As long as you keep your nose clean, this will be just the kind of exposure we need."

I blinked. Then I forced a smile to match his.

Of course.

How could I have not thought of this? It made perfect sense. Naturally my father would see this as an opportunity to enhance the public perception of our family. The country would be watching, which meant so would Indiana voters.

My mother moved closer to my father, slipping her arm through his and giving him a gentle squeeze. "It will be a wonderful opportunity for *you*, sweetie," she said to me, but if she was trying to give my father a hint to rein it in, it wasn't working.

"It could even give us name recognition among the younger voters," my father went on, standing a little taller like he always did when he talked politics. "It could encourage them to hit the polls in November. The eighteen-to-twenty-five demographic is nearly impossible to reach. This may do it, Blake. It's genius, really."

He grinned like the Cheshire Cat. But I smiled back

anyway. Maybe this was what politics was all about: two people pretending they were on the same side to get exactly what they wanted. "I couldn't agree more, Dad," I said. "The possibilities are endless."

My mother smiled wider, happy we were all in agreement. My father smiled at me with adoration I hadn't seen on his face since I was a little girl. "You know, Dad," I started, unable to help myself. "You haven't looked at me like this in years."

My father's features went cold. He must have heard what was beneath my words, and judging by the look on his face, he didn't like it. Not at all.

"Yes, well. You haven't earned that look, have you, Blake?" He smiled like he hadn't just said something awful, and my stomach turned. "And let's not forget everything I've just told you. While you're in LA for this contest, you won't do anything—and I mean, *anything*—to embarrass me or tarnish this family's image. Because if you do," he said, "the consequences will be unimaginable."

chapter nineteen

I stood outside Audrey's apartment building in my rain boots. The air was cold and the sky was dark with the promise of a storm. I texted Audrey:

I'm standing outside your place. Not to be a stalker but
I know you're there bc I can see thru your window. Can
I come in?

It was less than ten minutes after my father's warning. I'd told my parents I'd forgotten a book at school and needed to go back.

Audrey: I'm not going to leave you out there all night
w/ Roger and Nicorette, so yeah, come in.

I waved to Roger—Audrey's apartment complex's super who shaved his legs and wore sandals year-round—and his Chihuahua, Nicorette, and walked along the sidewalk, careful to avoid the spray from Roger's bright green hose.

I shoved open the front door. Audrey's apartment

building didn't have a lobby like the ones you see in the movies, and there wasn't an elevator, either. A row of bronze mailboxes lined the side wall. The floors were covered with dull white carpeting, and the walls were painted a flaking, dusty pink. I hadn't been there in years, but the details flooded back like it was yesterday. I remembered the cracks that ran over the wall along the stairs in a diamond shape. When we were ten, Audrey told her dad that the cracks looked like a spiderweb, and he picked her up and stuck her in the middle and said, "Now you're Charlotte." We laughed as she giggled and squealed to be put down.

I made my way up the stairs to apartment 313 and rang Audrey's buzzer. The smell of fresh bread seeped from below the door, which meant Audrey's mom was cooking. I was nervous, but not as much so as I thought I'd be. At least Audrey had invited me inside. That wouldn't have happened a few months ago.

The door stuck against the frame, and Audrey's mom had to yank hard to open it. She stood there with her brown curls piled high on her head and pinned back at the sides with bobby pins. "Blake," she said, looking not altogether happy to see me.

"Hi, Mrs. McCarthy," I said. And then, quickly, I added, "Audrey invited me in. Is that okay? I know it's dinnertime."

"Don't be silly," she said. "Come inside." She gestured across the living room with a long wooden spoon. "Audrey's in her room."

I thanked her and moved past the flowered sofa and

the glass coffee table covered with gold-framed pictures of Audrey's dad. I didn't need to ask why they'd never moved from their apartment to a nice house, even now that they could afford it. I knew Audrey and her mom well enough to know that moving would feel like leaving Audrey's dad and the place they had spent their life with him behind.

I knocked on Audrey's door. I was surprised she hadn't come out to let me in, but then she said, "Pass code," and I realized she'd done it on purpose.

I knocked to the beat of the *Friends* theme song, and Audrey started laughing. She swung the door open, wearing black leggings and a Pearl Jam T-shirt that I was pretty sure was Aidan's. "You're lucky you remembered it," she said.

I shut it behind us and said, "You're lucky I was clever enough to make up such a good pass code."

We moved to her bed and sat opposite each other. It was an old habit, and it happened before I realized it. I grabbed a fluffy white pillow and held it in my lap, toying with the white tassels.

"My parents suck," I said.

"Tell me something I don't know," Audrey said, rolling her eyes. But she said it like she was on my side.

"My dad has managed to make this reality show all about how it could benefit his campaign for governor," I said. I ran my hand across the pillow's soft cotton. I felt more relaxed just being in Audrey's room with the familiar yellow walls and Radiohead prints. She'd even kept her HANG IN THERE poster with the furry gray kitten falling off the shelf. It had to be over a decade old. Programming manuals were stacked next to her computer, and her father's worn leather Bible rested beside her bed.

She looked at me expectantly, like she was waiting for me to say more. When I didn't, she unscrewed the top of a Mountain Dew and took a few swigs. "He's so predictable," she said.

"The thing is, I want to go—I want to do this, to prove myself." I tucked a dark strand of hair behind my ear. "So it doesn't really matter what he thinks, I guess. At least he's letting me go."

Audrey nodded like that made sense. "I want you to be careful there," she said. "You know how dangerous Public is—and they're behind the show."

"Come with me," I blurted. It came out different than how I'd practiced on the drive over. I held my breath as we stared at each other.

"What? Where?"

"To LA," I said. "I'm allowed to bring one person to the reality show as long as they're over eighteen, too. It's just a few days out of school and you're already into college and practically have a job lined up, anyway. You'd have your own room in a separate guesthouse. It could be like a vacation." I took a breath. I needed to tell her exactly how I was feeling, how ever since today with Leo in the woods I'd realized that she was trying to help me, not take something away from me.

"I trust you, Audrey," I said. "You were right about

Leo. He's hiding something. I'm not sure what it is, but I realized today that you were trying to look out for me, not ruin what I thought I had I with him." I tried to read the look on her face, but I couldn't tell if she was horrified at the LA idea or just surprised. "I mean, whatever, if you don't want to—"

"I don't know, Blake, I . . ." Her voice trailed off. "When would we even go?"

"We'd leave on Friday. And it's only for a long weekend because it's filmed live. So we'd only need to miss Friday and Monday of school, and you know my uncle will sign off on it."

Audrey wasn't exactly a fan of my uncle Aloysius, the principal of Harrison. Still, she was smiling a little, and I could tell I almost had her.

"You and me," she started, "you're sure this is a good idea? We're not exactly Brad Pitt and George Clooney."

"How do you still make Brad Pitt relevant to any conversation?"

Audrey shrugged. "It's true," she said. "Things got so bad last semester."

"Things got so bad a long time ago," I said, and Audrey nodded. I held the pillow tight to my chest. I wasn't used to feeling so vulnerable, and it kind of made me want to throw up, but it was now or never. "I feel like you never forgave me after my dad said that awful stuff about your dad," I said.

A flush rose to Audrey's face, and the words hung heavy

in the air between us. I knew how painful that whole thing was, and the last thing I wanted to do was remind her of it. "I'm sorry," I said, "I—"

"It wasn't just that, Blake," Audrey said, and I heard pain mixed with annoyance, like I was too dense to understand what really happened. "I mean, *that* was beyond awful," she said, "but *you* were being awful, too. You were being so nasty to everyone at school."

"But I was taking such good care of you!" I blurted. "Didn't that count for something?"

Audrey pursed her tiny lips. "Of course it did," she said. "It was why I held on to you—to us—for so long."

Embarrassment streaked through me. The way she said it made me sound like a charity case.

"But then I just couldn't anymore," Audrey said, her voice a whisper.

I hated the warm tears that spilled over my cheeks. I hated letting my guard down. But everything between us still felt so raw, like a fresh wound reopened. I could feel the pain of her letting me go like it was yesterday. "So you just gave up on me?" I asked. "How was that okay after everything we'd been through?"

Audrey took my hand. "I'm sorry," she said, holding me tight. "Please try to understand how tired I was, and how sad. I wasn't okay without my dad. And I couldn't deal with the shit you were doing. It didn't seem right. And I didn't have the energy to try to fix you."

I sniffed. "You couldn't have fixed me, anyway," I said,

wiping my eyes. I'd watched enough Oprah reruns to know I was the only one who could fix myself. "And I'm sorry I did those terrible things," I said. "They weren't right. I don't know what's wrong with me, Audrey, I really don't."

"Come on," Audrey said gently, squeezing my hand. "We all mess up. We all make mistakes."

"I'm trying to fix mine," I said, meeting her gaze. "I promise."

Audrey gave me a small smile.

"But I'm still going to be a tiny bit bitchy, as the need arises," I said.

"Fair," Audrey said, really smiling this time.

I took a breath. "I know I can't make you trust me; I know I have to earn it. But I will. You'll see." My voice was quiet. "And right now . . . I need you."

Audrey took a deep breath. "If my mom says yes, I'll do it," she said, nodding. "I'll go with you."

I covered my mouth, trying to mask the squeal escaping it. "Thank you, thank you!" I said, still teary as I reached my arms around her shoulders. "You won't regret it."

Audrey shrugged as I pulled away. "It'll be kind of fun to see the look on the Public people's faces when I show up," she said, smiling. "And it will get me points with Infinitum for keeping close tabs on our enemy." But then her expression turned serious. "Public is smart. And they're dangerous. The stuff they were up to last year—who knows what else they're capable of. Promise me we'll be careful."

"I promise," I said. "Of course we'll be careful."

171

But I felt invincible with Audrey by my side. And really, what could they do to us? It was just a reality show: the kind of test I could handle. Entertainment, really. A title for which I'd been born to compete. And one I was set on winning.

Part 2

THE PRETTY APP LIVE

chapter twenty

I'd like to say that I forgot about Leo over the next four days, or that I didn't stare at my phone, waiting for a call/text/email/photo/anything. But of course I couldn't forget him. Not even close. Not even when Audrey and Lindsay came over and Audrey played on my computer while Lindsay picked out every single outfit she wanted me to wear during the show. She'd put together stuff in my closet I'd never even thought about pairing, and she brought some of her own stuff, too, like a lace-back cardigan she got at the Barneys Warehouse sale when she was in New York City for her fashion internship. She scanned the outfits laid out before us, each marked with fashion notes she wanted me to remember, like: *Wear this vintage pendant as an exit necklace with your backless Cushnie et Ochs gown, so it lightly bounces on your bare skin when you* turn and walk away from people, leaving a devastatingly glamourous impression.

I didn't forget about Leo when Joanna, Jolene, and Xander came by with a pink stuffed bear clutching a balloon that said, GOOD LUCK!, either, and I didn't forget about Leo as I walked on eggshells around my father, or when my uncle Aloysius sent me a singing telegram on behalf of Harrison High School, or when Nic came by with flowers and an envelope that she made me promise I wouldn't open until I needed it.

"How will I know when I need it?" I'd asked her.

"You just will," she said.

Still. As much as I wanted to, I couldn't bring myself to contact Leo. I didn't want to be stubborn about it, but it didn't feel right. He'd left me, and he'd done it without any real explanation. I felt pathetic for reliving our last kiss in my mind, the way his perfect lips devoured mine, the way his scruff felt against my cheek. I felt pathetic for holding on to his promise that he'd come back to me. But I couldn't help it. It was all I had.

On Friday, Audrey and I spent the first half of the plane ride to Los Angeles playing Rummy 500 and obsessing over reality show strategy. Things were feeling so new between us, and yet familiar, too. Sometimes I'd feel nervous and try to say the right thing, but mostly I was just myself.

Lindsay had made me a list of reality show dos and don'ts, like:

DON'T make out with any member of the camera crew or production staff.

DO make them think you might. You'll get more camera time.

DON'T sleep in mascara. They'll get a.m. shots and you'll look like something the cat dragged in.

DO cry in a pretty way. One or two tears. No sobbing.

DON'T wear anything that has brand names or mega patterns on it.

DO try and mention my blog if you can.

DON'T forget to eat to fuel your body and maintain your strength. But like going to the bathroom, eating is best done away from the cameras. There's a reason there aren't pics of fashion editrix and reality star Carine Roitfeld grazing at the craft service table.

DO befriend the hair and makeup people. These people can make or break how you look under the glare of harsh lights. Talk to them about astrology—they LOVE astrology.

DON'T wear short shorts.

DO remember that after reality shows end,

endorsements begin, so maintain an active social media presence and curate categories that brands like to have ambassadors for—fashion, beauty, health, home. Rent a puppy if you think Purina may be looking for a new celebrity to star in its campaigns. Try and have its coloring complement yours.

Audrey said to just focus on smiling and being myself. She was dressed for the plane in her dark skinny jeans and the gray hoodie with black wings on the back that she wears when she wants to feel brave. I was wearing an outfit Lindsay called *What Would Heidi Klum Fly In?*, which turned out to be well-worn ankle boots over skinny black leggings with corduroy patches on the knees, and a lightweight gray cashmere sweater. I fell asleep once, and when I woke, Audrey was bent over her computer poring through a slideshow of photographs.

"What's that?" I asked, my voice filled with sleep.

"Oh, nothing," Audrey said quickly. She closed her laptop before I could get a good look. "Can you move your long-ass legs so I can pee?"

The air felt different when we landed in Los Angeles, and I don't mean the temperature, or the smog. I had the distinct feeling we were somewhere wild and new, in a place where anything could happen.

Audrey and I practically ran down the Jetway into LAX airport. The chilled air smelled like espresso and chocolate.

"Is that Liam Hemsworth?" Audrey asked, pointing to

a guy wearing a black-and-white-checked scarf talking on his cell.

"Don't point," I hissed at her. "I think it's him. We have to play it cool," I said. But then, as we stepped closer, something came over me. "Liam!" I screamed.

I swear it felt involuntary, like breathing. It just happened.

"Oh my God, *Blake*," Audrey said, practically tripping over herself as she tried to steer me out of his path, like maybe that could save us.

"Is it him?" I asked.

"I think it's him," she hissed.

Audrey pulled me behind a plant.

"Holy crap," I said, "what's wrong with me?" I wanted to be embarrassed for myself, but Audrey was laughing so hard that I couldn't help but give in and start laughing, too.

"*We have to play it cool?*" she repeated. "Did you seriously say that and then scream his name?"

"I think I did," I said, laughing harder, trying to catch my breath. "But I think he thought we were hot."

"Or insane," Audrey said, giggling. We finally settled down, and Audrey said, "I'm glad you got that out of your system. They're probably going to have celebrity judges for your show." She elbowed me gently in the side. "You can't do *that* on live TV when you see them."

When we stepped out of the gate area and into the main concourse, I started taking it all in, just like Nic had made me promise. *Keep your eyes open to how different it is out there. Things won't always be like they are here.* But I felt thrown as

I did what she'd said. My eyes were open, and what I saw was the most beautiful population of people I'd ever seen in one place. Everyone was tanned and toned with shiny hair like mine. Each person was more beautiful than the next. I couldn't stop staring, and my giddy mood suddenly evaporated. This wasn't what I'd expected; I wasn't used to blending in, to not looking special.

I tried to steady my breathing, tried not to give away how shaken I felt, but I knew Audrey sensed something. "You okay, Blake?" she asked.

"Yeah," I said quickly. "Just a little nervous, I think."

My ankle boots tapped the tile, and my thoughts went somewhere dark.

I was the most beautiful baby in the nursery, according to my mother. I was the most beautiful child in elementary school, according to school pictures. I was the most beautiful girl in junior high and high school, according to anyone who ever laid eyes on me. I was the most beautiful girl in any room I'd ever been in, and I was the most beautiful girl I'd ever seen in real life.

And now I most definitely was not.

I was a pretty face in a sea of pretty faces, many of them more so than mine. My entire reality felt like it had shifted over the course of mere minutes.

"Blake?" Audrey asked as I slowed to a stop. A brunette girl whizzed past me wearing white capri pants and a suction-tight black top. Her tan looked airbrushed, and her nose was perfectly sloped and sized, like mine. Her dark eyes were even bigger than Nic's, and her lips were heart-shaped and glossy. A blonde in a maxi dress followed her, holding a Starbucks coffee and chewing gum, which sounds like a gross combination, but the girl was so beautiful that it looked perfectly natural, like an ad for chewing coffee-flavored gum. Another woman dressed like Jennifer Aniston in a white tank and boyfriend jeans appeared makeup-free, but her skin was glowing even more than mine did after an application of highlighter powder. I turned to see an African-American girl and a redhead in line at a juice bar. I could only see them from the back, but their bodies matched the Pilates instructor from the video I halfheartedly leg-raised along to every few weeks.

Where *were* we? Was this what all of LA looked like?

Even the men were tight-skinned and tanned and gym-bodied. And the ones who weren't looked like sharks, like they could eat you alive with one phone call to your agent.

"Are you sure you're okay?" Audrey asked. She pried her headphones from where they'd caught on her T-shirt.

"Um—I'm . . ." I fumbled, unable to say the words out loud to her, because I knew how shallow they sounded. I'd built my entire life on the foundation of my own beauty, my own aesthetic superiority, and now that foundation had just cracked like chapped lips. "I'm fine, I really am," I told her. "I think I just need some fresh air."

Audrey slipped her hand in mine and we stepped onto the motorized rubber walkway, not saying anything. The shops passed in a blur: Hugo Boss, Kitson LA, Harley-Davidson.

We descended an escalator, and when we got to the

bottom Audrey squeezed my hand and said, "*Look*."

Standing next to the baggage claim was a man with shaved white hair wearing a suit and holding up a sign that said DAWKINS.

"Oh my God," I said. "That has to be for us, right?"

Audrey's face was ashen. "It's definitely for us," she said. She slowed her steps and checked out the guy before he could see us. "Blake," she said. "It's going to be okay, I promise. We have each other, remember?" She lowered her voice. "But it's weird that we're tangled up with Public again. Don't you think? It just seems . . . *off*."

It wasn't what I was thinking about right then. I gestured to the mass of bodies around us, my anxiety climbing sky-high. "Have you not noticed how attractive everyone here is?" I asked her.

Audrey looked around and then shrugged, like she didn't give a crap. "Yeah," she said. "It's LA. This is where the beautiful and famous people live. Most of them have to look like this to get jobs." She shook her head. "Can you imagine if your job was based on how you looked?"

Um, *yeah*.

"Why didn't anyone warn me?" I asked, my question shrill and ridiculous even to my own ears.

Audrey adjusted the white drawstring on her hoodie. "What's the big deal?" she asked.

"You don't get it," I said. I didn't want to be sharp with her—I'd only just gotten her back as a friend. But this wasn't something she could understand. "You have so many other things going for you. But this is all I have, Audrey."

"Your looks?" Audrey asked, acting dumbfounded. "How can you even say that?"

"Because it's true."

"*Blake*," Audrey said. She put her hands on my shoulders. I wanted to squirm away, but I didn't. "Listen to me," she said. "There's a lot more to you than your looks, but your stupid father warped you into thinking that's why you're valuable. He's wrong. You're valuable even without any qualities at all. Like, as a person, you idiot. You don't have to do anything other than just be."

"Are you the Dalai Lama now or something?"

She rolled her green eyes like I was the dumbest person on earth. "Fine," she said. "You want me to name your other qualities?" Her hands bore down harder on my shoulders, like she needed me to hear this. "You're one of the most loyal people I know, and you're a really amazing friend when someone's on your good side. You're funny. People listen to you when you talk, because there's something magnetic about you. And you're great on camera—you could be an entertainment reporter, or a journalist someday. What more do you even want?"

"I want more friends," I said. I could've listed a lot of things I wanted: for my dad to love me unconditionally, for Leo to show up at the baggage claim and say he couldn't live a Blake-free life, for my ass to always stay this high. But *more friends* seemed like a good place to start.

"Then try being nice to people," Audrey said in her

exasperated voice, the one she'd used on the airplane when a toddler threw Cheerios at her.

"Fine," I said. "I'll try. But I hate it here. I want you to know that."

"We haven't even left the airport," Audrey said. "Maybe you should spend this beauty contest figuring out that beauty isn't everything, and then you'll be able to hang in LA like a normal person."

"You know you're not normal, either, right?" I teased her, suddenly feeling a little better.

"Yeah, but I figured that out a long time ago," Audrey said, grinning. "Now let's go tell that scary bodyguard man that you're Blake Dawkins."

"The one and only," I said.

We crossed the tiled floor to where the man stood beneath a glowing EXIT sign. Pilots breezed by us with luggage and name tags, one of them telling a joke as the others laughed.

"Hello," Audrey said to the man as we stepped closer. "I'm Audrey McCarthy, and this is Blake Dawkins."

The man's smile looked more like a twitch. "Pleased to meet you," he said. "I'll be your driver. Let's get your luggage, shall we?" He helped us lug our suitcases from the baggage carousel, doing a double take when Audrey pointed to a pink fluffy duffel featuring Rainbow Brite.

"You need to get new luggage before college," I said as Audrey smirked. "You don't even like pink."

We followed the driver through sliding glass doors to

the curb, where a sleek black town car was parked. The air was as warm as an early summer day in South Bend, but not as sticky. A boy on a skateboard whizzed past us singing an Eminem song. A statuesque woman who looked like Uma Thurman pushed a stroller with a towheaded toddler. She met another woman at the curb and gestured to the neon-colored lollipop the toddler was sucking. "It's organic," she said.

The driver opened the curbside door, and Audrey slipped inside. I followed, sinking into the smooth black leather. Two water bottles rested in a console between our seats. Audrey twisted one of the water bottles open with a huge grin on her face, like she was used to this kind of treatment even though I knew she wasn't. She lifted it and said, "Cheers to our big LA adventure." I was so glad she was with me. I felt lighter just seeing her pixie-perfect face across from mine.

"Cheers," I said, tapping her water bottle with mine. It made me think of my brunch at Bubby's with Leo in Chicago. I wondered what he was doing, and who he was doing it with. I wondered if he was trying to forget about me just like I was trying to forget about him.

chapter twenty-one

Audrey and I stared out the window as we zoomed along the LA highway past palm trees, apartment buildings, and In-N-Out Burger joints.

When the driver slowed to curve onto a winding street called Hillcrest, I had a feeling we were getting close. I'd imagined the Pretty App campus so many times, and now I was finally about to see it. I had to sign a release form saying I was aware that there would be cameras in every room except the bathrooms, and that I was subject to being filmed at any time. It made me nervous, but I figured I had signed up for that. And I wanted to go through with this, I really did.

The town car moved slowly up the road past beautiful Spanish-style houses with white and yellow stucco fronts and red-tiled roofs. I'd never driven up a road so steep. The houses seemed to be built into the side of a small mountain.

"Look," Audrey said. I followed her gaze to the white HOLLYWOOD sign, bright and shiny in the distance. And then I saw a camera crew filming shots of the famed sign from a park a hundred yards away. "This is so LA," Audrey said. "Let's take a picture of you for Lindsay's blog with the Hollywood sign in the background." We waited until the driver slowed, then rolled down my window. I pointed to the sign and smiled, my nerves fluttery as everything started to sink in. I was in LA, about to be on a television show, and I had no idea what to expect.

The driver eased the car around a wide circle surrounded by white fir trees. A small sign marked 17 HILLCREST pointed to a gated driveway. The driver swiped a fob over a keypad on a gray plastic pole, and the gate swung open.

Audrey and I exchanged glances. "Just take a deep breath," she said, and I did. We only drove a few yards before an Olsen twin–size woman dressed in all black nearly crashed into our car. "Stop, Jerry! Wait here!" She was shouting so loudly that we could hear her even though the windows were closed. She waved a clipboard wildly over her small, dyed-red head.

Our driver—Jerry?—rolled down the window and said, "I've got a guest drop-off." He jabbed his thumb over his shoulder, indicating Audrey.

The woman looked annoyed. "Guest pick-up!" she barked into her radio. Then she shoved her head into the car between the window and doorframe into a space so small I was sure she'd get stuck. "*Hi*," she said, grinning like we'd caught her stealing something. "I'm Marsha, and you must be Blake."

I nodded, too afraid to speak. The thin lines on the woman's face put her around thirty-five. Two splotches of blush dotted her sunken cheeks.

"I'm one of the producers here on *The Pretty App Live*," Marsha said. She seemed so thrilled about it that I wondered if she was being fake. "So you can direct any and all questions about filming to me. General concerns and problems can be written down on an index card outside your bedroom door, which we may not get to depending on our production schedule. Right now we're going to leave your friend here, where she'll be picked up by an escort and taken to the house on the *Pretty App Live* campus that she'll be staying in along with the other guests and the legal guardians for our under-eighteen contestants. You're free to visit her there."

She was talking about Audrey to me like she was a vet and Audrey was my cat.

"Uh, okay," I said, and then I turned to Audrey. "That's okay, right?"

"Sure, Marsh!" Audrey said in a fake-cheery voice, sticking up her thumb. "Sounds A-OK!"

I tried not to smirk. Marsha gave Audrey a tight smile, and then returned her gaze to me. "Blake, as soon as the car crosses that yellow line, you're on SBC Network and Public property."

"Get it?" Audrey said. "*Public property*?"

Marsha looked at Audrey like she hated her. Then she

turned back to me and said, "When you cross the yellow line, please know that you're subject to being filmed at any time of day and night, with the exception of when you shut the door to go to the bathroom. If you forget to shut the door to the bathroom, you are subject to being filmed." She smiled like that tidbit was normal. "The cameras may follow you anywhere on the *Pretty App Live* campus, including the guesthouse where your friend is staying. So please don't be alarmed when you see them," she said. "The crew is going to cut footage from your arrival to open up tonight's live premiere. The show is debuting a new format, where our team will work around the clock to have already-shot footage available alongside live performance." Marsha forced a smile filled with glistening white teeth that definitely weren't the ones God gave her. "So relax and enjoy yourself," she said. The mole on the top of her lip looked like she'd eaten a chocolate chip ice cream sandwich and forgotten one of the chips. She had to work her neck into a right angle to get her head out of the car.

"Whoops, watch your pea head," Audrey said when Marsha was out of earshot. Then she turned to me. "What the hell was up with that lady? And why was her head so small?"

"I have no idea," I said. Audrey opened her mouth to say something else, but right then someone opened the car door on my side. A skinny guy introduced himself as a production assistant and explained in great detail how my new microphone and amp would work.

I clipped the microphone onto my collar, and then a

knock on Audrey's window made us both jump. We turned to see a hot guy with dark brown hair wearing what looked like a safari uniform. He gestured to a Jeep Wrangler and tipped his khaki-colored hat. "You ready for a ride, little lady?" he said to Audrey.

"Now this is more like it," Audrey said, kicking her legs out of the car and waving to me from outside. "You're going to do great," she said as the driver rolled up the window. "Call me if you need anything," she yelled through the glass, holding an imaginary phone to her ear.

I raised my hand in a wave. "Thank you," I mouthed, and she nodded.

My nerves were crackling as the car coasted around another bend and a gleaming white mansion came into view. It was Spanish-style, just like the others on the street, but even larger and more grand. A fountain sprayed water into a lagoon-like pool where a black swan swam among ducks. Bright green cedar and cypress trees shaded an immaculately landscaped lawn. Shrubbery lined a white-stone walkway, and light pink rosebushes grew wild along the sides of the mansion. Wooden beams framed each window in dark contrast to the white stucco exterior. It was so breathtaking I almost didn't notice the camera crews set up at the entrance to the long walkway.

The car slowed and stopped near the cameras. A buzz came over the driver's radio, and he pressed a button to hear Marsha's unmistakable high-pitched voice. "Jerry? Tell Blake to exit the vehicle without claiming her luggage or bringing any personal items. I'd like her to proceed to the entrance of the mansion as though she does not have any bags with her. And have her wait for my go. Do you read me?"

"I read you," Jerry grunted. Then, to me, he said, "They'll bring your luggage when the shot's over," which I already kind of knew. You never see the *Bachelor* contestants exit the limo hauling a suitcase.

I looked out the window to see Pia Alvarez. I was momentarily starstruck even worse than with the Liam Hemsworth look-alike. Pia had flowing, golden-brown hair and deep-set, dramatic eyes the color of a hazelnut. She wore tight black leather pants and a matching leather corset. She had to be sweating, but she looked amazing. Her green-gray eyeliner lifted up into a slight cat-eye, and her lips were a matte, '50s-movie-star kind of red.

"You ever see a celebrity before?" Jerry asked, and I heard a twinge of a southern accent in his words for the first time.

"Only at concerts, really," I said. Unless Airport Liam Hemsworth had been the real deal. "Not up close, like this."

"I'll put the window down on my side so the camera won't see us but so you can hear what's going on out there," he said.

Pia seemed to be listening to something someone was saying into a mic in her ear as a skinny guy adjusted the lighting on her face. Pia nodded and then smiled into the camera. "Our next contestant is arriving now," she said. "Blake Dawkins is the daughter of gubernatorial candidate

Robert Dawkins, and a senior at Harrison High School in South Bend, Indiana. Where's that?" Pia asked sweetly, scratching her head like she'd been stumped.

"Cut!" a man called. I turned to see an older guy in his forties stride toward Pia. He had a dark beard streaked with gray, a tan face but a pale forehead—like he played golf on the weekends and wore a hat.

"You can't make fun of small towns, Pia," the man scolded her.

South Bend. *Small?*

"Oh," Pia said. "Okay. Sorry. Let me try it again."

"Yes, that's the idea," the man said, clearly annoyed. He strode back to his chair. "In five, four, three, two," he said, and then he held up his index finger and pointed it at Pia.

"Our next contestant is arriving now," Pia said. "Blake Dawkins is the daughter of gubernatorial candidate Robert Dawkins and a senior at Harrison High School in South Bend, Indiana."

"Blake is a go!" Marsha shouted over the radio.

"That's your cue," Jerry said, sounding bored.

"I should get out of the car? And walk to Pia?" I asked. Why weren't they explaining more of this?

"I'd just do whatever seems natural," Jerry said. "But what do I know? I'm just the escort."

Pia was staring at the car. It was now or never. I couldn't stay in the car the whole time. I reached forward and shoved open the door. A camera was suddenly in my face, but instinct told me not to look directly into the lens.

Whatever seems natural, Jerry had said. I could be natural.

It was just like acting, which I'd loved, and which I'd wanted to take classes in when I was younger. My parents forbade it, because they said acting wasn't a proper hobby for a young lady. But I'd been acting ever since I could speak, when Nic would write plays and make me perform them for hours after school and every weekend.

"Hi, Pia," I said as I made my way up the white-stone steps. My shoulders were back, and my gait was relaxed. There were no crowds around, so what did I have to be nervous about? I'd had eyes on me my entire life. What were a few million more?

I walked along the path to where Pia stood. "I'm so excited to be here," I said, and Pia looked taken aback that I was talking to her.

"That's great . . ."

"Blake," I said, in case she'd forgotten. I flicked my shiny, jet-black hair over my self-tanned shoulder. This camera stuff was even more fun than I could've imagined when I'd practiced. I kind of liked the lens in my face. It was like having a friend who always wanted to hear what I had to say. "This contest means everything to me," I said. *A whole new life. A way to show people that I can be important, that I can do good things.* "It's a way to show people the new me."

"Well, that's great," Pia said again, looking like she wasn't quite sure how to get a handle back on the conversation.

"And I love your new single, 'Man-Child,'" I said. Then I hummed a few bars, because I actually have a sort-of okay voice. I looked over and saw the director grinning into his video monitor. *Love this girl,* he mouthed to another woman who stood next to him. So I hummed a few more bars and then sang the chorus. *"Oh, Man-Child, will you ever grow? Or will you always be a child at play?"* At this point, Pia seemed to get her groove back and joined in, and we both sang: *"Man-Child, Man-Child, please don't break my heart on a swing set,"* and then Pia starting clapping. "You've got pipes, Blake Dawkins," she said.

I smiled wide for the camera. "Thanks, Pia," I said. "That means a lot coming from you." And then I took off along the walkway because I figured my job there was done. I swung my hips just so: suggestive, but not like a hooker. This was way easier than I'd thought it would be. All I had to do was tell myself to act confident, and it happened.

"Cut!"

I turned to see the director heading in my direction. He strode past Marsha, Pia, and another guy holding one of those black-and-white clapperboards you see in *Us Weekly* pictures taken on movie sets. "That was fabulous, Blake," he said. He extended his hand. "I'm Rich Gibbons, the director here on *The Pretty App Live.* You're a natural."

"Oh, thanks," I said, a little more nervous now that the camera wasn't on.

"I'd like to get a few more shots of you exiting the town car. And I love that sound bite about how you want America to get to know the new you. Maybe you could look up at the mansion and have a tender look on your face, like this really is going to be the place where the New Blake gets her start."

"Sure," I said, smiling so he'd know I was game for anything. The advertisements running on TV for *The Pretty App Live* said the entire country would vote for their favorite contestants. That meant I needed to get as much time in front of the camera as possible.

The crew filmed me exiting the car at least six times (so much for reality TV), each time with varying expressions of hopefulness on my face. When we were finished, the driver brought me my luggage and Marsha glued herself to my side. "You're going to enter the mansion now, Blake," she said, and I thought, *Well, yeah*. Then she combed back a flyaway strand of dyed-red hair. It was the kind of red that probably looked good on the bottle, but looked a little purple in person. "And you're going to be introduced to the six other contestants who've already arrived," she said.

"Okay, great," I said. "Thanks, Marsha."

"Good luck," she said, like I might need it.

chapter twenty-two

Two deep breaths later, I grabbed a scalloped bronze handle and pushed open the massive wooden door. Three men dressed in black held cameras on their shoulders and aimed them in my direction. Camera lights shone in my face.

"Hello!" I called out, because for some inexplicable reason it was easier to do all of this when I was being filmed. I'd spent so many years doing some kind of *acting*: acting like I didn't care every time one of my tests came back with a *C* or a *D*, acting like the daughter my parents wanted, acting like I was the biggest bitch in school who wasn't afraid of anything, even when I was.

This wasn't really hard compared to all of that.

"Is anyone here?" I asked sweetly, hearing my melodic voice echo in the cavernous main hall.

I peeked into the first room, smiling as the cameras

followed my every move. A long oak table held twelve elaborate place settings: Antique china sets with varying patterns were arranged next to crystal wineglasses. Silver candlesticks in the shape of tree branches held tall white candles. Renaissance-style paintings were framed in gold, and dark wooden beams crisscrossed the white stucco ceiling. It was like staring at a page in *Elle Décor*. It was unlike any other home I'd ever been inside.

I moved into the next room, and that's where I saw the six other contestants sprawled on plush white leather sofas in front of a faux fireplace.

I might've had a panic attack were it not for the camera lenses staring me square in the face. Every single one of the contestants was breathtakingly beautiful. I'd purposely avoided looking at their pictures online, and I know how stupid it sounds that I was surprised, but I thought this was supposed to be a contest of high school girls who just happened to be pretty, like me. But these girls were in an entirely different league: They were even prettier than the ones you see stomping down the runway. They were the kind of models you saw in *Vogue* lounging in a dark forest wearing couture, the kind of girls who looked like movie stars, the kind of girls picked to ride a white horse in a flowing dress while her boyfriend sniffs her, like in the Ralph Lauren perfume ads. (Even though anyone who's ever ridden a horse knows that all you can smell while riding a horse is the horse.)

"Hi, I'm Blake," I said. I scanned each of their perfectly symmetrical faces, their collection of charming noses, wide eyes, shining manes of perfectly styled hair. And I could tell even while they were seated that at five feet nine inches, I was the shortest one in the room, and at one hundred and thirty pounds, the largest.

The girls sized me up, too, but they didn't seem at all worried.

"What's up, Blake? I'm Casey Clark from North Carolina," said a girl with teeth whiter than Chiclets. Her barely existent roots were the color of peanut shells, but her platinum highlights were so well done you hardly noticed.

"I'm Delores Abernathy," said a girl with auburn hair that spilled over her shoulders in fat waves. Her boobs were Ds and her eyes were periwinkle (and possibly enhanced by color contacts). She was the kind of girl who could make farts sexy. Or the name Delores.

"I'm Sabrina Ramirez," said a girl with hair almost as dark as mine. She was dressed up more than the others in a red cocktail dress. Her long legs were tan, and her open-toed heels showed off neon-pink toenails, which didn't quite go with the dress, but as Lindsay had told me when she'd picked out the same polish color for my toes, "Hot pink looks youthful, and that's the whole point. America wants something beautiful, something better. You have to give them hope, Blake," she'd said. She'd made Audrey and me laugh, but I could also tell she was kind of serious from a style perspective.

"I'm Betsy Greenberg!" said an enthusiastic girl with wide-set eyes and limbs longer than most NBA players.

"Amy Samuels," said a nervous-seeming girl with a

southern accent. I saw freckles peeking through her foundation. Even dressed down with two braids falling over her shoulders, she was so stunning that I had a hard time looking away.

"Cindy Manger," said a girl with full lips and a platinum-blond bob like Gwen Stefani's.

Every single one of them was more beautiful than me. If LA didn't kill me, it had to make me stronger. "Nice to meet you all," I said. And then I made my way to the plush white sofa and took a seat. Up close, I noticed that I was also the only contestant with any clogged pores, which never mattered at Harrison, because kids there had actual zits.

"Amy here was just telling us how corn grows," the girl named Sabrina said as the cameras filmed her. She gestured toward Amy, who wore a jean overall top and skirt. Sabrina rolled her eyes at me and stifled a fake yawn, and Cindy laughed, both of them clearly making fun of Amy. The cameras panned to get my reaction, so I gave Sabrina and Cindy a *you're lame* look. Because here we all were in the same situation: on national television competing for something we all really wanted. To pick on someone felt sort of cliché. Which, if I was being honest, was kind of applicable to my entire mean-girl high school routine. "I hate corn on account of how bloating it is, but I'd love to hear about it," I said to Amy, who gave me a grateful smile. Then she described in painstaking detail how important it was to plant the seeds two to four inches apart.

We all made small talk while the cameras rolled and filmed the entrance of Maddie Foss, Delia Lee, and Jessica

Torres with their perfectly styled hair and cheekbones so high and sharp they looked like weapons. Then came Charisse Fuller, who looked like a six-foot-tall version of Kerry Washington. The final entrance was Murasaki O'Neil from Minnesota, who told us to call her Mura, and who looked vaguely familiar, like maybe she already was a professional model.

As I stared around the room at everyone's face, something became alarmingly clear: I was the odd woman out. I was pretty, sure. Beautiful, even. The best-looking girl at Harrison High School. But I wasn't a supermodel in the making. This room was a beauty pageant on crack: Every single one of these girls could have a career modeling. Or in movies. I knew my own limits (how could I not? I'd been raised in a family that reminded me of my limits on a daily basis), and the next Gisele Bündchen I was not.

My heart picked up speed. What the hell was happening? Because even if being from Harrison High like last year's contest winners got my Pretty App profile an extra look, it wouldn't have gotten me here. Not with this crowd—no way. It would take something more. It would take a reason. A motive.

I let my mind go to the places I hadn't let myself imagine, and maybe an outsider looking in would say how stupid and foolish I was for not figuring it out earlier. And I guess I *am* pretty freaking stupid when it comes to ignoring everything my father could be doing behind my back. Maybe it's self-preservation, but I can't go there when it comes to him. I can't reconcile that the same man who used to read me stories at bedtime is a lying, deceitful monster.

Our next contestant is arriving now. Blake Dawkins is the daughter of gubernatorial candidate Robert Dawkins, and a senior at Harrison High School in South Bend, Indiana.

It had struck me as odd when they had mentioned my father during my introduction outside the limo, but now it felt like a puzzle piece slipping into place. How could I have missed it?

We need to rehab your image, Blake.

He'd said that so many times over the course of his campaign. There were the photo ops of us volunteering across town, and the lectures about what I wore and what I posted online. But *this*? Cheating to get me into a beauty contest? He'd always done whatever it took to secure money and power, but I hadn't even realized he knew anything about the Pretty App before I was announced as one of the nation's winners. He'd certainly never mentioned it, and I'd figured it was just like any other app for teenagers: something he barely noticed. And then, when I'd won, I figured he jumped on board to support me when he realized everything it could do for his campaign. But that was back when I thought I deserved to win. That was back when I thought the prettiest girls in their respective high schools would look like me. But now that I was here and realized I didn't belong, it was obvious that he'd gotten Public to pick me. It wasn't even that far-fetched: My father was already a huge investor, and he was likely soon to be a very powerful political ally. Why wouldn't Public want to strengthen that bond by giving him exactly what he wanted?

A chill coursed through me. He'd done this to me—his own daughter. And now here I was, with no way out. I tried to breathe, tried to make sense of what was happening to me, while a camera was fixed on my face.

I watched Cindy smooth her platinum hair and arrange her boobs when the cameras weren't watching. I held back tears as a cameraman filmed Betsy pouring seltzer into a champagne glass. She held the glass up and said, "Here's to the most beautiful girls in America," and I swear she looked at me sort of funny right before she took a sip.

I tried to take shallow breaths so I wouldn't cry. My father had used me as a pawn. I'd seen more beautiful people today than I'd ever seen before in my life, and I couldn't compete with them. I didn't *want* to compete with them. I didn't want to embarrass myself on national television in front of millions of Americans who would see that these girls were far more beautiful than I was. I didn't want to lose a contest for the one thing I thought I was good at.

Don't cry. Please, don't cry.

But it was happening. The tears were coming. They were rolling hot and thick down the sides of my cheek.

"Blake?" Amy said gently. "Are you all right?"

Sabrina glanced over. "Oh my God," she practically shrieked. "What happened to Blair?"

"It's *Blake*," Amy said.

The cameras whirled to face me. One of the men stepped so close I could smell his Old Spice deodorant as he lifted his camera to get a better shot.

Tears blurred my vision, and I knocked over Betsy's seltzer-champagne as I did the only thing I could.

I got to my feet and ran.

chapter twenty-three

Out the heavy wooden door, down the white-stone walkway, and across the grass I flew. My tears came fast and furious now, and I nearly stumbled over some sort of intricate stone labyrinth at the edge of the lawn.

I heard the camera people barreling behind me, one of them shouting, "Go right! I'll circle around!"

"Blake!" Marsha's voice. A near-wail. "Blake! Stop!" I turned to see her trying to keep up with the cameras, and I made out Amy, Betsy, Mura, and Sabrina standing on the front porch of the house, watching the commotion with their hands over their mouths.

I ducked my head and kept going. Faster and faster I ran, wishing I'd tried harder in gym class so my legs wouldn't already be burning with the exertion.

There were a bunch of cypress trees straight ahead of me. I didn't know where Audrey was staying, but it seemed like a safe guess that she'd be somewhere past the woods. It was the same direction her safari-man driver had taken her in the Jeep. Worth a shot.

I barreled through a cluster of trees, wincing as their branches scratched my arms. I heard a crash behind me and realized the camerapeople were closer than I thought. I tried to follow what looked like a dirt trail, but suddenly I was face-to-face with a wall of trees and no sense of which way was the right direction. "Crap," I said beneath my breath. My lungs felt like they were on fire.

"Blake!" Marsha screamed again. The director in his army-green vest and black cargo pants emerged through the trees first. When had he joined them?

"Hi, Blake, it's me, Rich Gibbons."

No shit, Rich. "I don't have amnesia," I said.

The camerapeople shoved through the trees, followed by Marsha, and then all five of us were standing on a small patch of dirt. A gray-haired woman held the camera closest to me. I hadn't seen her back at the house. The cameraman was panting, but the woman had barely broken a sweat. The cameraman adjusted his lens and crouched to film me from a different angle. The woman wasn't staring through her lens. Her camera was on, and it was pointed in my direction, but she was staring at me, considering me.

"Blake, tell us what happened back there," Rich Gibbons said, his voice filled with concern, like Maury Povich.

I didn't speak. I couldn't. I'd been tricked enough, and I wasn't about to fall for this.

"Tell us how you're feeling," Marsha said.

Don't say anything.

I stared down at my *What Would Heidi Klum Fly In?* ankle boots. If I quit the show now, Audrey and I could jump on a plane tonight. I could show my father that I was in charge and that I wasn't some meaningless player in one of his power games.

The camerawoman broke the silence. "Let me talk to her alone," she said. Rich Gibbons looked annoyed at first, but then he glanced from the camerawoman to me and nodded. He beckoned Marsha and the cameraman back toward the trail. I watched as they retreated, the branches *swish-swish*ing in protest as they pushed them aside.

The gray-haired woman turned off her camera. She peered over her shoulder like she was trying to make sure they couldn't hear her. Gold studs dotted her earlobe. She turned back to me, staring with clear blue eyes. She reminded me of a tough grandmother.

"Look, Blake," she said. "They're maniacs, obviously. But they can use any of the footage we've already shot. They can show you crying in the house, and then bolting into the woods like Little Red Riding Hood."

I smiled a little, and then so did she.

"So if you want to say something," she said gently, "you may as well do it. It's just me and the camera. At least we can show you how you really are."

I sniffed. She seemed honest. "Okay," I said, nodding.

She lifted her camera gently and then gestured with her hand to let me know we were rolling.

"Hi," I said softly, my voice raspy from crying. A part of

me wanted to blurt out that my father had deceived me and arranged for me to be here. But Public was still in charge of what aired—they'd never show it. And even if we were live, like the show would be tonight, could I really do that to my father? No matter what he'd done to me, he was still my dad. I loved him no matter how broken our relationship was.

"I guess I just got a little overwhelmed in there, seeing all of those girls," I said. I took a deep breath. The woods smelled smoky, like there was a barbecue nearby. "They're all more beautiful than I am. And I suddenly felt sure America would see that I didn't belong here, that I'm just ordinary. And that's the thing: I *don't* belong here." It was the truth, at least. "I guess that's why I'm so upset."

The wind blew a dark strand of hair across my face, and I didn't bother fixing it. I wasn't the most beautiful anymore. What did it matter?

"I know this is a pageant to be a Citizen Ambassador and a spokesperson for my generation," I went on. "And I really want that. And maybe I don't deserve it, because I haven't always been a good person. But I'm trying harder now." It felt strangely good to admit my vulnerability. Painful at first, and scary, but then satisfying. Like a bikini wax. "And I thought that being an ambassador would be a chance to set a good example. So I guess when I was sitting in that room with all of those beautiful girls, I realized that I was the odd one out, and that meant winning this contest was further away than ever."

I let go of a breath. I looked away from the camera at

a spot over the camerawoman's shoulder, feeling my gaze relax. A moment later, I turned and looked into the camera again. "But I'm really appreciative that I even got this opportunity," I said. "I've always wanted to see LA. And now I have. So I'm grateful."

I put my hand up to say good-bye. Then I turned and walked deeper into the woods, away from the camera, away from the contest.

chapter twenty-four

Audrey's guest quarters weren't hard to find. Half a lacrosse field later, I emerged from the woods onto a bright green lawn. Sprinklers misted crystal sprays of water with rhythmic *pfffst* noises. A more normal-size house with red shutters sat perched on a hill. The Jeep that had picked up Audrey was parked next to two town cars, and the safari-man who had driven her stood at the top of the driveway holding a clipboard. He was talking to two middle-aged women. One looked exactly like a forty-five-year-old version of Sabrina Ramirez, the contestant who wore the tight red cocktail dress and made fun of Amy. It had to be her mom. The other woman didn't look familiar, but her white T-shirt with TEAM MURASAKI O'NEIL on the back gave her away as Mura's mom, or legal guardian of some sort. The safari-man looked up as I crossed the lawn, but he didn't seem concerned. If he'd been alerted about my escape, he wasn't acting like it.

"I'm looking for Audrey McCarthy," I said, trying to sound like everything was fine.

The two women sized me up as the man gestured with his pencil toward the house. Sabrina's mom said to Mura's mom, "Blake Dawkins," in the tone you'd use to say you'd caught chlamydia.

"First room at the top of the stairs," the safari-man said. Then he tipped his wide-brimmed hat like he was a cowboy and we were in the Wild West instead of LA.

I bolted up the steps. I swung open the first door without knocking, and Audrey whirled around. The room was painted sky blue. Posters for SBC's latest hit series lined the wall: *Igneous Rock Man*, *A Tale of Two Hookers*, *Four Guys Being Really Funny*. A small window looked out onto the pristine green lawn, and Audrey sat at a chrome desk in a futuristic-looking ergonomic chair. The same slideshow of random female faces I'd seen on the plane paraded across her laptop.

"We're getting out of here," I said. I was done being weepy; now I just wanted to get this over with. "If we go right this second, there's a chance the cameras won't get it on tape."

Audrey didn't move. She stared at me like I'd suggested we'd run off to Vegas and marry each other. "Audrey, *come on*," I said. I grabbed her gray hoodie and a leather-bound journal from the bed. Rainbow Brite's worn round eyes stared up at me as I stuffed Audrey's things into the duffel bag. "Blake," Audrey said, rising from the ergonomic chair. "What happened?"

They hadn't made Audrey sign anything, so even though we were subject to being filmed if the cameras followed us, I didn't think there were hidden cameras or recording devices in the guesthouse. But I still shut the door in case anyone was listening.

"My *father*," I whispered.

Audrey cocked her head. "*What about him?*" she whispered back mock-dramatically.

"He did this," I said. "He was the one who got Public to pick me. He's the reason I'm here."

I expected Audrey to draw back in shock, or swear, or act in any way that expressed horrification. But she just pursed her lips a little. Blood rushed to my face. "*You knew*," I said.

Audrey threw up her hands in surrender. "No," she said, shaking her head. "I didn't know anything. I swear, Blake. But after what happened last fall between your dad and Public, how conniving they were together . . ." She paused, staring hard at me. "I suspected."

I held my breath as I considered Audrey, standing there in her tattered gray tank top dotted with tiny skulls. I wasn't going to make the same mistake that I did when she tried to tell me about Leo. I wasn't going to assume she was trying to do something behind my back. That wasn't Audrey.

"Why didn't you tell me?" I asked instead.

She shrugged her slender shoulders. "It was just a hunch," she said. "I didn't have any proof." She toyed with

211

a white rope bracelet on her wrist. "And I didn't want to hack emails to find out," she said. "I got myself into enough trouble with Public doing that before." Her green eyes blinked. "Plus, I guess a part of me thought that maybe your dad did it to do something nice for you."

I let out a strained laugh that sounded like a cackle. "Yeah, right," I said.

Audrey shrugged again. "I'm not saying it was right. But maybe in his own strange way, a part of him thought he was giving you something you'd want."

It felt weird standing there in the middle of the floor, having a conversation like this when all I wanted was to bolt. But I had a feeling she wanted to tell me something. The air between us felt heavy with it.

"My mom did that once," she finally said. "Right after my dad died. Do you remember those art classes I took?"

I nodded. They were on Saturday mornings at the South Bend Museum of Art. I always asked her to show me what she'd made, but she never did.

"My mom was desperate to get me out of the house," Audrey said, "and she knew I'd never take art classes, so she told me that she and my dad had talked about how fun it would be to take art classes together as a family. She and I took a few classes, and then later I found out that they were taught by this art therapy counselor who specialized in grief. I was so pissed I didn't speak to her for days. But then I finally realized she was doing it because she honestly thought it would be good for me."

I stepped closer to her. I wanted her to know I understood, but this was different. "My dad isn't like your mom," I said carefully.

"But he's the only dad you've got," Audrey said.

I let go of a breath. Maybe she was right, but I still didn't know how to make it okay. "So I'm just supposed to be all right with the kind of stuff he does?" I asked, feeling my chest tighten.

"No," Audrey said. "But you can't change him, either." She shrugged. "Parents are flawed. Maybe it's just about loving them anyway."

I'd never heard anyone say it like that, and I wasn't sure what to make of it. "But *I'm* still allowed to hate your dad," Audrey said, smirking.

I laughed. "Yeah. You are," I said. I collapsed onto the bed and patted the spot next to me.

When Audrey sat, I gestured to her laptop. "I want to know what that is." The screen had gone dark, hiding the slideshow of women.

"That's a computer," Audrey said.

I rolled my eyes. "You've been working on something."

Audrey's cheeks went red. "If I tell you about it, you can't tell anyone," she said.

I crooked my pinky into a hook. "Pinky swear," I said, just like we used to.

Audrey sat up straighter on the bed. She was cross-legged, and her hands grabbed her knees. "It's an app," she said. "I think I'm gonna call it Get Real Beauty. It's a

213

photo-sharing app, like Instagram or Flickr, but you post photos of yourself where you *feel* beautiful, like, say, if someone took a picture of you helping an old lady cross the street." Her cheeks flushed even brighter. "Obviously that's cliché, but you get what I mean. And you're supposed to post photos of yourself without makeup on, so the focus is on real beauty. I mean, of course the no-makeup thing is on the honor system, but the test group of people are really responding to it so far and sending in a ton of pics. It's supposed to be a way to show what we all really look like. Real beauty, not this fake crap where people get all dolled up or use the Pretty App's filters and post their prettiest profile pic. It's kinda my answer to the Pretty App," she said. Her shoulders tightened and shot up close to her ears. I could tell how nervous she was. "What do you think?"

"It's freaking brilliant," I said.

Audrey clapped her hands together. "I'm so glad you think so. Infinitum knows about it. And if it gets enough traction, they'll put money into it."

"Can I help you?" I asked. "I could do anything."

Audrey shrugged. "Sure," she said. "Maybe you can do PR with Lindsay or something."

This was perfect. It wasn't a reality show on national television, but it was worth something—something *good*. I could feel it.

I checked my watch. "We should get going," I said. "If we change our flights, we could get home tonight. And then tomorrow I can get started helping you with your app." I could barely contain my excitement. For Audrey to let me in on her app and accept my help meant she trusted me again. This stupid trip had been worth it even if that was the only thing that came out of it.

"*Sit,*" Audrey said as I started to climb off the bed.

I did what she said, and Audrey curled her knees to her chest. "We're not going anywhere."

"You weren't there, Audrey. You didn't see these girls. They all look like models. Like Miranda Kerr when she was young, but better. There's no way I even make it past the first round."

"So you're gonna give up? Just like that?"

"I'm not giving up," I said. "I'm not even supposed to be here." But even as the words came out of my mouth I knew that what I was doing was the definition of giving up. Audrey didn't say anything, probably because she knew it, too.

"Don't make me do this," I said. "Please."

Audrey considered me for a little while, and then looked down at the alternating black and silver polish on her nails. I waited for her to say whether or not she'd go with me, but she didn't. Instead, she said, "Last year Lindsay told me she wanted me to have a chance at something big. For me, that was the Boyfriend App." She looked up. "Maybe this contest is yours."

"Even if my dad bought my way in?"

"Even if your dad bought your way in, it's still up to you what happens here."

I ran my fingertips over the corduroy patches on my leggings. "Maybe it's a chance for me to lose everything," I said.

Audrey shrugged. "I think that's the way it goes with big chances."

"So now you're like a motivational speaker?"

"I'm basically Lindsay," she said, smirking.

"Your outfits aren't as good as hers."

"No one's outfits are as good as hers."

"True."

"Look," Audrey said. "All I'm saying is: You're Blake Dawkins. Blake Andrea Dawkins. Even your initials spell *bad*. Since when do you back down from a fight?"

I sat up a little straighter on the bed. Maybe she was onto something. Just because my selfish father tried to throw me to a den of reality television show wolves without caring what a fool I might look like didn't mean I had to give up. And I was good at TV—I could use that to make up for what I lacked in looks.

"You think I have a chance?" I asked her.

"I *know* you have a chance," she said.

I steeled my shoulders. Then I lifted my chin and pursed my lips just like I did each and every morning on my walk into Harrison High School. At the end of the day, I was still *me*. And maybe I'd become more of a softie over the past week or two, ever since Leo showed up, ever since Audrey and I made up, ever since Nic revealed her secrets and pulled me back in, but Audrey was right. I was still Blake Dawkins.

Blake Andrea Dawkins.

And maybe that meant there was only one thing I could really do.

Win.

chapter twenty-five

FOR IMMEDIATE RELEASE
THE PRETTY APP LIVE *PREMIERES #1 IN ITS TIMESLOT*
Public is thrilled by the overwhelmingly enthusiastic response to the Pretty App and The Pretty App Live, *a joint production with SBC Network, announced Alec Pierce, CEO of Public Corporation. Join hundreds of thousands of others who've taken part in the* Pretty App Live's *interactive fan site filled with quizzes, contestant profiles, live video footage, and much, much more. Download the Pretty App and visit ThePrettyAppLive.com today for your inside look at the hottest reality show on television.*

3:46 p.m.

LiveTvJunkie.com

With the live premiere only hours away, it seems

America has already found her sweetheart. Blake Dawkins's weepy video footage has made her a fan favorite, as thousands of viewers ask: How can this sweet, beautiful girl think she doesn't belong?

But what will tonight bring? Check out this video of Ice Queen Sabrina calling Farm Hand Amy a "manure-shoveling cowgirl." We predict high drama as the most beautiful young women in America compete for the title of Prettiest.

3:52 p.m.

EntertainmentNet.com

Will Danny Beaton's arrest preclude him from judging tonight's the *Pretty App Live* beauty pageant on SBC? It appears not. After being taken into police custody at 4:27 a.m. today and being charged with disorderly conduct, public urination, and animal endangerment (a surveillance video shows him peeing on a pigeon near the Mulholland Fountain in Los Angeles), the pop star is rumored to be out on bail. Minutes ago this tweet appeared on his authenticated Twitter account. @DannyBeaton: who'z pumped 4 tonight's live premiere of The Pretty App Live? Tune in at 9 pm EST to see me and the beauties hit the stage. #PigeonsSuck

3:59 p.m.

TeensBlogToo.com

By Xi Liang

We already have a favorite *Pretty App Live* contestant
here at TeensBlogToo. (That is, if she shows up for the
competition!) How can you not love Blake Dawkins?
She's so insecure! Can't even believe how emotional
I got when she started crying and ran away from the
other girls. And then her confession in the woods about
how she hasn't always been a good person? I totally
know how she feels! We've all made mistakes, Blake!
Your honesty makes you beautiful.
Keep being real, Blake Dawkins, and you'll get my vote!

4:06 p.m.
RealWomenSoundOff.com
By Betty Collins
Give me a freaking break! Why is America falling for
Blake Dawkins's "poor me" routine? Oh yeah, Blake,
the rest of us fatties and uglies feel so sorry for you,
you gorgeous piece of crap!
I'm so sick of these entitled types whining about their
misfortunes. Blake Dawkins is ready for Hollywood
with her 2-bit sob story.
Love, Betty

4:09 pm
Twitter.com
@JoannaMartin: @BlakeDawkins we are so proud of
you! America loves you, just like us! @JoleneMartin
@XanderKnight

chapter twenty-six

At five that evening, after obsessing with Audrey over the online responses to *The Pretty App Live*, I tore through the woods and across the lawn toward the mansion. Marsha sat on the front steps. Her headset was lopsided, and she was chewing on something that looked like a straw. When I got closer I saw it was a Pixy Stix.

"Blake," Marsha said, perking up. She dumped the powdered pink contents of the Pixy Stix onto the grass. "You decided to stay and compete?"

I nodded. "And I'm sorry I ran off like that," I said. "It was stupid." The wind had picked up, and the cool breeze felt good on the back of my neck. "Am I still eligible?"

Marsha let out a bitter laugh. "You couldn't get kicked off now if you tried, baby doll." She smirked at me. "Reality TV loves a train wreck."

I'd watched enough reality television to know exactly

what she meant, and it stung. *A train wreck.* That was how she saw me?

"You're the one solo-eating soggy Pixy Stix," I said before I could stop myself.

Marsha raised her eyebrows. She tucked a strand of red hair behind her ear, and pink sugar dusted her fingertips and left a trail along her cheek. "I can't stop eating these ever since I quit smoking. Don't ever start."

"Good advice," I said.

"Anyway, if you listen to what people are saying online, your little maneuver actually turned out to be pretty smart."

I couldn't tell if she was annoyed or impressed. She had one of those scrunched faces that was hard to read. Mostly she just looked constipated.

"I won't do it again," I said, feeling completely unprepared for how this was all turning out.

Marsha stood and brushed grass from her black jeans. "Come on," she said. She pushed through the heavy wooden door and I followed. The dining room was still set like the Queen of England might visit. "You're a little late for the Dressing Room, which is where you'll be expected at five p.m. sharp every night before the show." She led me down a long, marble-tiled hallway. A cameraman appeared and started following me.

Marsha opened the door to a space the size of three classrooms with floor-to-ceiling mirrors just like in the Martins' basement. A waist-level shelf ran along the perimeter like a ballet bar. Twelve stations were set up, each with a black leather chair, two curling irons, a hair straightener, and so many beauty products that the room looked like the makeup department at Macy's. My luggage and garment bags were waiting in the only empty station. It was like they knew I'd show up.

The eleven other contestants stared at me: Delores with her periwinkle eyes and auburn curls, Casey with her whiter-than-toothpaste teeth, Delia with her weapon-sharp cheekbones. I tried to smile, but my mouth wouldn't cooperate. I didn't want to feel so nervous. Audrey had told me to pretend that these girls were any eleven girls at Harrison, but it's not like I felt comfortable at Harrison, either. Maybe I could pretend I was at Notre Dame with Audrey, or in Chicago with Leo. They were the last places I'd felt peaceful.

"You all remember Blake," Marsha said.

"Hi, Blake," Amy, Maddie, and Betsy said, but the rest of the girls just stared at me. Sabrina looked like she might start laughing. I beelined for my station between Amy and Maddie.

Marsha checked her watch. "You all have five minutes until the makeup artists arrive and we start filming. Use this time to change into your dresses, unless you want that filmed for national television."

She turned on her heel and left us alone. I felt the heat of the girls' stares on my back. I tried to act casual, stuffing my luggage beneath the makeup counter at my station, but I heard their whispers. I unzipped the garment bag holding a sleek black Yigal Azrouël dress. Lindsay had let me borrow it after she assured me it was *sophisticated yet provocative, like Angelina Jolie.* Just looking at it draping perfectly on the hanger made me feel a little better.

Amy cleared her throat and I flinched. I didn't want to talk about what had happened with anyone. "Wow," she said. When I turned, I saw she was staring at my dress.

Maddie from Wisconsin whistled her appreciation. "Last season's Yigal Azrouël capsule collection?" she asked.

I nodded. Maddie would've been Lindsay's favorite. She was by far the most fashionable besides me, and that was only because Lindsay had picked out all my outfits.

"So what happened, Blake?" Sabrina asked in a singsong voice from across the room. I turned to see her standing next to Cindy, who wore a white fluffy robe with her initials over her ample chest. "Yeah, what *was* that?" Cindy asked, chomping gum and smirking. "A mental breakdown?"

The mean girls. I thought it before I even realized what I was thinking. And then I thought something else: *They're just like me.* Or at least, the way I was before things started changing. Too bad they didn't realize that I knew all of their secrets. Or at least, the most important one: *Beneath every mean girl is an insecure girl.*

I smiled. It was kind of funny, actually. I knew *exactly* how to deal with them. If I lied and told them it was all a strategy, they'd be thrown off their game.

But I didn't want to lie. I didn't want to play by the mean-girl rules. It was too easy: I could take these two beauty queens down faster than they could say *double-sided breast tape.*

"I panicked," I said instead. This honesty thing was so

refreshing. "I mean, you're all so beautiful."

Nine of the girls smiled appreciatively. Sabrina and Cindy looked suspicious. But what did it matter? I didn't need to win them over. I suddenly liked having the majority on my side, instead of the only two Ice Queens in the room. *Blake Dawkins: woman of the people?* Wait until I told Audrey.

"You girls ready to strip?" I asked, and a few of them laughed. I pressed a button on my phone and Beyoncé's "Single Ladies" blared.

"All the single ladies, all the single ladies!"

Ten of us whooped and did our best Beyoncé moves while we took off our clothes and slipped into our evening gowns. Sabrina and Cindy rolled their eyes. The thought struck me, not for the first time, that mean girls were usually so busy being cooler than everyone that they missed out on the fun.

"Will you buckle me?" I asked Amy as Beyoncé sang about her Deréon jeans.

Amy hooked the bronze buckle on the back of my dress. And then she said, "Hot stuff," and we laughed. I turned to look at myself in the mirror. I'd scrubbed my face clean because I knew we'd be getting our makeup done. Still, I wasn't used to seeing myself without makeup, and it made me think of Audrey's app. Every day the first thing I did was put makeup on, and I didn't take it off until I was about to get into bed at night. I looked different without my usual dose of concealer, mascara, and blush. Almost like a stranger.

225

"Girls! You better be dressed!" said Marsha as she swung open the door. When she saw we were all clothed, she said, "Good." And then, "Rich?"

Rich Gibbons entered wearing a black turtleneck and khaki chinos. "Ladies, ladies, ladies," he said. He smiled at us like he had the best news of his life. "The cameras are about to start rolling. You'll be in hair and makeup for an hour, and we'll continue to use the footage online and in promos as we've done throughout the afternoon." Rich turned and grinned at me like he and I were in on it, like we'd planned the effect my footage would have on the show's viewers. I felt a few of the girls look at me, and I wanted to shout out that it wasn't true, that it wasn't my intention. "We'll be live as soon as we arrive at the amphitheater. Marsha can answer any questions you have from here on out, right, Marsha?"

"Right, Rich."

"Good luck, ladies," Rich said. And then he left the room. Commotion sounded from the hallway. I could hear his voice giving the same kind of spiel to whomever was outside.

"Please be seated, ladies," Marsha said as two cameramen and the gray-haired woman stepped into the room. Two dozen men and women dressed in black followed, wearing apron-like pouches around their waists stuffed with varying sizes of makeup brushes and hair sprays.

A petite woman with sleepy brown eyes and long, blond wavy hair like Brigitte Bardot's made her way over to me. "I'm Jamie," she said, smiling. "I'll be your makeup artist."

She extended a small hand with short manicured nails painted gray, and I shook it.

I saw one of the cameramen filming Sabrina out of the corner of my eye. "I'm so excited!" Sabrina said into the lens. Then she smiled like she was posing for a Glamour Shots photo session. Watching her was nothing like watching Amy, whom they filmed next. "I'm from Cynthiana, Kentucky, and I have four brothers and sisters," Amy said. "And I'm born on the cusp of Capricorn and Aquarius." She paused and laughed a little to herself. "Anyway," she said, her southern accent charming, "what else do you want to know?"

"How about what you hope to gain from this competition?" the camerawoman prompted her. I knew from studying a few behind-the-scenes videos that the director or person interviewing you usually got cut out of the footage. That's why you were supposed to repeat the question in your answer. Maybe Amy knew it, too, or maybe she was just a natural, because she said, "The main thing I hope to gain from this competition is the new house prize. Our house is pretty small for all seven of us." I watched as she smiled sheepishly. There wasn't a fake bone in her body.

The camera spun around to catch me staring at Amy. Thank God I was smiling. I couldn't help it: I liked her.

I gave the camera a little wave. And I figured they'd want me to talk about what I wanted out of the competition, too. I knew better than to say I wanted to be a TV host. That'd be like when the *Bachelor* contestants say they want to be actresses. Still. I *was* trying to be more honest.

"Well, I'm interested in TV," I said as my makeup artist smoothed foundation over my skin. "In how it all works. And I like talking on camera so far. But I guess it's more than that," I said. The camerawoman nodded behind the camera. She used her hand to make a beckoning motion, like she wanted me to say more. "I want a fresh start," I said. "I want to do something that matters. I haven't done that yet in my life—not even at all. I'm going to college in the fall, and I don't want to be like I was in high school. So I was thinking this show could be my chance to show everyone that I'm different. That I can be good." And then I thought of Lindsay, and said, "That I can be the kind of person America needs right now."

The camerawoman put her hand up. She shook her head just slightly, but in that good kind of way that someone does when you've done something better than they thought you would. She looked up and winked at me before crossing the room to film Jessica and Mura.

"That was *so* good, Blake," Amy said. Her hair person had put rollers all over her head. She looked like the Kate Upton version of a Muppet.

"So was yours," I told her.

"Hold still," Jamie said. She brought an eyelash curler close to my lids and squeezed. When she was done, I asked Amy, "So what kind of house would you want them to build for your family?" I felt stupid asking it, but I wanted to know. I already had a nice house. Maybe if I won, I could give the new home part of the prize to Amy. Not like Public would ever go for that.

Amy shrugged. "Nothing special," she said. "Just more bedrooms. We only have two now."

Two? For five kids?

I tried not to let surprise show on my face, but I could tell by the way she glanced away that I had.

"My parents sleep on a pull-out sofa in the living room," she said. "Us three girls sleep in one bedroom, and the two boys sleep in the other one. It's not that bad, actually," she said, and something in her voice made me believe her. "Except my sister talks in her sleep about nonsense stuff and wakes everyone up."

I laughed. When we had finished getting our hair and makeup done, Marsha lined us up like cattle. "We'll be transporting you now to the Westbrook Theater in a stretch limousine provided by Pepsi," she said, smiling as the cameras filmed her. She looked us all over, her gaze settling on me when she said, "I hope each one of you is ready for the most important night of your lives."

I hadn't felt the buzz of something so good since my date with Leo. Maybe this night could finally help me put Leo out of my mind. Maybe it could help me forget how crazy I was about someone who had never even been my boyfriend.

chapter twenty-seven

Nothing could've prepared me for our arrival at the Westbrook Theater in Hollywood. Dramatic pillars held up a white-brick façade with a fabric banner that announced THE PRETTY APP LIVE in sparkling gold letters. The theater itself was so grand—bigger than Harrison High School, bigger than any building at Notre Dame— that it felt like arriving at the Oscars. An actual red carpet extended from the curb to the entrance. Amy gasped in the seat across from me. "Oh my God, oh my God," she said beneath her breath.

Hundreds of people gathered on the sidewalk. The limo pulled to the curb, and I breathed a sigh of relief when I made out velvet ropes sectioning off a space for us. The last thing I needed was a crowd-anxiety attack.

The limo honked as we parked in front and the crowd cheered. They waved handmade signs like: SBC MAKES

AMERICA PRETTIER and DANNY BEATON PICKS THE PRETTI-EST ONE OF ALL! There were no cameras in the limo, which is probably why Cindy felt okay yawning and sounding practically bored when she said, "This theater is a knockoff of the Palais Garnier in Paris." She stuck her hand into her silver-sequined dress and adjusted the sticky tape holding her boobs in place.

Mura fidgeted with a bobby pin in her glossy black hair. "It reminds me of the theater where they film *American Idol*," she said. "I was cut right before the top twenty-four contestants were announced."

I knew she looked familiar.

"Don't forget your lyrics tonight," Sabrina said, smirking. Her dark hair was long and loose. Curls the size of toilet paper rolls bounced over her toned shoulders.

"There's going to be singing?" Amy asked, looking petrified. Delores's mouth made a concerned *O*, and Casey looked like she might be sick. None of us had any idea what was happening tonight. We were only told to dress in the evening-wear option of our choosing, and to exit the limo one at a time with at least thirty seconds between each contestant.

"I was being metaphorical, you idiot," Sabrina said.

"She's not an idiot," I said.

"I'm pretty sure you both are," Cindy said.

"I'm pretty sure you can stick it where—" I started, but just then the limo's door swung open and flashbulbs popped in my face like something I'd only seen on Hollywood shows like *Entertainment Tonight*.

Marsha stood next to the row of photographers and beckoned wildly for me to get out of the limo.

Just pretend you're a movie star, I told myself. I took a breath. *Go!*

Pop! Pop! went the cameras as I swung my legs over the side of the car with my knees pressed together like I'd seen Jennifer Lawrence do. I waved to the cameras with a twisty wrist instead of a jiggly one because I'd read somewhere that those photographed better. I jutted one hip forward. I positioned my fingers in a curve over my right hip bone and angled my left shoulder back. (*Us Weekly* was proving to be my most useful subscription.) I smiled for the amount of time I figured was good—twenty seconds maybe?— and then started walking down the red carpet like I knew exactly where I was going.

"Sabrina!" I heard behind me. I knew I should keep walking, but I couldn't help but turn and stare as Sabrina exited the limo. Cameras flashed. Someone yelled "Over here, Sabrina!" and I figured the woman was cheering for her, but then she screamed: *"Why do you hate farmers?"*

Sabrina didn't break. She went on smiling like they'd asked her what shampoo she used.

"America's heartland is the reason you eat!" the same shrill voice yelled again.

Sabrina hurried along the red carpet away from the crowd. Amy exited the limo next and the crowd went wild, screaming way louder than they'd done for Sabrina and me.

I turned and made my way to the entrance, climbing

the steps and slipping through an open door into the Westbrook Theater. I stood in the lobby, taking in the pristine white marble and bright red velvet curtains. I moved past the box office into the theater itself, where thousands of seats cascaded toward the stage in neat rows that fanned in a semicircle. The ceiling was domed and painted like I'd only seen in photos of the Sistine Chapel. It was breathtaking. People dressed in black rushed back and forth, barking orders into headsets and saying things like, "Please assure Bradley that this is a peanut-free environment." I stood still, admiring the perfection of the theater and the swirl of activity. Someone grabbed my arm, and I flinched when I saw a man dressed all in black with a headset like Marsha's. But then I relaxed when I saw how fabulous he was. Clearly someone who understood the importance of exfoliating meant me no harm. The man wore a black boa around his neck, and his neatly trimmed silver facial hair made his crystal blue eyes and dark lashes even more dramatic. "I'm Francisco," he said. "And I'm here to make sure you have anything and *everything* you need." He smiled so mischievously that for a second I thought he meant drugs. But then he said, "I live to be at your service, gorgeous. So just snap your fingers and I got your back. Water. Snacks. Makeup touch-ups." He whipped out a mini-pack of almonds that read LESS THAN 100 CALORIES! and a shiny pink gloss from his pocket. "I always carry lip balm," he said. "Nothin' worse than a beauty queen with cracked lips."

"I'm Blake," I said, grinning.

"You don't think I know who you are?" Francisco asked. "America loves you, gorgeous." He glanced over my shoulder and hushed his voice. "But you better watch out for Amy. Right now she's your stiffest competition."

I nodded. He was telling me something I already sensed.

"Let's get you to the green room," he said, flicking the loose end of the boa over his shoulder.

Francisco ushered me to a room that wasn't green. The beige walls were covered with framed, signed headshots from stars like George Clooney, Taye Diggs, Olivia Wilde, and Hayden Panettiere. Bowls of M&M's and Tostitos sat next to a row of apples. Comfy-looking tan couches lined the room. Francisco stood next to me as the other contestants filtered in. A few times he whispered things like, "saggy lower lids," and "closet kleptomaniac," as a new contestant entered, and I knew he was doing it to chill me out, but it wasn't working. My nerves were starting to race as the reality of what I was doing sank in. I was about to be on a live show in front of millions of Americans. I was about to compete in a beauty pageant with eleven other girls who were more beautiful than me. My phone was buzzing with texts from Audrey, Joanna, Jolene, Xander, and almost everyone else I knew:

We r so proud of you!

Everyone's watching!

Give it your best shot—you can totally win!

Lindsay texted me saying that evening wear with visible bra lines was quite possibly the end of civilization, and to check mine.

Even our priest had texted: Let go and let God. From Father Doyle.

I was grateful for the support, but all of the excitement wasn't calming me down. And every time the phone buzzed I wanted it to be Leo. I couldn't stop thinking about whether or not he'd watch the show tonight. Why had he told me that everything he felt for me was real if he was just going to drop me like a stone?

Marsha entered once we were all inside the green room. "The general public are taking their seats now," she said. The way she said *general public* made them sound like bedbugs. "We'll be live in T minus ten minutes."

The small room had filled quickly with contestants and handlers, and the tight quarters weren't helping my nerves. Plus, there were no cameras filming, which meant I didn't need to act okay. I tried to take a few deep breaths.

"You feeling all right, Blake?" Cindy asked with fake concern.

Sabrina chomped mint gum. "Yeah, Blake, you okay?" She could barely contain her snarky giggle.

"You should spit that gum out," I said sweetly. "It causes gas in the intestinal tract, which leads to bloating and farting. You don't want to smell like a toilet, do you, Sabrina?"

I smirked. I still had it.

Sabrina glared as Francisco maneuvered me into a corner near the snacks. Mura and Casey had their own versions of Francisco at their sides, chatting away and answering their questions. "So you really don't know what we'll be doing tonight?" Casey asked a woman in a black T-shirt and leggings. "I really don't, sweetie," the woman said. "Our job is just to make sure y'all are where you're supposed to be. Last year the network ran a show and one of the contestants had a panic attack and hid beneath a catering truck. Smelled like exhaust the whole time," she said, shaking her head.

Casey nodded, wide-eyed. Mura said, "You have to have nerves of steel for this business. I've been singing and doing pageants since I won the Minnesota Dairy Princess title at age four." She chewed the inside of her lip. "It makes my parents so happy."

My phone buzzed, and I almost didn't think of Leo. I saw it was from Audrey, and clicked on a video attachment. Audrey had taped herself jumping up and down and singing the theme song from *Friends*. I started laughing as she sing-shouted: *"I'll be there for you! 'Cause you're there for me too-ooo-oo!"*

Marsha's voice broke through Audrey's. "Please put your personal belongings in the wicker basket, Blake," she said.

"Sure," I mumbled. I locked my phone and tossed it in with the rest of them. Marsha's purple-red hair was clipped up in silver mini-barrettes. She was talking back and forth with Rich Gibbons over the headset, frowning at whatever he was saying. Finally she put her hand over the receiver part. "Ladies, we're about to go over your entrance," she said. "Then we'll mic you and escort you to the stage."

"This is it!" Francisco whispered. "Do you have to pee or anything? I can make a case for the ladies' room if you need it."

I shook my head. I was so nervous I could barely feel the lower half of my body.

Marsha wheeled a table into the room with a three-dimensional scale drawing of the theater. A dotted line demonstrated where we'd walk downstage to meet the judges and answer questions. "There's an obvious red carpet for you to walk on," Marsha said. "Not even an idiot could mess this up."

Once Marsha was done telling us how to position ourselves, our handlers helped us snake the microphone wires under our dresses and secure the amps to our backs. I clipped my mic to the patent leather collar on my dress, glad I'd picked black as Cindy complained about how obvious hers looked against the silver sequins of her dress. Amy's hands were shaking so hard she couldn't clip her mic, so I helped her snap it into place on the strap of her dress. When I turned over the fabric, I could tell by the stitching that the dress was handmade. "Did you make this?" I asked softly. I didn't know Amy that well, but something told me she wouldn't want everyone to know. She nodded, and her face made a mixed expression: Her smile told me she was proud, but the pink that rose to her cheeks said she was a little embarrassed, too.

"It's beautiful," I said, and she smiled wider.

Marsha lined us up in alphabetical order, and we left the green room and paraded down a long, narrow hallway lined with more framed headshots. The hallway seemed to get skinnier as we walked toward the stage, like it was closing in on us. The lights dimmed, and Marsha put a finger over her mouth and went: "*Shhhhh!*" even though none of us were talking. Everyone except Sabrina, Maddie, and Mura looked like they wanted to run. Even Cindy looked a little green as we stepped into the wings of the theater. The red velvet curtains shielded us from the stage, but in the inches below the curtains I could make out bright spotlights circling wildly on the stage floor. Pia Alvarez's voice echoed through the theater: "Good evening! And welcome to *The Pretty App Live!*" she said, and then the theme song they'd been using online and in promos blared. It was a mashup of Danny Beaton lyrics and an upbeat melody like the kind you hear on commercials for cleaning products, the ones that show a mom looking elated to be mopping her floor.

"*The Pretty App Live* promises to go where no beauty pageant has ever gone before," Pia's lilting voice announced. "Over the course of our three-day live television event, you—*America*—will use your own Pretty App to decide which one of our twelve beauties is most deserving of our crown, a crown that means one year of selfless dedication as a United Nations Citizen Ambassador and a commitment to prettifying the nation through service and education, through kindness and dedication, through passion and hard work." Pia paused, and the music swelled again. "Let's meet our contestants!" she screamed over the music, and the audience went wild. The noise was deafening. Marsha shoved Delores closer to the curtain. Then she nudged me onto a piece of yellow tape and shouted in my face, "*Stay on your mark until I say so!*"

When the audience finally quieted down, Pia said, "Our first contestant is from Jersey City, New Jersey. Please welcome Delores Abernathy!"

"Delores, you're a go!" Marsha screamed. And then she flicked Delores on the shoulder. Delores turned and shot her a filthy look, but Marsha didn't seem to notice. She was too busy grabbing me from my mark and manhandling me toward the spot where Delores had just been standing. The curtain closed, and I could hear the crowd clapping and cheering. A video came on—I couldn't see it, but I could tell from the soundtrack of Delores' voice: *"I'm Delores Abernathy, and if you vote me as Prettiest I won't let you down. My track record of community service is unbeatable. I volunteer at a nursing home where I read* Cosmopolitan *magazine to little old ladies. That's just me! Delores Abernathy!"*

I definitely hadn't made any kind of application video like Delores's. I stared at the back of the red velvet curtain and felt my legs go wobbly. My stilettos chattered on the hard stage, and for the first time in my life I wished I were wearing sensible shoes.

"Our next contestant hails from South Bend, Indiana," Pia said. "Blake Dawkins is the daughter of gubernatorial candidate Robert Dawkins."

The way they announced my dad again made my blood boil. It was like I couldn't do anything important—get into Notre Dame, make it into this contest—without his help.

Marsha's hand felt freezing on my shoulder. "Do I go?" I asked her.

"Shhh!" she hissed in my face.

She listened to something on her headset and nodded, but I couldn't tell if the nod was meant for me, so I just stood there until she screamed "Go!" so close to my ear it started ringing in protest.

Then she held open the curtain and I stepped into the spotlight.

chapter twenty-eight

The theater was packed with thousands of people cheering and shouting and holding up signs and cell phones. Hundreds of squares of bluish light floated in the dark auditorium. I concentrated on the red carpet beneath my feet and heard Marsha's voice . . . *Not even an idiot could mess this up!*

A memory came over me so quickly I could hardly keep my footing: I saw my father rip open my report card in ninth grade . . . I saw the way he looked at me like he was disgusted . . . and then I heard his cold voice say, *What kind of idiot gets a D in Earth Science?*

My legs weakened as the memory grew stronger. They felt weighted down by a force, like the carpet was quicksand beneath me. I slowed my steps, terrified. I had to stop or I was going to fall. I could feel it: I was going to collapse in front of everyone.

I froze. A sea of faces stared at me. Thousands of them. I couldn't make out details with the spotlight in my eyes—only the shapes of the bodies and faces and the stillness that came over them as they sensed my fear.

My breathing became fast and shallow. I was about to hunch over and put my head between my knees when I saw them: the cameras.

Big. Black. Insect-like.

Familiar.

I couldn't explain it—I still can't. Nothing about it made sense, but it was like I trusted them to show the person I wanted to be: *Confident. Smart. Maybe even kind.* It was like all I had to do was perform for them, no one else. It was like I was the most alive I'd ever been while in front of them.

It was like I was born to be on camera.

Blood filled my legs again. My breathing slowed. Even the stilettos felt sturdy.

I started moving. Cheers from the audience pushed me forward like a hand on my skin, a singular, beloved voice, beckoning.

I was back.

"Blake!"

"Blake Dawkins!"

"We love you!"

"You go, girl!"

The cheering got louder as I made my way down the red carpet past Pia and stood to the left of Delores. The cameras followed my every move, and I smiled into the one angled up at me from the base of the stage in the orchestra pit. I put my right hand on my hip just like Delores had done. And Delores was still grinning like it was her turn, so I decided to do that, too.

Just stand still and smile, Blake.

Breathe.

Smile.

Breathe.

My legs still felt a little unsteady, but mostly okay. Delores and I stood a few inches apart, like Rockettes, and I felt the ridiculous urge to grab her waist and kick my leg.

Music played behind me. I turned to see my image projected high above the stage on a massive screen. Mascara streaked beneath my lashes. The video started playing, and tears welled in my eyes on the screen. It was the footage they'd taken of me in the woods when I'd bolted from the mansion. My voice echoed through the theater: *"I know this is a pageant to be a Citizen Ambassador and a spokesperson for my generation. And I really want that. And maybe I don't deserve it, because I haven't always been a good person. But I'm trying harder now. And I thought that being an ambassador would be a chance to set a good example. So I guess when I was sitting in that room with all of those beautiful girls, I realized that I was the odd one out, and that meant winning this contest was further away than ever."*

The screen went dark. I snapped my head around to face the audience. I was a little embarrassed about how emotional I'd gotten, but that faded when the audience erupted with applause. Some of them actually stood up. I grinned as I watched them, struck by the reality that I might not ever get to do anything like this again. There I was, standing on a breathtakingly beautiful stage, staring out over thousands of people and being broadcast to millions more. How had this happened?

My father.

The answer entered my mind like a slap. What if there was truth to what Audrey had said? Was there any way my dad had seen all of this in his mind and thought about how much I'd love it? He was the one who'd said being a TV person was insubstantial, but he was the one who'd made this happen. Was this all about him and our family's image, or was part of this his way of giving me a chance at the one thing I might actually be good at doing?

I smiled at the audience and said a quiet thank-you, and then Pia's voice interrupted the cheering. "Our next contestant is from Duluth, Minnesota. Mura O'Neil is a junior at Saint Agnes High School and an accomplished singer-songwriter. She enjoys long walks on the beach and helping other teens achieve their full potential."

Mura emerged from the wings wearing a skintight white dress. She paraded down the carpet like this was what she did every Friday night. Mura's video consisted of her bringing down the house with an improvised version of "You're Gonna Love Me" on *American Idol*, and then being rejected and throwing her microphone into a plant.

After Mura came Sabrina, prancing as confidently as a Golden Globe winner en route to accept her award. Cindy appeared next, looking nervous as she stood next to Sabrina. Maddie sauntered across the stage after Cindy, followed by Betsy, Casey, Delia, Jessica, and Charisse. Amy was announced last. She strode down the carpet looking a little scared, but mostly adorable, and it struck me that she was the most beautiful one of us all. I couldn't really differentiate the most beautiful at first among the eleven of them, but the more I got to know Amy, I was sure it was her.

Pia strode to the center of the stage. She wore an emerald-green evening gown that draped over her slender frame in billowy waves. The red soles on her pyramid-studded shoes gave them away as Christian Louboutin, and her fifty-six-carat diamond necklace had been donated by Neil Lane (they'd shown footage of Pia visiting his store earlier and Neil picking it out especially for her; now a bodyguard stood in the wings of the stage to watch the necklace. Apparently the diamonds had to be in his sight the entire time, unless Pia was peeing).

"And now it's time to reveal our esteemed panel of judges," Pia said.

I squinted into the darkness. I hadn't seen any judges. I wondered if they were going to walk down the carpet like we had.

"Our first judge needs no introduction," Pia said into her white microphone. "His concerts sell out theaters across America, and he is beloved by millions of fans. Please welcome Danny Beaton!"

A spotlight beamed down from the ceiling and illuminated Danny Beaton sitting in a plush velvet chair at a chrome table ten yards away from the stage. The glow from his spotlight made it clear that another judge sat next to him, but it was impossible to see who it was.

The crowd shrieked as Danny waved. He ran a hand through his fauxhawk and flashed a grin for the camera.

"And now, for the judges you *didn't* know about," Pia said, a sly smile creeping over her face. "Public Corporation and SBC Network decided that a teen contest must be presided over by teen judges. So they combed the nation for the best and brightest teenagers! We have talent: a pop singer and a Hollywood star. We have wealth: a teen entrepreneur estimated by Forbes to be worth eight hundred million dollars. We have smarts: a genius with the highest teen IQ ever recorded. And we have looks: an internationally recognized swimsuit model who's graced the covers of major magazines. Without further ado, let's meet our judges!"

The crowd went wild again. I couldn't wait to see who the movie star was. If only Ryan Gosling were still a teenager . . .

"At the age of eighteen, our next judge is already a two-time Golden Globe nominee and the star of the upcoming film *Spiderman Takes Back the Night*. Please welcome Bradley Searing Jones!"

A spotlight shined down and I couldn't help but scream along with the audience. Bradley Searing Jones was even hotter in person. (Shorter, too, but still hot.) Jolene was obsessed with him, and I smiled when I thought about her and Joanna clapping and cheering back home. I felt homesick just thinking about it. Maybe I could get Bradley's autograph for Jolene—she'd freak.

When the crowd quieted, Pia said, "Our next judge invented QuickieClips, the undergarment lifesaver that revolutionized how we all wear our bras. After being featured on 'Oprah's Favorite Things,' she sold her company to Target for forty-seven million dollars. *Forbes* has named her the richest self-made teenager in the world. Please welcome Shilpa Singh."

The spotlight illuminated a tiny girl with black, blunt-cut bangs and red-framed glasses. She wore an off-the-shoulder 1980s concert T-shirt. Billy Joel's face stared at me from the shirt as he banged away at the piano. "Thanks, Pia! Thanks, America!" Shilpa shouted into the microphone. And then she waved frantically at the cameraman crouched in front of the table.

My gaze went back to Pia. I wanted to watch how she did this—how she sensed when the audience was ready for her to move on, when it was time to quiet everyone down so she could say her next line. The perma-smile on her face made me wonder if TV hosts needed to do special facial exercises.

Pia put a hand up and said, "Get ready for our next judge! At age sixteen, she became the youngest model to ever appear on the cover of *Glamour*. Two years later, she's made a career modeling for magazines like *Sports Illustrated* and *Maxim*. Please welcome Carolina Samuels!"

The light fell on gorgeous, blond, six-foot-tall Carolina Samuels. She wore a sky-blue sequined top that plunged between her boobs, which were entirely fake. Triangular gold earrings the size of Doritos dangled from her ears. She had a sideways, tricky smile, the kind that makes people think *be careful,* and then makes them forget they ever thought it.

"Hi, Pia!" Carolina said. She waved, and I saw her nails were painted red, white, and blue.

Pia smiled back like she was a grandmother and the judges were her brats at a playground. The audience went on clapping until Pia signaled she'd had enough. "And now, for our fifth and final judge, I'd like to introduce you to a bona fide boy genius with the highest IQ score ever achieved by a teenager. He was instrumental in the creation of the Public Party network after being recruited by Public Corporation at the age of fifteen for his unparalleled tech skills! Please give a warm welcome to Leo Bauer!"

No.

She couldn't have just said—

No way.

The light landed on Leo and my stomach fell someplace far and deep. My mind tried to make sense of Pia's words and Leo's face but I couldn't—it was like seeing him through a kaleidoscope, disjointed and blurred. Something had to be wrong with me. I was hallucinating. The pressure had cracked me.

He was looking at me. Leo was looking at me. His gorgeous face was tilted sideways and he was studying me, his eyes asking if I was okay.

I am not okay.

The muscles in my legs went soft. My body felt like a ball of yarn unraveling and I wondered if I was going to fall.

He's real. This is happening.

Leo turned to Pia and smiled. Some people might have thought he looked nervous, but Leo wasn't the type to get nervous, not even for something like this. Even after just one date I knew him well enough to know what I saw written on his face: guilt. It snapped me back into the moment. Leo was here. Leo was a judge. Leo worked for Public.

I couldn't let myself pass out and I couldn't run away again, no matter how much I wanted to. I couldn't let Leo and his lies derail this night—there was too much at stake. I scanned for a camera and found one, focusing on the square lens and the red light on the black plastic. I smiled as Leo said something about it being an honor to be here.

Ignore him. Pretend he's not even there.

I went on smiling into the camera like my lungs weren't on fire with every breath, like my heart wasn't being torn into pieces. How could he do this to me? How could he play me like this? Was that the whole point—was that why he was at Harrison? To get close to me? To somehow trick me into competing in this contest? *Why?* It didn't make sense: I didn't need any extra push to come here. I would've competed with or without Leo's encouragement.

My mind raced. How could I have been fooled so easily? First by my father, now by Leo. How dumb could I be?

Stupid, stupid, stupid me.

The words echoed like a nursery rhyme. How was it that I could be so on edge, so fearful all the time, and yet miss the biggest betrayals?

What kind of idiot . . .

My father's voice was back. I shook my head to try to clear it. Danny Beaton was saying something, but I couldn't pay attention. And then Delores was talking to Danny Beaton and the judges. But the words sounded like they were coming from the far end of a hallway. I couldn't focus. All I could hear were my dad's words again . . .

"Blake?"

I heard my name, but blood was swirling so fast in my ears it was hard to tell if I heard my father's voice or some other deep, cold, male voice.

"Blake Dawkins?"

Silence.

Pia cleared her throat.

"Do you need me to repeat the question?"

I turned. It was Danny Beaton talking to me.

"I think I get it," someone else said.

I blinked. Leo's voice this time.

"I understand what she's demonstrating for us," Leo said, nodding. "*Silence.* It's the biggest threat to safety among teenagers. When a teen doesn't speak up about a crime committed, how can the perpetrator be charged? That's what you're trying to say, isn't it, Blake?"

Teens. Crimes. Silence. That's what they were talking about?

"Yes," I said, my voice shaky. "That's what I'm trying to say. Thank you for understanding."

"Well, he *is* a genius," Danny Beaton joked, rolling his eyes and making the audience laugh.

Leo ignored Danny. "Go on, Blake," he said. "Tell us more about your concerns about silence in the face of injustice."

My insides went fluttery with nerves. I didn't want to blow this. I'd already lost Leo—I didn't want to lose this, too. "When teens don't speak up about injustice, they become powerless," I said, my voice shaking the tiniest bit. "No one can help them unless they know about the injustice or crime committed."

Most of the audience murmured their assent. At least I'd answered the question; at least I hadn't stayed frozen. I could do this.

I *would* do this.

"And what about you, Mura?" Bradley Searing Jones asked. "What do you think is the greatest challenge facing teenagers today?"

My heart was wild in my chest. It didn't make sense. I was so sure what we'd had was real. It's not like we'd had a lot of time together, but the little time we did have together had felt like something true, something important.

"Many teenagers do not have access to organic food," Mura said.

Amy let out a little gasp from her position at the end of the line.

"Do you have something to say, Amy?" Bradley Searing

Jones asked. I followed his gaze to see Amy's brow furrowed.

"Well, I mean, many teenagers don't have access to any food at all," she said.

The audience cheered and blurted things like, "That's right!" and "Damn straight!"

Mura reddened. "I'm just saying that I think nutrition is one of our greatest challenges to overcome as a nation of the United States of America."

"And I'm just saying I think it's poverty," Amy said. "Many crimes—not all—are committed out of financial desperation."

"And that makes them okay?" Sabrina spat.

"I didn't say that," Amy said.

"Ladies, ladies," Danny Beaton said, like we were skittish thoroughbreds and he was trying to calm us. "This is an interview session, not a debate. Wowza," he said, wiping his brow. "We have some hot ones tonight!"

The audience cheered. I stared out at them, trying to un-blur their individual faces, trying to do anything that would distract me from the reality of Leo sitting ten yards away from me, but it didn't work. I wanted answers. I wanted to freeze everyone else so it was just Leo and me, so I could ask him why he'd done this.

"And what about you, Maddie?" Shilpa asked. "What are the concerns you have for the future of this country's youth?"

"My fashion line, Lean and Green, donates point zero

five percent of its proceeds to helping teens who have lost their way," Maddie said. "When a girl feels good about her clothes, she feels good about herself." She grinned at Carolina. "Right, Carolina?"

"So you think if teens had better clothes, it would solve all their problems?" Leo asked.

"I mean, it couldn't hurt," Maddie said.

"Right," Leo said, looking like he wanted to stab himself with a pencil.

Carolina frowned at Maddie, and then turned to Charisse. "And how about you, Charisse?" she asked. "What would you say to America's youth if you were an ambassador on their behalf?"

Charisse smiled warmly. Her smooth mocha skin glistened under the lights, and she looked radiant in her teal strapless dress. "I'd tell American youth that kindness and generosity count. We need to support each other. I'd ask American youth what they're doing for their fellow classmates. What are they doing for their communities? We can't exist in a vacuum. We have to think outside of ourselves." Charisse looked down the line at all of us, and asked, "When was the last time any one of us helped another classmate?"

Not even the nearness of Leo could distract me enough to ignore Charisse's question, and I felt myself flush with guilt. I hadn't done anything for anyone else in a very long time. I thought of the tutoring table Audrey had set up in Harrison's cafeteria. She tutored every Friday after school

253

on a first-come-first-served basis, and she was so smart that she could help anyone with any subject. Her dad was the one who always told us how important it was to use what we were blessed with to help others. So what did that mean for me? I was pretty; that was all. How was I supposed to use *that*?

It felt like a cop-out even as I thought it. And then something niggled at the edges of my mind . . . if this *thing*—this on-camera business—if this was what I was good at . . . if I had a chance to host some kind of TV show . . . maybe that was the thing I could use for good?

Maybe the shock of seeing Leo and the stuffy stage air were getting to my head. But what if I were onto something? What if I could make it happen?

Someone shouted, "I love you, Charisse!" and the audience started clapping. Charisse smiled like she'd won the contest, and maybe her answer was so good that she had.

In the midst of the cheering I turned and let my eyes fall on Leo. He stared back at me, and then his glance darted to the two cameras positioned nearest him. One filmed Charisse, and the other filmed the audience's reaction.

He turned to me, his gray eyes pleading. His hands gripped the edges of the table as he mouthed: *I'm sorry.*

chapter twenty-nine

The rest of the night passed in a blur.

Casey, Betsy, Delia, and Jessica fielded more questions about teen issues, and then each one of us had to talk about our journey to *The Pretty App Live*. Most of the girls talked about fund-raisers and send-off parties, about saying good-bye to siblings and interviewing on local news stations.

Leo watched me carefully, and I wondered if he could sense the myriad responses floating through my mind. *Well, first, a boy was sent to my high school who I promptly fell in love with. When I won the contest, I asked him to come here with me. He disappeared, and it turns out he's a judge and an employee of Public Corporation. Meet Leo, everyone!*

Instead, I said, "I was fortunate enough to have the support of my friends and family." Even if I only had, like, three friends. "And my former best friend, Audrey, came with me as my guest. We haven't been friends for three years, and now it's like we're starting all over. So, really, that's been the best part of my journey so far."

The audience applauded, but not as much as when Amy told them that her journey involved sleepless nights while she and her mother sewed all of the evening gowns she'd be competing in. I felt myself losing the audience's favor, but there were so many other things to worry about that it was hard to focus on that. I suddenly didn't care as much. Plus, my response about Audrey was the truth. I wasn't about to start making things up to win this thing, especially now that I knew what it felt like to be lied to over and over again.

At eight p.m. California time, Pia dismissed us by saying, "America, we hope you've enjoyed meeting the nation's most beautiful teens. Remember, live footage will play all day tomorrow on SBCnetwork.com and Public's Pretty App before tomorrow evening's show. So tune in to watch the contestants prettify LA's 405 by picking up trash and roadkill! See them interacting with underprivileged children at a local inner-city school. Vote all day—as many times as you like—via the Pretty App or by calling 1-866-VOTENOW or texting 85637. Six young women will be cut tomorrow night. Make sure your favorite stays! Standard text messaging fees apply."

The lights faded, the cameras dropped, and all at once the auditorium felt like the life had been sucked out of it. A handler escorted Pia from the stage, and another went to escort the judges. Bodyguards appeared at the edges of the orchestra pit—maybe to keep the audience members away from Danny Beaton and Bradley Searing Jones. I couldn't look at Leo, but I felt his eyes on me. Marsha stomped onto the stage and started yapping about our transportation arrangements. I'd never been so happy to see her; I just wanted to get out of there. And there was no way I could stay at the mansion tonight, even if it meant more exposure and online footage. I had to get to Audrey.

The judges walked by us in a single line. A few of the contestants said, "Hey, Danny," or, "Hi, Bradley," but not me. I stared at Marsha like she was Barack Obama delivering his inaugural address, like something so important was happening that I couldn't bear to look away. I could feel Leo staring at me, and I swore I even heard him say, "Blake," but there was too much commotion going on to be sure. Maybe I'd just imagined it. Maybe I'd just imagined everything about us.

Maybe nothing between Leo and me had ever been real.

chapter thirty

Jolene: We can't wait to see you! We are so nervous we can't even imagine how you feel!

Xander: What channel is this shit on?

Joanna: Xander's kidding. We're obviously watching right now. And Pia Alvarez is totally flirting with Danny Beaton.

Jolene: Ah! You're walking on stage now! You look so beautiful! I love your dress.

Joanna: Seriously you look insanely good.

Xander: Dude you look hot.

Jolene: BRADLEY SEARING JONES is a judge? Ahhhh oh my God can you please introduce us?!

Joanna: What the hell? Leo's a judge?!

Jolene: OMG best surprise ever!

Xander: Dude ur boyfriend's famous.

Jolene: Did you know about this? You're such a good secret keeper!

Xander: Still think he's a prick.

That night, after scrolling through my texts, I changed into pajamas at the mansion and waited until the cameras were filming Cindy, Sabrina, and Betsy playing strip poker (while most of the other girls bad-mouthed them, except for Casey and Amy, who brought their Bibles down and sat at the strip poker table for a Bible study) before I took off my mic, slipped out of the mansion, and raced to Audrey's house.

I wanted nothing more than to call Joanna, Jolene, and Xander and tell them everything. But I was too worried the word would get out that I'd been in the dark the whole time. What if the bloggers caught onto the fact that Leo had been at our school and that he'd tricked me? What if I got disqualified for knowing a judge?

The safari-man was guarding the front door of Audrey's guesthouse again, and when he saw me, he didn't say hello. Instead, he took out his radio and said, "Blake Dawkins is entering the guesthouse."

Inside the house, Mura sat next to her mother in the living room. Her mom was holding a notebook and sounded like she was giving Mura notes on her performance. "You'll need to make up for *all* of this tomorrow," she said to Mura, who looked on the verge of tears.

I couldn't stop shivering, no matter how warm the LA

night air was. I moved past Mura and her mom and hurried up the stairs. I banged on Audrey's bedroom door. She swung it open, her face a mixture of shock and concern.

"OkayOkayOkay," she said quickly, pulling me into the sky-blue room. She checked the hallway behind me, looking a little paranoid. When she didn't see anyone, she guided me to the bed and sat me on it. "First things first: You were amazing tonight. You're meant to be on TV. You're a total natural. And you look even more beautiful on television than you do in person. How that's even possible, I have no idea, but it's true." She exhaled, visibly trying to calm herself. "Second. What the hell was *that*?! Did you have any idea about him?"

"*No*," I said. I didn't know what else to say. I needed Audrey to say something that would fix this.

"I don't get it," she said. She squeezed next to me on the bed. "Why didn't he tell us he worked for Public? Why was he at Harrison?"

"I was hoping *you'd* know," I said, desperation making my voice thin. "You're the smart one. I thought you'd figure it out."

Audrey's lips pursed. "It must have to do with your dad, right?"

I shook my head. "When Leo showed up at my house that morning to take me to Chicago, my dad got this crazy look on his face. It was like he recognized Leo from somewhere. Maybe he'd met him before through Public and that's why he let me go on the date in the first place, but I don't think he knew they'd sent him to Harrison."

Audrey did what she always did when she needed to think: She ran both hands through her dark pixie cut like she was shampooing it. "When Leo got to Harrison, he zeroed in on both of us," she said. "He became friends with my friends. He asked you out on a date. I didn't think anything of it, because my friends are awesome and you're, well, you're *you*. But what if he was there to spy on us? To make sure I didn't cause any trouble with another stupid Public contest, and to make sure you were on board with competing on *The Pretty App Live* to go along with whatever crazy plan they had with your dad?"

We stared at each other. She was right—I knew she was right.

"You figured me out," said a low voice.

My heart lurched. Audrey and I whirled around to see Leo standing in the doorway with one hand on the white wooden frame.

"And now you're spying on us again," Audrey said, her words a growl.

"Get out," I said. I moved to the door to slam it but Leo stepped inside the room. "I mean it, Leo," I said. "Get out!" I knew how childish I sounded, but I couldn't do this with him. Not now. Maybe not ever.

"Blake, *please*," he said, his voice charged with emotion. He stood a few inches from me, and all I could think about was everything I felt for him.

"You tricked me," I said.

"I tried to tell you," he said.

"That's bull."

"I told you as much as I could." Sweat had broken out on his smooth, tan forehead, and he swiped it away with the back of his hand. "I told you I worked for a tech company."

"Yeah, but not Public! And you acted like you were just a regular transfer student when you were really there under the weirdest pretenses ever. That's a *lie*, Leo. You're a liar. And you made me feel something for you! You *used* me."

He took a step toward me.

I put my hands up. "No," I said. "Don't come any closer."

The worst part was how much some pathetic part of me wanted the opposite of what I was saying. *Stay. Explain this to me. Tell me everything between us was real.* "I want you to leave," I said, my voice choked. I was trying so hard not to cry that my insides felt like a teakettle about to scream. "Please, Leo," I said, finally unable to hold in my tears. My words were raspy and broken. "I'm asking you to go."

A door slammed downstairs and feet pounded the steps. "They're upstairs!" someone shouted, and my stomach twisted as I recognized the older cameraman's voice.

Leo's face tightened. He took a step backward. "Blake, if that's what you want," he said. "But I—"

"You have to *go*, Leo," Audrey said, her voice urgent. "You'll make it worse for her if they catch you up here." Leo looked at me one more time, his gray eyes heavy and pleading. Then he slipped through the open doorway and moved down the hallway until he was only a shadow against the wall, and then nothing. Audrey hurried to the space where he'd been standing and shut and locked the door. I heard his footsteps on a back stairway, and I said a silent prayer that the cameras wouldn't catch him. Audrey turned to me, her green eyes wide. She wrapped her arms around me and held me while I cried.

chapter thirty-one

Blake Dawkins
By Nina Carlyle
Excerpted from TeensBlogToo.com

Blake Dawkins is not who she's pretending to be.
This whole "new chance to show I'm good" thing?
It's manufactured, just like her perfectly plucked
eyebrows.

It's time someone showed you the real Blake
Dawkins, the one who torments the less fortunate
members of the high school social strata, the one who
only looks out for herself, the one who has escaped
any repercussions for her behavior (besides everyone
in our school hating her guts except for her two evil
friends) because her father runs the town and her

uncle is the principal of our school. Blake Dawkins
wants a new chance? I say it's too late.

FACT: Blake Dawkins cheated on her first love,
Xander Knight, with his best friend and teammate,
Woody Ames.

FACT: When she was fourteen, Blake called me
"the fat slob on a sled," plunging me into years of
insecurity and image issues.

FACT: During the Pretty App contest, Blake and her
two best friends created an Ugly Page to torment an
innocent Harrison High School student.

Just thought all of you should know exactly who you're
voting for.

BLAKE DAWKINS IS A MONSTER.

chapter thirty-two

I spent the early part of the morning texting with Joanna and Jolene, letting them console me about Nina's post, wishing everything they said about it not being a big deal was true. But I knew it wasn't. By nine, Nina's *TeensBlogToo* post had circulated the internet like a bad cold. There were 15,043 retweets on Twitter alone. Reality show viewers from South Bend to South Beach reblogged and commented en masse on the article, calling me a liar and a cheat, and saying I never deserved to be in the contest in the first place.

The worst part was how right they were. Even I felt horrified when I read over the things I'd done—and I was the one who had done them. What was wrong with me?

I sat in the bedroom I'd been assigned to in the east wing of the mansion with Amy and Charisse. Three four-poster beds with way too many plush pillows lined the walls. The window was cracked and fresh air filtered into the room along with twittering sounds from the birds that jumped from branch to branch on a massive oak tree. On the mauve carpet, our suitcases were splayed open with underwear, bras, leggings, and makeup falling out of them like afterthoughts. I sat in front of one of the three laptops and kept my back to Amy and Charisse while I scrolled through the comments on Nina's post:

Blake Dawkins sounds ugly on the inside. That alone should get her kicked off tonight.

This girl sounds like a total nightmare. Thanks, Nina, for showing us the real Blake Dawkins.

So typical. A girl who's only acting nice to win. Can't wait to vote against her tonight.

Who does sh*t like that? Bitch!

I didn't need Lindsay to tell me I couldn't survive a PR fiasco like Nina's post. Tears spilled over my cheeks as I stared at the computer. I didn't want Amy and Charisse to know I was crying—and there were cameras posted in two corners of our bedroom that could catch everything. But then my shoulders started shaking, and all I could think was: *Serves you right for everything you've done, Blake. Serves. You. Right.*

I dug into my suitcase to find Nic's letter—the one she said to save for when I really needed it. But then I felt a hand on my shoulder. "Blake?" Amy asked gently.

I swiped my tears away and turned to see her sweet face. The way she was looking at me with such empathy made me cry even harder. She set down the *Us Weekly* with its headlines speculating Danny Beaton and Pia Alvarez were dating (IS THE POP PRINCESS PREGNANT WITH BEATON'S BABY?) and rushed to my side. Charisse watched the two of us without emotion, like we were onstage performing a play and she wasn't interested in the outcome.

Amy knelt next to the chair. "Don't worry about the stuff they're saying online," she said.

"You saw it?" I asked, mortified.

"Some of it," she admitted. "My friends sent me a few links. But I told them that I've spent time with you and that you're really nice, and to make sure they wrote comments saying stuff like how you weren't a witch."

Charisse rolled her eyes behind Amy.

"You did?" I asked. Was she serious?

"Sure I did," she said. "Just check out Garrett B.'s comment on *TeensBlogToo*."

I scrolled through the dozens of comments until I found it. Garrett B. wrote:

I happen to know secondhand that Blake Dawkins is a real nice person deserving of another chance. Plus, she has an amazing rack.

Amy reddened. "I didn't tell him to write the part about your boobs," she said.

I smiled a little, but then my eye caught the comments below Garrett's:

The funny thing is that Blake's the ugliest one there! So now that we know she's mean, too, it's time she gets the boot.

Sayonara, mean girl.

And she walks kinda weird, too.

She's totally the ugliest!

There were so many times I'd said worse stuff to other Harrison kids, so cavalierly, so utterly unconcerned about how it would make them feel. I was everything Nina had said and more. I tried to look away from the computer, but I couldn't tear myself from the comments parading down the page.

And how stupid did she sound when she answered that question about the issues facing American teens?

She basically froze and that judge tried to save her. Haha. She's mean, stupid, and the least pretty person in the contest.

So true! She's by far the worst looking. Let's vote the stupid ugly mean girl off!

The irony stared me in the face: I'd spent years tormenting the kids I'd thought were somehow less than me. But all of that time *I* was the freak. I was the monster. The more comments I read, the harder I cried, until Amy could barely hold onto me. "Blake, please, calm down," she said.

"I'm a monster," I said, sobbing. I took a breath and tried to calm down, or at least lower my voice. "I blew this contest. And it was the one thing I thought I had that could redeem me. Now everyone knows the truth about me."

"You didn't blow anything," Amy tried. "It's not over till it's over."

I sniffed back tears, not wanting to admit what I was about to say. "Amy, all those things that girl Nina wrote about me are true." I fiddled with the thin gold band on my index finger. "You should know the truth about me, too," I said. Here Amy was defending me to her friends, not knowing everything I'd done.

Amy considered me. Her light blue eyes were rimmed with thick black lashes, and she had a way of looking at you that made you feel like she could really see you. A little while ago, that would've made me feel uncomfortable. But now, I prayed she *could* see me, or at least see the somebody I wanted to be.

Amy glanced up at the two cameras positioned in the corners of our bedroom. She angled herself so that she was facing away from them. "Once I stole tampons and candy," she said in a hushed voice. She tucked a lock of curled blond perfection behind her ear. She looked nervous, like I was going to tell on her or something.

"What kind?" I asked her.

"Tampax Pearl," she said.

I laughed a little. "I meant the candy," I said, and then she laughed, too.

"I think Good and Plenty," she said, "but I forget. I was only fourteen." She glanced over her shoulder at Charisse, who was busy folding her half-dozen lace thongs into triangles and rearranging them in her suitcase, and then at the cameras again. She lowered her voice to say, "My family hit on hard times a few years back. My father lost his job, and our food budget meant no coffee, no snacks, and definitely no candy. Quitting candy cold turkey felt like how they describe withdrawal in health class. I swear I had the shakes."

I smiled at her. But it wasn't the same. She wasn't bad like me. She was pure goodness. "Stealing candy isn't as bad as hurting someone," I said.

"We all do things we feel bad about," she said. "And when we do, the only thing to be done is to move forward in a different direction."

I wanted to believe her, but what if what I'd done was so bad that there was no way to make up for it, no way to redirect my course?

"My mom is sick, Blake," Amy said in a low voice, "and we don't have health insurance. Remember how I told you I want the new house part of the prize because I share a room with my sisters? That's not really why. I don't care about sleeping in the same room as my sisters. I kind of like it, actually. What's really going on is that we're about to lose our house. And I'm scared we'll all get separated and have to live with different relatives." Her voice was so quiet I could barely hear her. "I'm telling you this because I trust you," she said, leveling her light eyes on me. "So tell me: How can everything this girl says about you be true when you're the only person here who's shown me kindness? Maybe that girl was writing about an old version of you, but the past is past."

I looked into Amy's clear blue eyes, wishing I could fix everything she needed. "Is your mom going to be okay?"

"I don't know. I really don't," Amy said. "I hope so."

My tears had stopped, but now hers had started. I wrapped my arms around her shoulders. "I hope so, too," I said, pulling her tight against me. I felt a hollowed-out space within me that was ready to be filled with something different. Everything Amy had said played through my mind on repeat, like each and every word could save me. What if she was right? What if I could start over?

I pulled Amy closer, rubbing her back as she cried. "It's going to be okay," I said over and over again, praying my words would come true.

chapter thirty-three

"That's right, ladies! Roadkill. America's thirty-second most common cause of automobile accidents is now your number one priority."

The late-morning California sun bore down on us twelve contestants lined up along Highway 405. Delores fanned herself next to me. Cindy got teary-eyed and said, "The poor creature." (The cameras weren't even filming her: That's just the first thing that came to her mind when she saw the skunk. Maybe animals were her soft spot?)

I was trying not to look at it, but the skunk smell was so strong you couldn't really pretend it wasn't there. The whole situation was ridiculous enough to distract me from the awful (and mostly true) things being said about me online. I was trying to focus on everything Amy had said this morning, but it was difficult to remember when I saw how a bunch of Harrison kids had joined in the fun, posting random pictures of me captioned with the mean things I'd said or done to them since the start of high school. I knew deep down that Amy's words were true, but why was it so hard to hold on to the truth when bad stuff started happening?

"Squirrels, rabbits, deer, skunks, possum," the roadkill woman said. Her white-streaked hair was tied back with an actual rubber band, not the kind they make for hair. She wore a blue-gray jumpsuit uniform with ETTA stitched above her uniboob. Sun glinted off her aviator shades and the buckles of her combat boots, and she wasn't smiling.

A cameraman zoomed in on Etta as she waxed on about the safety of handling most forms of roadkill. "Lots of folks in other parts of our fine country actually like to eat roadkill," she said. "Waste not, want not! Hell, PETA even says right on their website that roadkill is a superior option to the neatly shrink-wrapped plastic packages of meat in the supermarket."

My stomach turned. She couldn't be serious.

"But it seems roadkill isn't good enough for fancy, high-falutin, Los Angelenos," Etta said as she passed out shovels. "They'd rather eat at Spago." Etta thrust a heavy wooden shovel in my direction, and I grabbed the handle, trying not to think about what we were about to do.

"And that's where you ladies come in," Etta said. Her grin revealed a shiny silver tooth. "Let's Prettify America!" she bellowed into the camera.

Delores nudged me. "Check out Sabrina," she said.

I craned my neck to see Sabrina dry heaving dangerously

close to the highway as another cameraman filmed her. Cars whizzed past. Sabrina's hair blew wildly in the breeze, and she tried to gather it away from her face, but it was so long and luxurious that she couldn't quite get it all in her grip.

We spent the next few hours in our jean shorts and SBC Network–issued *The Pretty App Live* tank tops (white tanks, hot pink lettering across the chest) shoveling up roadkill and plopping it into the back of a yellow dump truck that drove ahead of us with lights flashing. Earlier that morning, Rich Gibbons had reminded us that America would be watching streaming video of everything we did, and that we should think about presenting ourselves in the very best light to win their votes. Viewers could vote all day, and as many times as they wanted. The voting didn't cut off until the very last second before they announced the winner. Even though America seemed to hate me, and I was pretty certain I'd get voted off tonight, I still tried to smile for the camera and say upbeat things about the roadkill. Might as well try my best till it was over.

When the camera people went on break (union rules) Mura picked up an animal and said, "This is what America wants?" Then she smiled into an imaginary lens. "I'm going to bring this squirrel home and grill it tonight for dinner," she said cheerily, like she was doing a commercial. "Roadkill is an excellent option for a low-cost meal high in protein!" We all laughed as she flung the squirrel into the back of the truck.

A few hours and several obsessively thorough showers

later, a limo carried us to a public school in downtown Los Angeles. Mura sat in the back of the limo, breathing into a brown paper bag while Casey and Jessica rubbed her back. We should have known: the cameras are never off.

While the regular camera crew ate their lunch, one of the assistant producers had whipped out his buyPhone and filmed the whole Mura roadkill-as-what's-for-dinner episode. The video clip had spread across the internet, along with headlines like BEAUTY QUEEN EATS ROADKILL. Someone from her hometown had submitted a photo of Mura holding her two hamsters and captioned it: ARE THEY NEXT?

It felt like a war zone online, like if anyone captured a photo or video of you doing something embarrassing or scandalous, they got off on spreading it. I'd spent all of high school reading gossip blogs without thinking twice about what it would feel like to be the celebrity behind the gossip. Now I knew.

"Welcome to Clearview Elementary School," Marsha said as our limo pulled in front of a gray concrete building. The camera people filmed us lining up single file and passing through a metal detector. They followed us down a long hallway and through an open classroom door. My heart squeezed when I saw the judges. Leo stood between Shilpa and Bradley Searing Jones as the three of them watched Danny Beaton sing his new song, "Girl, You Amaze Me," a cappella for a classroom of rapt eight-year-olds. Carolina leaned against a blackboard with arithmetic scrawled in yellow chalk. Leo examined his fingernails, looking bored out of his mind. I had no idea he'd be here, and now I was a thousand times more nervous than before. The emotion racing through me from the events of the last twenty-four hours felt like way more than I could handle, but I had to. I didn't want to live up to Marsha's *train wreck* label. I was the one who wanted a career in Hollywood, and I knew I could do this.

I took a breath, and when Danny finished, I smiled and applauded along with everyone else as the cameras scanned the twelve of us contestants.

Pia appeared from behind an easel. "Here are the *Pretty App Live* contestants now!" she said, grinning. Leo's head snapped in my direction. His hair was wavier than usual and a little mussed, like he'd spent the morning at the beach. He watched us file into the classroom, his eyes never leaving me. His presence felt like a force, like I was being pulled in his direction and there was nothing I could do to stop it.

"Good afternoon, contestants," Pia said, tucking a golden-brown strand of hair behind her ear. M&M-size diamonds dotted her earlobes. (Probably another gift from a famous jewelry designer.) "Please meet Mrs. Cesarz's third-grade class." Pia wore a plaid jumper that looked like a private-school uniform and seemed weirdly out of place. Most of the kids wore ripped jeans, T-shirts, and beat-up sneakers or flip-flops. "Today, you'll be painting a mural over the vandalism that the school endured last week," Pia said, her voice dipping into *this is super serious* mode. "The mural will represent hope, forgiveness, and all the ways *The Pretty App Live* is prettifying America!"

We all smiled at the cameras and the children, who looked much less excited about us than they had about Danny Beaton.

Pia led us outside and the judges followed. There was a smudged yellow-chalk mirror image of 22 + 22 = 44 on the back of Carolina's vest from where she'd been leaning against the chalkboard. Marsha raced over and tried to beat it off, and Carolina snapped, "Be careful! It's cashmere!" I tried not to notice how close Leo was standing to me, but I couldn't help it. His nearness felt like warmth on my skin.

"Our thanks to Benjamin Moore Paints for their generous donation," Pia said to the camera, gesturing to the dozen or so cans of paint that lined the sidewalk. Black spray-painted letters spelled racist words on the wall of the school. The third graders looked anxious, seeming embarrassed that we were seeing it. One little girl started to cry, and Amy went to her side. "It's okay," Amy said, kneeling so that she was at the girl's level. "What's your name?" she asked.

"Cara," the girl said.

"I babysit a little girl named Cara back home," Amy said, and the girl grinned. "You do?" she asked. Amy nodded, and the camera caught her giving the little girl a hug. Of course Amy was good with children. No surprise there.

Marsha passed out paintbrushes. I watched her hand one to Leo, who thanked her. He met my glance just for a breath and then busied himself examining his paintbrush.

"I think we should paint a rainbow," Charisse said. "Do you kids like rainbows?"

I rolled my eyes. Of course they liked rainbows. Who didn't?

"Or puppies," Cindy said, sidling next to Charisse like they were a team. Sabrina stood next to me, looking pissed.

"Or cutesy little babies," I said. "C'mon, ladies! Have some imagination. I say we do a rock-and-roll scene. What do you kids think?"

The third graders cheered. "Like Metallica!" a little boy shouted. "My dad listens to them."

"Or Yanni," another girl said.

"Um, *no*," Sabrina said to the girl.

The kids flocked around us and started shouting their ideas for a rock-and-roll mural. Cindy and Charisse looked annoyed, but Amy was grinning. "Whatever makes you kids happy," she said, moving close to Sabrina and me with a smile that said *I don't care that you called me a Manure-Shoveling Cowgirl, Sabrina. We're all in this for the sake of the children.*

I tried to blend in with the kids, using my paintbrush in broad strokes and pretending I didn't care when a little girl painted a black streak along my brand-new AG jeans. "Sorry!" she said, and I tried to smile forgiveness through clenched teeth. Children were not my strong suit.

"Can I make a butterfly?" a little boy asked me.

"Um, this is sort of an indoor scene," I said, working with my brush to make a microphone stand.

"So?" the little boy asked.

The camera was filming both of us.

"Butterflies don't usually hang out inside," I said,

279

forcing a smile. I used my most gentle voice, but the boy suddenly looked like he was going to cry. America hated me enough already: I could *not* make a little boy cry. "But maybe your butterfly flew in through a door to see the concert," I said. A laugh sounded next to me and I turned to see Leo. I ignored him, pouring my attention back onto the little boy. "Want me to help you?" I asked, and the boy nodded. We worked together for a few minutes, outlining the wings and talking about different kinds of butterflies. As far as children went, he was actually pretty cute. Leo finally left to work somewhere else, and I was almost starting to enjoy myself when I heard Sabrina growl, "What the hell?"

I followed the direction of her paintbrush to see Delores painting a near-perfect picture of James Hetfield, the lead singer of Metallica. His black T-shirt read METALLICA in white letters, and Delores was in the process of giving him light blue jeans with rips on the knees. The portrayal was so accurate it could've appeared on his *Wikipedia* page.

"Incredible," Leo said softly.

The hair on the back of my neck stood up at the sound of his voice. I hadn't realized he was close again. I turned to face him. Nearly everyone had flocked to watch Delores, and we were standing by ourselves. "Please, Leo," I said. "Don't make this harder."

I smelled his perfect boy smell and let my eyes fall on him. I didn't want to get emotional on camera—I'd done that enough already—but just being there with him and hearing his voice made me choke up. Warm California air stirred between us as I tried to breathe. A lone child tottered past to get closer to Delores.

Leo reached down and turned off his microphone, and then so did I.

"I'm not trying to make anything harder," he said. His dark blue shirt was untucked and a streak of white paint raced along his jaw like a lightning bolt. "I'm just trying to talk to you." His voice went so low I could barely hear him. *"I'm just trying to tell you that everything that happened between us was real."*

My heart quickened. His words felt like everything I'd ever needed to hear, and for a split second I worried I'd made them up. Hot tears stung my eyes as I took a step away from him. "Then why did you do this to me?" I asked, the words coming out softer than I meant them to. I wanted to be strong: I wanted to tell him that what he'd done wasn't okay.

"It was a mistake," Leo said, closing the distance between us. I wanted to lean my head against his chest and feel him fold his arms around me. I wanted to tilt my chin and let him kiss me. But I couldn't. Not in front of everyone, and not with everything that had happened. "I've wanted to explain this to you, Blake, you have to believe me. But it's not like I can do anything over the phone—I can't text, I can't call. Public can easily access my phone," Leo said quickly, keeping track of where the cameras were.

I opened my mouth to say something, but Leo wasn't finished. "I went to Harrison as part of a job," he said, his voice urgent, like he was going to tell me this no matter what. "I'm nineteen, but I never actually graduated high school, so it was easy to get in as long as I had an address in the school district. I was supposed to watch Audrey, to keep her from doing what she'd done last time, which was basically almost bring Public down." He glanced around us, and then dropped his voice again. "That was the big priority. But you were there, too, and they wanted me to make sure you'd compete in the contest after your dad suggested that it would be in 'everyone's best interests' for you to make the finals. Public wants him happy. I'm sure you know that." Leo lifted a hand like he wanted to touch me, to hold me, to make sure I understood what he was telling me. Instead, he dropped his hand to his jeans and stared at me like maybe, if he wished it hard enough, I would somehow magically be okay with his explanation.

But I wasn't.

"My dad fixed the contest. And you set me up," I said.

"It's not like that."

"It's exactly like that."

"Okay," Leo said, stepping the tiniest bit closer. "Maybe it is like that. But I didn't know you when I signed up for this. I thought it was going to be like any other job."

"Do you always fool people on your jobs?"

"That's not what I meant."

I knew it wasn't, but I didn't want to admit it. I didn't want to give him anything right now.

"There were so many chances for you to tell me," I said.

Because really, that was what made me the most upset: Leo had lied to me, and then he'd kept up the lie until we were face-to-face on national television. "If everything you felt for me was real, like you said it was, then you could've told me."

"I know, Blake, trust me, I know. And I tried a few times. I really did. I swear."

"But you didn't," I said. I turned toward the kids cheering on Delores. I watched Pia study cue cards, and Marsha come up beside her and gesture to Sabrina and Amy. I couldn't make out what she was saying.

No one seemed to notice us, but if we kept on talking like this I knew they'd get suspicious sooner or later. I tried to keep my face neutral as I turned back to Leo, like we could be talking about any old thing, not betrayal and heartbreak.

"I should've told you," Leo said, his gaze intense. "I'm sorry. But can you try to understand why I didn't? Visiting Harrison and being on this reality show is my last gig for Public. It was supposed to be simple." He ran a hand through his hair. Seeing him agitated put me even more on edge. "But then things got out of control," he said. "I didn't expect to fall for you."

My breath caught. Leo reached out his hand. I wanted to take it, but I couldn't move. I couldn't speak. I couldn't do anything at all, really.

Applause sounded from the crowd that surrounded Delores. My heart was pounding as I took in Leo's face.

I didn't expect to fall for you.

"But you lied to me, Leo," I said, unable to keep the emotion from my face this time. "You lied to me just like my dad did. How am I ever supposed to trust anything you say?" My words were choked with tears, and when Leo started to defend himself, I didn't let him. "My entire life, the one man who was supposed to be there for me never was. My dad prioritized his career over me at every turn. And now you've done the exact same thing. You made a job more important than me."

"That's not what I did, I—"

"It's exactly what you did," I said, my voice trembling. "And now we can't go back."

We stared at each other. I could feel the air between us warm with everything we felt and everything we wanted. Leo looked like he needed to say more, but the crowd around Delores was dispersing, and the cameramen circled wide to film all of us. Leo and I instinctively turned away from each other, using our paintbrushes to fill in nonexistent cracks in the mural as the cameras came closer.

A black town car pulled into the parking lot behind the cameras. Rich Gibbons got out, yakking on his cell phone and making wild hand gestures. Was he in on it, too? Was my reason for being here a secret kept only between Public higher-ups and my dad, or was the network involved?

Tears fell as I ran my paintbrush over the mural's stage. I'd tried to be better, and where had it gotten me? I'd been played by my father. I'd been played by Leo. I'd been humiliated and exposed in front of the entire country. Everyone watching the show would know who I really was:

Blake Dawkins. Queen Bee. Glamazon. Prettiest Girl in Harrison. Bitch.

chapter thirty-four

That night, Marsha lined us contestants up in the wings of the stage. The cameras shot a few minutes of us waiting there, and then Marsha instructed them to take their positions in the auditorium. I tried to take a few deep breaths. It was one of the few times we'd been free of the cameras all day, and thank God, because I had a wedgie. As much as I loved the cameras, they made certain things really hard, like adjusting your underwear, yawning, getting something out of your teeth, or—God forbid—farting.

I stood behind Delores, who was still on some kind of paint high. "Did you see the footage of me painting James Hetfield online?" she asked me, flushed and grinning. "I've already gotten calls from two different art schools."

The trash-talking online about me had only gotten worse, and I was feeling so awful that old instincts flared within me: instincts to bring someone else down instead of lift them up. Mean girl instincts.

I took a breath. *No.*

"That's incredible," I said, realizing it was true. "You're an amazing artist."

Pia's voice broke through our conversation from beyond the velvet curtains: "Good evening, America!"

"Thanks, Blake," Delores said over the audience's applause, smiling sweetly. "And you're awesome on TV. A natural, really."

I wasn't expecting her compliment, and it made me feel so good that my grin widened to match hers. Marsha cut between us and said, "Girls, shut up! Your mics are about to go live." She shook her head like we were idiots, and Delores started laughing, and then so did I. I didn't usually get along with other girls all that easily, but I'd done it in the last few days. First with Amy and a little with Maddie, too, and now Delores. And maybe I could still do it at Notre Dame if people could just see past everything they'd heard about me.

"Please welcome America's most beautiful teens!" Pia shouted, and then the curtain flung open and Marsha screamed at us to start walking.

Delores paraded into the bright white lights and I followed. My heels trod the red carpet walkway and I contorted my arm into a Miss America wave just like Delores did. I heard Mura curse under her breath behind me. She hadn't been quite right since the roadkill incident went viral. I took my place at the end of the stage and kept my eyes from straying in Leo's direction. The warmth of the spotlight coursed over my body and cast an ivory glow onto my billowy white, Grecian-style dress.

"Who will survive tonight's elimination round?" Pia asked as we all lined up. She smiled sweetly at the audience like she was selling Girl Scout cookies.

The massive screen lowered from the ceiling and played a montage of today's events. Most shots focused on Delores's painting and Mura's roadkill declaration. I cringed when the audience started laughing. I could feel Mura shrinking beneath their ridicule, and then I did something without thinking, something I wouldn't usually do. I reached for her hand and took it. Her palm was soaking wet. I didn't dare turn to look at her.

"Roadkill Beauty Queen!" someone shouted from the front row. I squinted to look closer, and it was hard to be sure because of the lights, but I swore it was Sabrina's mom.

Mura's grip tightened on mine, and then completely relaxed. And then she dropped to the floor.

"Mura!" Sabrina cried from beside her. A gasp sounded across the auditorium.

I knelt to the ground where Mura's olive skin was eerily white beneath the spotlight. I picked up her head and put it into my lap. Then I brushed away the pieces of black hair sticking to her forehead. Maddie elbowed past Sabrina and Cindy and arranged Mura's flowing emerald-colored dress to cover her skinny legs.

"We need a doctor!" Pia screamed into her microphone, which turned out to be unnecessary, because two paramedics flew onto the stage carrying a stretcher, which struck me as a tad dramatic.

Mura's eyes fluttered open, and she glanced worriedly at Maddie and me. "It's okay, Mura," I said.

"You just passed out a little bit," Maddie said. "It will probably help your ratings."

"Oh my God," Mura moaned. I tried to tell the paramedics she seemed okay, but they were rolling her onto the stretcher.

"It's procedure," one of them said, brushing my hand away from Mura's.

The paramedics hiked Mura into the air and started carrying her away, but Mura sat up straight and waved to the audience like she was Cleopatra and the stretcher was a chariot. The audience went wild.

"She's okay!" Pia shouted. "*Thank God.* Mura's okay!"

Mura waved with both hands now, and the audience screamed.

"We love you, Mura!" a voice shrieked as Mura was carted off the stage.

I moved closer to Sabrina to fill in the spot where Mura had stood. Sabrina was smiling out at the audience, but it didn't really feel right to grin like that, so I just stood there.

Pia's voice went quavery as she said, "I too suffer from vasovagal syncope." The lights dimmed, and Pia's eyes watered. "It's a difficult diagnosis," she said. "It basically means unexplained fainting."

"That happens to me, too!" Carolina said from her perch behind the judges table. "Every time I do the cayenne pepper and lemon juice cleanse, I pass out at least once a day."

Pia nodded sympathetically.

"Maybe you should try eating solid foods then, Carolina," Leo said.

"That's not the point of a colon cleanse, *genius*," Carolina snapped.

Danny Beaton laughed and said, "Pia, I think we better get this show on the road. I'm ready to send some of these ladies packing."

"How generous of you," Leo said. He and Danny glared at each other.

"The show must go on," Pia said cheerfully. "Even in the face of vasovagal syncope." The lights around Pia brightened, and a small boy emerged from the side of the stage carrying a large gold envelope. Upon closer inspection, I realized he was the little boy from the school who'd wanted to draw butterflies.

"Please welcome Oliver Daniel with the results of our nation's votes. Oliver is a student from Mrs. Cesarz's third grade class at Clearview Elementary School"

Oliver's big brown eyes widened as he crossed the stage toward Pia. He thrust the envelope into her hand and bolted back in the direction he'd come from.

"Are you all ready for tonight's first elimination round?" Pia shouted.

I felt less nervous than I thought I would as the audience cheered. I knew I'd be voted off tonight, but at least I could go back home to my regular life, and even if it wasn't perfect, it was still far away from the charade of pretending to belong in this contest, and far away from Leo and the feelings I was desperate to leave behind.

Pia tore open the envelope. Her eyes scanned the list, and she smiled to herself. I couldn't decipher the satisfaction on her face. Was it what she'd wanted? What she'd expected?

"Murasaki O'Neil!" Pia shouted, staring directly into the camera. "If you're watching right now from the ambulance or the ER, I want to personally tell you that you're safe! You've made it through the first round of eliminations."

The audience cheered for Mura and held up signs. Some of the signs depicted small animals. One read: ANIMAL MURAderer! and pictured a drawing of Mura chasing a small raccoon with a fork.

Pia's hair was curled '40s-style, like Veronica Lake's. She used her pinky to adjust a wayward strand near her temple and said, "And now for the contestants with the highest number of votes this week: Sabrina Ramirez, Charisse Thompson, and Blake Dawkins!"

What?

"Ladies," Pia said, "please take your places on the white chairs. You're safe tonight."

I froze—momentarily stunned. How was that even possible? Tens of thousands of people were hating on me around the country. They'd declared their disgust on every social media outlet known to man. And *Sabrina*? Where was Amy on that list? I knew that Hollywood was an industry that often rewarded bad behavior, but America seemed to have fallen in love with Amy. I turned to see Amy's face. She looked on the verge of tears. I quickly looked away, embarrassed to see her like that. My heart pounded as I tried to figure out what was going on. There were still two more spots—maybe Amy would stay.

I made my way numbly to the plush white chairs at the edge of the stage. I tried to look excited about being safe, but really my mind was churning. What if this was part of my dad's plan with Public? What if it wasn't just about me participating but about me *winning*? Was it possible? Could they—would they—skew the votes?

They could. They would. I suddenly felt sure of it.

"Mura, Sabrina, Charisse, and Blake, you've made it through tonight's elimination round," Pia said. "Congratulations!" She turned to the remaining eight contestants. "There are two more spots left in the top six. Which of you have made America fall in love with you? And which of you have left them cold?"

My stomach turned. It was bad enough that my dad got me here. But for Public to rig the results so I'd win?

I tried to breathe as Pia prattled on. I needed to talk to my dad. I needed the truth, no matter how scared I was to hear it.

"Amy, Maddie, Delores, and Betsy, please come and stand on my left side," Pia said. The four girls walked stiffly toward Pia. Amy and Maddie were looking down at their feet. Amy looked like she was going to be sick. Delores and Betsy held their heads up and smiled.

"Jessica, Casey, Delia, and Cindy, please stand on my right," Pia said.

Pia looked at the group on her right, and then to the group on her left. "Only one of you on each side of me is safe," she said. She turned to Jessica, Casey, Delia and Cindy. "Cindy, you're safe!" The audience burst into applause. Pia clapped, too, and then she said, "Jessica, Casey, and Delia, pack your bags. You're going home tonight."

"No," Casey said, and Jessica started crying. Delia looked pissed.

"We're so sorry to see you go," Pia said without seeming sorry at all. Her head snapped in the direction of the other group. "Delores, Betsy, and Maddie are going home, too. Good-bye, Delores," she said in a cold monotone. "Good-bye, Betsy. Good-bye, Maddie."

Delores let out a small shriek. She shook her head and then immediately started sobbing. Betsy joined her and so did Maddie. Bodyguards emerged from the curtains. "Why?" Delores cried into her hands as the bodyguards escorted all six of them offstage.

Amy watched the whole thing, looking bewildered.

"That's right, Amy," Pia said smoothly, her smile back in place. "You're safe. Congratulations!"

Relief washed over Amy's face. She looked like her life had just been spared as she raced over to join our group, and after everything she'd told me last night I understood why. We all exchanged hugs and platitudes, letting out little shrieks of excitement. I squeezed Amy's hand and whispered in her ear, "You did it!"

"Told you it's not over till it's over," she said.

"America," Pia said gravely. "These are the candidates you've voted as your top contenders. Consider them carefully. Only one will be Public's Pretty App Prettiest Girl in America."

As Amy hugged me tight, I caught Leo's glance over her shoulder. After tonight's results, I was surer than ever that Public was working behind the scenes to manipulate the show.

I know Public has rigged the contest, I thought. *I know you helped them do it.*

chapter thirty-five

"This way!" Audrey said a few hours later, yanking me behind the cover of azalea bushes. "Couldn't you have changed into something a little less glow-in-the-dark?"

I was still wearing my billowy white gown, and the fabric made me look like a ghost moving through the darkness. "Lindsay didn't exactly pack me a getaway outfit," I said, and Audrey grinned. Our breathing was heavy as we edged along the line of the trees leading away from Audrey's guesthouse. It was nearly one in the morning, and we'd waited until the producers and the camerapeople left, presumably to call it a night. Still—I was freaked out. If we got caught sneaking off campus it was grounds for me to get kicked off the show. But we had to get away: We needed somewhere safe to talk. What if there were secret cameras or listening devices hidden in the walls at Audrey's?

Our feet scuffed over the white stones that lined the driveway. Audrey's sneaker snapped a twig and the sound made me jump. I grabbed her hand, and we moved faster and faster until we were sprinting across the lawn.

Audrey let out a squeal when we reached the edge of the driveway. "I think we're safe," I said, breathless. We raced down the neighborhood's hilly road past white stucco houses and palm-tree-lined sidewalks. We came to an intersection, and we were silently waiting to cross when a Jeep Wrangler zoomed down the hill. "Crap!" Audrey said when she saw it. It looked like the safari-man's car. Headlights blinded us. The Jeep zoomed past us, and I made out the silhouettes of two women. "It's not him," I said, giddy with relief.

The traffic light changed, and we ran across the street. On the other side of the intersection, beneath the streetlamps, Audrey looked at me in my evening gown and burst out laughing. "I think you're dressed just right for In-N-Out," she said, pointing to the burger joint. I glanced through the window and made out three or four diners, and plenty of empty tables. "It's perfect," I said.

We pushed open the restaurant's door. Red-and-white tiles covered most of the walls. A white painted border cut through the tiles, stenciled with red palm trees swaying in an imaginary breeze. A neon-yellow sign shone with cursive letters that read QUALITY YOU CAN TASTE. The air smelled like french fries and Windex.

We ordered our food and took it to a table in the back.

Audrey listened to everything I suspected my dad and Public of doing, and then she was quiet for a few moments. Finally, she swallowed a bite of her burger and said, "I know they played you, and I get why you want revenge. But you don't want to mess with Public. They're dangerous. They almost ruined my entire future last year, Blake. Or at least my chance of getting into college."

"It's not just me," I said. I picked up the grilled cheese I'd ordered from the In-N-Out Secret Menu, a tip I got from Lindsay's *Blake and Audrey's Guide to Los Angeles*. The guide was so extensive that I'd asked Audrey when Lindsay had spent time in LA, but Audrey had said, "Never. She just knows stuff."

The sandwich smelled like plastic-wrapped single-sliced cheese, the kind my mom never let us get at the grocery store. "They took advantage of Leo, too," I said. I bit into the deliciousness of the preservative-laced food. Maybe I couldn't forgive Leo, but I could still be pissed on his behalf. "And Amy should be the one winning this contest, not me. I shouldn't even have made it past the first cut." Amy's private words to me in the green room after tonight's show raced through my mind: *I wasn't even in the top votes category. I'm not going to win this thing, am I?*

"Yeah, well, some companies do bad things," Audrey said. "Don't you watch movies? Half of them are about big bad companies and their dark, dangerous secrets."

"So we're just going to do nothing?"

Audrey jabbed her french fry in my direction. "That's

exactly what we're going to do," she said.

I snatched the fry from her fingers and popped it into my mouth. "This doesn't sound like you," I said between bites. "You were the one who told me to fight."

Audrey pursed her lips. "That's because I believed you could win this contest with or without Public's scheming," she finally said. "But I don't know if we can win against Public, and I don't want to put us in jeopardy just because your dad and Public have morality problems."

"So you agree with me—you think they're cheating?"

Audrey shrugged. "It's possible." She dipped two fries in ketchup. "The Pretty App voting application allows users to vote more than once from the same IP address. So you could write a script that casts multiple votes automatically."

I thought about Leo. If this was what Public was doing, it was something one of their employees—someone like him—had programmed. Did he know about it? Had he been the one to do it?

"So how do we prove it?"

"I can't prove it without illegally hacking their systems," Audrey said. She looked down at her hands and let go of a breath. "I don't want to do that again, Blake. Please don't ask me to."

"I wouldn't," I said, meaning it no matter how disappointed I was. I'd already lost everything; maybe there was some way to make things right and I just had to find it. I picked up my cell. "I'm calling my dad," I told Audrey.

Her eyes went wide, so I said, "You know I at least have to ask him."

My mom had left me a voicemail after last night's premiere saying how proud they were of me, but I hadn't heard anything from them today about the footage shown online from the roadkill pickup and the school's mural. Maybe they'd seen Nina's awful letter on *TeensBlogToo* and were too disappointed to talk.

"Blake?" My father sounded strained on the other line. It was the middle of the night South Bend time. No doubt I'd woken him. "Are you all right?" he asked.

"I'm fine, Dad," I said, fumbling for the best way to do this. "I'm sorry to call so late, but I was wondering if I could talk to you about something?" I asked, my voice question-marking and squeaky.

He cleared his throat. He didn't say anything, so there was nothing for me to do except blurt it out. "Did you and Public arrange for me to win the contest?" I asked. I met Audrey's glance across the beige plastic table. She was staring at me with a french fry frozen in midair, her dark eyebrows furrowed with worry.

My dad was silent.

"Is she okay?" I heard my mother ask in the background. "Tell her not to worry about all those lies people are telling about her. Tell her we saw the show and we loved her dress." She sounded like she knew something was wrong and was trying to fix it.

"Where would you ever get an idea like that?" my father

snapped, suddenly very awake. And then he laughed to himself. "Did Audrey come up with it?"

"No," I said, annoyed that he'd even suggested that. Did he assume I couldn't figure it out on my own? "It's something I found out while I was here," I said. I tried to sound like I had proof, even if I didn't. "And I wanted to hear it from you."

My father's voice was muffled like his hand was over the phone. He was saying something to my mom, and then I heard a door shut.

"Now you listen here, Blake," he said. "Everything I've ever done for you has been for your benefit and for the benefit of this family."

He didn't deny it, which was basically the same thing as him admitting it. I knew my dad—if I'd accused him of something so bad as cheating on a national level and he hadn't done it, he would've been pissed and defensive. It was possible he'd act pissed and defensive even if he *had* done it. But for him to feed me some BS line that everything he'd done was for my own benefit and the benefit of my family was basically the same thing as him saying *I did it*.

"I want what's best for you," I heard him say, and even after everything he'd ever done, I still felt shocked that he'd gone this far. My skin went cold as I tried to make sense of his words rambling together. "I always have," he said. "And being beautiful is your strong suit, and I know you want this, too."

"Okay, Dad," I said, my voice shaky. "I think I understand." In his warped mind, me being in the public eye and winning a beauty contest was what was best for me and for our family, even if he had to fix the contest to make it happen. I felt one step closer to understanding how he operated.

It just didn't mean I had to operate that way, too.

chapter thirty-six

From: Blake.Dawkins@Public.com
To: Alec.Pierce@Public.com

Dear Public CEO Alec Pierce and to whomever else it may
concern,
I am aware that I do not belong in this contest. Please do not
crown me the winner or runner-up in tonight's final round of
competition, or else I will be forced to reveal what I know.

Blake Dawkins

My fingers shook as I pressed send. I whirled around to
face Audrey and covered my mouth with my hands.

"You did it," she said.

"I did it." I felt more nervous than ever before, but
relieved, too. I was doing the right thing—I could feel it.

It was almost three a.m., and we were back in Audrey's guest room. In-N-Out had closed at one thirty, and we figured now that I'd gone and formally accused Public, it wasn't like any hidden recording devices would even matter.

"So now what do we do?" I asked Audrey as I drummed my fingertips on the desk.

Audrey squished her butt next to me in the ergonomic chair and pressed refresh on my inbox. "We wait," she said. Then she ripped open a bag of M&M's and a box of Good & Plenty that reminded me of Amy's story about stealing the candy. She offered me some but I shook my head, too nauseous to even consider it. "What if they don't email me back?" I asked her. Email was the only contact information we had for Public—we figured Alec Pierce's address would be the same configuration as everyone else who used a Public email account. We'd toyed with the idea of talking to Marsha and Rich, but we were worried they might not even know about any of this. Public could be the only ones pulling the strings behind the scenes.

"They'll email," Audrey said, "or they'll figure out some way to get a message to you. They're not going to take a chance that you'll blow their cover. They've had enough PR fiascos this year, courtesy of me." She sorted the brown M&M's away from the colored ones, and the white Good & Plenty candies away from the purple ones, and shaped them all into an oval pile. "What?" she asked when I gave her a look. "I'm trying to avoid food coloring." She shoved the brown M&M's into her mouth and refreshed my inbox again.

Nothing.

"Maybe no one at Public is awake," I said at four o'clock.

"They're Trogs," Audrey said. "Trogs don't really sleep all that much."

Eleven minutes of me deep breathing and Audrey eating brown M&M's later, an email with the subject line *Are you sure about that?* popped up from an unidentified sender. I was too nervous to open it, so Audrey did. There wasn't any text inside the email, only a video attachment. I looked closer and my stomach dropped.

"No way," Audrey said.

I knew what it was the minute I saw the freeze frame, but Audrey pressed play anyway. The video of Nic kissing her girlfriend at Notre Dame came to life on my screen. We both scrambled to press stop, and then stared at each other.

"Public," I said, unbelieving.

"Bastards," Audrey said. Then she turned to me. "They've got you."

My throat felt like it was closing. "You really think they'd release this?"

"They'll show it to your dad at the least."

"How did they even get the video?"

"Maybe they just keep tabs on you and your family," Audrey said. "Maybe they have alerts in place for when any of you show up on the internet."

A pit formed in my stomach. "What if Leo did it?" I asked, my voice hushed. What if he'd taken the video down from the site and stored it somewhere to be used later, if needed?

Audrey covered my hand with hers. "We don't know that," she said.

"But what if it was him? What if he used me even more than I realized?"

"Blake, listen," Audrey said in her *calm the F down* voice. "We need to focus on getting out of here without getting your sister exposed."

"So now what? I just go along with this? I win the show?"

"If you don't, if you try to say something about not belonging here, they'll just accuse you of being a hysterical, hormonal, insecure teenager who feels undeserving of her crown. *And* they'll do something with the video. They have ways to beat you, Blake. This is Hollywood," she said, her green eyes narrowing. "It's way worse than high school."

I shook my head. If Hollywood meant deceit, backstabbing, and head games, then maybe I knew the rules, but I needed to figure out another way to play. "I should go," I told Audrey, wrapping my arms around her shoulders and thanking her for the millionth time for everything she'd done for me.

I left Audrey's and called Nic from the dark woods between Audrey's house and the mansion. I was sobbing by the time I finished the story about everything that had happened since I'd arrived in LA, about what I'd figured out and what I'd tried to do, and about what Public threatened to do with her video to stop me. Nic was crying, too, when I finished, her voice shaking when she said, "I wish I could be there for you."

I stopped pacing and sat on a patch of cold grass. "It's okay, Nic," I said, letting go of a long breath. I tipped my head back and took in the tiny stars dotting the clear night sky.

"It's not," she said. "This isn't the first time that I haven't been there for you. I gave up on you and me and everything that we had together, and I'm so sorry." She started crying harder, and I wanted to reach through the phone and hug her. "I'm so sick of holding on to this secret," she said. "I don't know how much longer I can do it. It makes me feel a thousand pounds heavier."

Nic and I were both still a mess when we said our goodbyes, and right when I was about to hang up, she asked, "Have you read my letter yet?"

When I said no, she made me promise I'd read it as soon as I could.

I crossed the dark grass to the white cobblestone walkway and made my way to the door. I nearly screamed when I saw one of the cameramen on the front porch. He was dressed all in black and silently filming my entrance. It felt gross, like someone had spied on me naked and alone and unaware. I swiped at the mascara that I was sure had smeared while I was crying, and held my head high as I passed him.

"Where were you tonight, Blake?" he asked, smirking.

"Taking a walk to burn some calories," I said sweetly, figuring it was the most boring thing I could possibly say, and therefore wouldn't be used on air. Two could play at this game.

I yanked open the front door and took the marble staircase to my room. The hallway was dimly lit, and I glanced around to check for cameras in the shadows. I eased the bedroom door open and slipped into the darkness. Amy and Charisse's bodies made long lumps beneath their peach satin comforters. Moonlight fell on Amy's delicate shoulder.

I dug into my suitcase and pulled Nic's folded letter from beneath instant nail polish remover pads and gummy bears. I pulled a blanket over my head and used my phone to illuminate her handwriting, which looked just like mine.

Dear Blake,

I'm so proud of what you're doing. You're leaving your comfort zone in South Bend and trying something new. It won't always be easy, but no matter what happens, just give it your best shot and don't forget I'll be rooting you on the whole way.

I always used to dream about what it would be like to finally get to LA. I'm really glad you're testing the waters first. Maybe when you graduate Notre Dame I'll already be out there, and you can move out, too, and we can get an apartment together or something. You never know. It sounds like both of our dreams might take us there. I'm just so proud that you're starting to make progress on yours.

I want you to know that you are my sister and that I have always loved you. But something is changing, and over the course of the past couple weeks, I don't only love you, I like you. I like the person I see in you and I want to get to know her better. I hope you'll give me the chance.

Love,

Nic

chapter thirty-seven

That's what the letterboard sign read at the Sunoco gas station where Sabrina, Cindy, Amy, Charisse, Mura, and I had set up a car wash for "charity."

I held my hose at an angle, my hands cramped from squeezing the metal handle. The spray had nearly cleared the dirt crusted on the banged-up bumper of a Ford pickup. A skinny guy with an Adam's apple that made him look like he'd swallowed a Ping-Pong ball leered at me in the rearview mirror. "This is humiliating," I whispered to Amy.

"Beyond," she whispered back.

We were wearing the red-white-and-blue bikinis that

had arrived outside our bedroom door that morning in a gift-wrapped box with a note that read:

CHANGE INTO THESE. THE LIMO WILL PICK YOU UP AT NOON. BE PRETTY! (OUTFIT CHOICE NOT OPTIONAL.)

Glitter sparkled on our bikini bottoms, and stars paraded across our tops. Amy complained that the stars were purposely positioned to cover our nipples and make us look like porn stars. She and I had picked flip-flops, Charisse and Cindy wore kitten heels, and Sabrina and Mura wore stilettos. The whole thing was mortifying. Not like I have a problem wearing a bathing suit in public, but wearing a bathing suit while giving a car wash to any creep who saw us and pulled off the highway?

"Want to quit?" I asked Amy, only half-joking.

"Wish it were an option for me, Blake," she said, scrubbing at a stubborn patch of mud on the license plate.

Hot sun beat down on us. We smelled like the coconut sunscreen the show had provided (and filmed us applying).

"Woo-hoo!" Sabrina shouted as she sponged up a Cadillac with tinted windows. Her butt stuck out straight, her body making a perfect 90 degree angle that I was pretty sure wasn't necessary for car-washing. Cindy, not one to be outdone, said, "It's so hot out!" as the camerawoman filmed her, and then sprayed water all over herself. Mura watched the two of them, and then rolled onto the hood of a Camry and scissor-kicked her legs in the air. She made a sexy face at the camera, almost as good as Jessica Simpson's in *The Dukes of Hazzard* car wash video. Her arm was bandaged at the wrist from her stay at the hospital, but it clearly wasn't bothering her. She shimmied up the hood of the car on her elbows, and then traced a soapy finger down the length of the windshield wiper.

"Hey! Why can't you girls do somethin' like that?" yelled the guy from the front seat of the pickup Amy and I were trying to clean.

Amy looked on the verge of tears. "I can*not* do that," she said to me. "My parents are already going to have a heart attack. I promised them there was no swimwear competition."

"Don't worry about him," I said, and then, when I was sure the cameras weren't filming me, I sprayed the man in the face with my hose.

"What the—?!" he yelled, yanking his skinny head back into the car.

Amy burst into giggles. The man sped off, and the cameras turned to film us laughing. I was almost starting to enjoy myself when my phone rang from my bag. We weren't technically supposed to carry our phones with us, and Rich Gibbons shot me a dirty look, but instead of turning it off, I excused myself to go to the bathroom. I curved around a Dumpster to the back of the gas station, where two teenage boys holding skateboards were arguing over gum. They took off when they saw me.

I yanked my phone from my bag and saw the call was from my dad. I was almost too nervous to answer—what if he'd heard about my email to Public?—but I did anyway.

"Did you know about this?" he asked, his voice hard

and cold. "Did you know about your sister?"

I racked my brain. *He couldn't mean . . .*

"Dammit, Blake! Did you know a video of your sister kissing a girl is all over her Public Party page?"

"*What?*" I asked. "No, no, no . . ."

"Yes, Blake. Yes."

Blood rushed to my feet. Why would Public post the video? I hadn't outed them—I hadn't done *anything*.

I tried to steady myself against the chipped, white wall of the gas station. Audrey had said Public was dangerous—that they could beat me—but I never, *ever* would've sent that email if I had known they'd do this to my sister. I sank onto the grass, flashing back to Leo at dinner that night in Chicago, asking me if I'd *really* want something like this. His words raced through my mind: *It's not exactly flattering most of the time.*

Had he been trying to warn me? Why didn't I listen to him? How could I ever have thought this would be worth it?

The skater boys were back, riding over the pavement and laughing. The wheels on their skateboards made gravel-crunching noises so loud I couldn't hear what my father was saying until they disappeared around the other side of the gas station.

". . . with no regard for what this could do to us," my father yelled on the other line. "Because that's your sister. Selfish. Selfish to the bone."

"That's not true," I said. "She didn't want to disappoint

you, Dad. But this is who she is. Samantha is who she loves."

My dad hung up before I'd finished my sentence.

I put my head into my hands. I heard more cars speed over the pavement, and then Danny Beaton's voice saying, "Good morning, America!" even though it was the afternoon, and even though it wasn't a funny joke. The last thing I needed right now was an encounter with Leo. I lifted my head, but I could only see Danny and Bradley's bodyguards from my position behind the Dumpster. I heard Carolina say she should show us how swimsuits were *really* done, and then Shilpa shouted that all of this was derogatory toward women.

I couldn't go back out there. I wanted to curl up into a hole and transport myself back to South Bend. I wanted to rewind time to before any of this had happened so I could make a different decision. If I'd known who Leo was, if I'd known all the ways he could hurt me, I could've been more careful. And if I had known what this contest could do to me, how it could make me feel like a fraud and hurt Nic, I never would've done it. It made me never want to feel like a fraud again. It made me want to fight against it with everything I had. When I thought back to how hard I had tried at Harrison to be the prettiest, the toughest, the queen bee . . . it all seemed so foolish. All I wanted now was to go home and be myself, or at least try to figure out who that person even was.

Regret pounded my body. I pulled my knees to my

313

chest and felt the gravel dig into my thighs, but I didn't think I could stand up yet. I needed to warn Nic and tell her how sorry I was that I'd done this to her. I picked up my phone, but then I heard Leo's voice:

"I can just go back here. I don't need a velvet-covered toilet-throne like Beaton, for Christ's sake."

A hot gust of air carried the smell of garbage to where I sat, making me even more nauseous. Leo rounded the side of the gas station holding a key on a splintered piece of wood marked MEN's. He stopped dead when he saw me, his red Converse scuffing against the gravel.

"Are you all right?" he asked, searching my face.

I scrambled to stand. I wiped my eyes, feeling more ridiculous than ever in my stupid bikini. My hands were sweating on my phone. "Did you do this?" I asked, my voice barely a whisper.

"Do what?" Leo asked, stepping closer. His light hair curled just above his ears. Freckles dotted the smooth, tan skin over his nose.

I backed up until I was pressed against the white paint, my bare back scratching against the wall. "Did you give Public that video of my sister kissing her girlfriend?"

"*What?*" Leo asked, his eyes widening. "*No.* Of course not."

He moved even closer, but I threw my hands up and he stopped.

"Blake," he said, "I would never do something like that to anyone, let alone to you or your sister."

The air got hot between us, but there was no way I was

going to lose myself this time. "This is what I meant, Leo," I said, my voice hard. "Don't you get it? I can't trust you. I *can't*." Even if Leo was telling me the truth about this, and about his feelings for me, I couldn't trust someone who'd lied so cavalierly, and so many times. I was too scared of getting hurt again.

Right then one of the camera guys rounded the side of the gas station. He didn't say anything; he just came way too close to our faces and filmed us. Leo took a few steps back. I adjusted the strap of my bathing suit from where it had slid over my shoulder, and wiped the tears from my face, but I knew it was too late, I knew exactly what this looked like. I tried to smile, but it felt fake and forced. I could see the cameraman grinning behind the camera, like he'd caught us.

Leo gave the camera a small salute. He jingled the key to the men's room. "Just hitting the bathroom," he said. "Not much to see here."

"Just going to get some gum," I murmured. I ducked my head and moved past the cameraman, worried that making excuses probably made us look even guiltier.

Rich Gibbons saw me and beckoned me over to the car wash. He seemed annoyed, but I still needed to call my sister. I swung right into the gas station's mart. It smelled like peanuts and cherry Life Savers. I ducked into a row with cheese Combos and dialed Nic.

"Hey!" she said. "I'm watching the streaming footage of your car wash! How ridiculous is that backbend move Mura just did? Is she a gymnast or something?"

"Nic, listen, I need to tell you something," I said, my breathing fast.

"Actually, I need to tell *you* something," she said. She sounded wound up, like she was on a sugar rush. "Samantha and I stayed up all night last night talking. Sam said there's no way we could let Public hold that video over your head. We went together to tell her parents about us this morning, and they were, like, shockingly supportive. I mean, mostly her dad just nodded and adjusted the volume on the TV over and over, but then he hugged us. And her mom asked if we eventually planned to get married and adopt a baby. Apparently she likes the name Hannah for a baby girl. Anyway. Surprised, but okay." Nic took a breath, and I realized I'd been holding mine, too. "Sam and I posted the video online, Blake," she said. "I mean, it's so tame, anyway. It's not like it's a sex tape. And now that we're out, what's a little kiss going to do?"

Something flipped inside of me as I processed what she was saying. It hadn't been Public. It hadn't been Leo. It'd been my sister and Sam being brave.

"Dad's friends at Public can't hold anything against you now," Nic said. "You can do whatever you need to do. Whatever you think is right."

"Thank you," I said as my mind raced with everything this meant. "I'm so happy for you and Sam. And I'm proud of you."

"Thanks," she said. "I think I may try to work on a documentary next about all of this, about what it's like to come out." She let go of a breath. "Dad's super pissed about the video," she said, but of course, I already knew that. "Mom won't answer my phone calls. But Sam's so happy, and the whole thing makes me so happy I haven't been able to sit still all day. No more secrets," she said. "No more lies."

A bell jingled. I turned to see Rich Gibbons and the cameraman busting through the door of the mart. "Film her head-on," Rich Gibbons said. The cameraman hurried to my aisle and filmed me standing there in my tacky bikini next to the Pringles and Combos. Rich looked on with a smug face. The girl behind the counter asked, "Can I help anyone?" and Rich shushed her with his thick, hairy index finger.

"I have to go," I told Nic. "I love you."

"I love you, too, Blake."

I dropped the phone into my bag and smiled at the camera. I wasn't about to give them anything else. "Better get back to the car wash!" I said cheerfully. I pushed past them, not bothering to check my compact mirror. I suddenly didn't care as much about my smeared makeup and screwed-up hair. My sister was okay—*more* than okay.

No more secrets. No more lies. That's what she'd said, and I'd heard the relief in her voice. What if it could be true for me, too? What if there was a way to get Public to crown the *real* winner tonight—whoever that might be? What if there was a way to get them to vote me off and set me free?

chapter thirty-eight

'd never felt so nervous as I did that night sitting in the green room at the Westbrook Theater. Maroon 5 was performing onstage, the song filtering through two black speakers positioned next to our snack table. I couldn't stop running through every possibility for tonight's show. If they eliminated Amy, should I say something? And what exactly should I say? I could make a case that she deserved to win for being the most beautiful, kindest, funniest . . . but who would listen?

> *"Beauty queen of only eighteen*
> *She had some trouble with herself . . ."*

The speakers blared Adam Levine's voice as I thought about Leo. No matter what he'd done, no matter what had happened between us, I needed to apologize for suspecting him of leaking the video. Maybe Leo wasn't perfect, but neither was I. Far from it. I had to get him alone before I left tonight for good and never saw him again.

Francisco handed me a lip gloss and I smoothed it on. "Smile, gorgeous," he said. "You look great."

Amy gave me a wink from across the room. She stood still as Marsha sewed a small tear in the strap of her dress.

Adam Levine finished singing, and sounds of the audience cheering blasted through the speakers.

"Girls, get ready," Marsha said, her words warped from the pin she was holding between her teeth. "We're heading to the stage in two minutes."

Charisse stared straight ahead like a robot programmed to take over the contest. "This is it," Sabrina said softly. It was the first time I'd seen her look scared since she'd gotten here.

"Good luck, ladies," Mura said. Her arm was still bandaged at the wrist. She'd told me earlier that it didn't hurt, but that her mom told her to keep the bandages on to win sympathy votes.

"Oh my God," Cindy said suddenly. She was staring at her phone. And then she started laughing.

Sabrina looked over Cindy's shoulder and suddenly didn't seem scared anymore. She grinned and said, "Oh, wow, Blake, you *so* don't want to see this."

I snatched the phone from Cindy. A video flashed on her screen and I saw the unmistakable pink feather boa and Mardi Gras beads that I'd wrapped around my neck in the Martins' basement. I was dancing sexily on top of the costume chest as Justin Timberlake's voice sang out:

"Look at those hips (Go 'head be gone with it)
You make me smile (Go 'head be gone with it)"

My low-cut V-neck had fallen way lower than I'd meant it to, showing nearly all of my boobs as I bent forward and shimmied with the boa. Beneath the photo, *Anonymous Harrison Student* commented: **and she's a slut, too!** which wasn't even fair, because the only three people I'd made out with since the start of high school were Woody, Xander, and Leo.

Chills raced through me. I looked practically naked, and my father was going to end me if he saw it. I suddenly felt the thousands of eyes on me again, like I'd felt the first day I got here, but this time it didn't feel good. The reality of all of those viewers seeing me like this made me want to throw up. My stomach twisted as I watched myself lean forward and blow the camera a kiss with my boobs practically falling out of my top. My legs felt like jelly and my head went funny, and I stumbled backward to sit on the chair. Francisco was talking to Mura's handler, and Amy was busy getting her dress fixed by Marsha. I opened my mouth to call for one of them but nothing came out. The room whirled around me as I tried to calm down. I tried to tell myself that this post was just like all the others I'd read, and I'd survived those. But this felt different. It felt like every icky, vulnerable sensation I'd ever felt when someone stared at me. It felt like *it*: the final straw that could break me.

I flashed back to the night I spent with Audrey a week ago on Notre Dame's campus. I remembered the fresh air in my lungs and the stars above our heads, and how I'd felt like I could be someone new there. And now everything circulating the internet declared me exactly what I didn't want to be. I tried to breathe as Cindy took her phone back, but I felt ruined. "Blake," Cindy said, quiet enough that Sabrina couldn't hear her. "It's just a stupid video."

But it wasn't. It was my reputation. It was everything I was trying to overcome pulling me *down down down* again.

"Sixty seconds, ladies," Marsha said. She pricked Amy's shoulder with a pin as she sewed and Amy flinched. Amy looked over at me and furrowed her brows. "You okay?" she mouthed.

I stood on shaky legs. *Get through tonight and then you can get home.*

But *home* was supposed to be South Bend. And my new home was supposed to be Notre Dame, and now I worried it would be just like Harrison: kids would hate me. Panic filled my lungs. I thought I'd turned my phone off, but then it buzzed, and I was so out of it that I answered without checking the caller ID.

"I know about your email to Public," my dad said on the other end of the line.

My entire body recoiled. "Dad, I really can't talk. I—"

"And I saw that video of you."

My heart stopped. I waited for him to yell at me, but he didn't.

"I'm going to do everything I can to get it taken down,

Blake," he said. He almost sounded like he was on my side, like he was going to right a wrong that had been done to me. "You're going to win this contest," he said, his voice steady, "because it's the only way to redeem yourself and our reputation." I heard him inhale. He sounded exhausted. "I'm sure you can see that now."

I froze. To hear it said like that by my own father felt like a knife in my gut. He hung up, and I started shaking.

Francisco sauntered across the room and leaned in close. "Gorgeous, you okay? You need water or anything?"

"I—I'm okay," I said. And then I did what I always did when I got hurt: I tried to steel myself. But it wasn't working. Too much had happened to me over the past few weeks. I'd fallen for Leo, I'd been given the biggest chance of my life—even if it was fixed—and then I'd lost Leo and fallen from grace. My reputation was in tatters. The country hated me, which meant the kids at Notre Dame would probably hate me, too. Everything I dreamed this contest could be for me had blown up in my face.

My heart beat wildly as I thought about what my father said: *It's the only way to redeem yourself.*

Was he right?

No matter how warped his logic sounded, a part of me realized that what he was saying was mostly true. If I won this contest, if I secured the modeling contract and became the United Nations Citizen Ambassador, I'd be practically famous, and then people would tolerate my past bad behavior. I'd heard countless stories about how cruel and diva-ish starlets could be, and people still worshipped them. Wouldn't it be like that for me, too?

Marsha lined us up. Francisco fixed a bobby pin holding my chignon in place. Marsha started ordering us down the hall, but I couldn't pay attention to anything she said as I fell in line behind Sabrina. My winning the contest was already preordained by Public and my father, and they were way more powerful than me. What if going along with their plan was the only way to save myself?

We reached the velvet curtains blocking the stage. Amy reached out and squeezed my hand. *You should be winning this*, I thought as I looked into her sweet, heart-shaped face. *I just don't know how to prove it. And now I'm really scared that I shouldn't.*

Pia's disembodied voice announced us, and then the curtain flung open and the six of us paraded onto the stage. My arm shot up into the Miss America wave that was becoming disconcertingly natural. I took my position at the end of the stage behind Sabrina. Celebratory jazz music played behind us and multiple spotlights flew over our bodies. This was it. The night for which we'd all been waiting. Out of the corner of my eye I saw that Sabrina was crying. Not sobbing or anything, just tears that trickled over her face as she waved to the audience. I wondered if she always used her hard shell to cover up everything she really felt and wanted. It was what I'd always done, and it was way easier than actually admitting that you weren't perfect, or that you felt things just like everyone else. It was exactly what I wanted to do right now. I wanted to close myself to everything real. I wanted to take the easy way out.

I wanted to win.

"And now let's welcome our judges!" Pia shouted. "Danny! Bradley! Leo! Carolina! Shilpa!"

Leo waved along with the rest of the judges, his free hand holding a jumbo-size Pepsi. He didn't look at me, and I hated myself for wanting him to. I hated myself for wanting to fix the pain he'd caused me by stealing glory that wasn't mine. I hated myself for wanting to ease the ache of all my past mistakes by hurting Amy. Wasn't that what I'd always done? Kept other people down so that I could be on top?

Leo stared straight ahead at the camera. He wore a dark gray suit that made his eyes look like smoky quartz. His blond hair was neatly combed back and he'd shaved. I wanted to put my hand against his smooth cheek. I wanted to tell him how sorry I was for what I'd said. I wanted him to know I was ashamed of the thoughts swirling through my mind, for not being able to be the good person he once saw in me.

Leo never looked at me, and I finally made myself stop staring at him. I glanced around the packed theater. Thousands of bodies jumped up and down, cheering, filming with their phones, and screaming out the names of the judges and contestants they loved. There were a few calls of *Blake!*, but mostly *Amy! Bradley! Danny!*

I wondered if Nina Carlyle was happy. She'd finally gotten to say her piece about me, and in a more public and damaging way than either of us probably ever could've imagined. Not that I blamed her. I deserved every word.

A few strains of the *Pretty App Live* theme song played,

and then a video montage came to life on the screen. Most clips showed our morning at the car wash and other drama that had happened at the house, like when Cindy threw a fork at Mura's bad arm at lunch and yelled, "Catch!" When Mura caught it, Cindy said, "Your wrist isn't broken, you faker."

"Ladies and Gentlemen," Pia said, looking like an Oscar winner in her fire-engine-red floor-length gown. She held a cream-colored envelope tied with a satin ribbon. "You've seen the contestants in action and you've cast your votes for the young woman you'd like to win this contest and become a Citizen Ambassador for our great nation." She whirled around to face us contestants. "Ladies, you've given this contest your very best. But only one of you can be voted Prettiest," Pia said as she untied the envelope's ribbon. She tore the envelope and stared at the thick paper inside. "I'm so very sad to see the first two contestants go." She shrugged and perked up. "But America has the final say," she said, the way you'd say *Oh well!* if you didn't really give a crap. She looked up and her eyes scanned all six of us. Finally her gaze settled on Mura and Cindy, who stood together at the end of the line. "It's time to say buh-bye to Murasaki O'Neil and Cindy Adams!"

Whoa. The audience let out a gasp, and I turned to see Cindy staring blank-faced at Pia. Mura had gone bright red. If Mura had had another microphone, she definitely would've thrown it. Her eyebrows furrowed and her fists clenched like a child's. I watched her count backward from ten, visibly trying not to lose it.

"Let's watch Mura and Cindy's journeys here on *The Pretty App Live!*" Pia said cheerfully, and then the overhead TV screen showed video of both contestants and their defining moments, which seemed slightly ridiculous seeing that we'd only been on this "journey" for three days.

Bodyguards escorted a crying Cindy and an enraged Mura from the stage. Charisse, Sabrina, Amy, and I stared at one another. My heart thumped against my chest. Mere minutes more and I'd know the final results. Being voted off was what I'd said I wanted—to Public, to Audrey, and to myself. So why did it suddenly sound so scary?

"Sabrina and Charisse, please stand on my right side," Pia said, her tiny nose crinkling as she smiled. Sabrina and Charisse did as Pia told them, looking petrified. "Blake, Amy, please stand on my left."

Amy reached for my hand as we took our places. "Good luck," she said, smelling sweet and citrusy. I squeezed her palm in response. I was too nervous to say anything, too guilty to look her in the eye.

The lights dimmed. A single spotlight landed on Pia and she smiled like the attention was finally where it belonged. "I'd like to introduce your top two finalists on *The Pretty App Live!*" she said. "Please give a warm round of applause for Amy Samuels and Blake Dawkins!"

The audience screamed, and my legs went wobbly. It was happening.

"*Amy! Amy! Blake! Amy!*"

"Good-bye, Sabrina and Charisse!" Pia said over the screaming.

I watched Sabrina. Her arms went rigid at her sides, and her bottom lip quivered for just a moment and then stopped. A small half-smile froze on her face. Her chin went up, her shoulders pushed back. I recognized everything she was doing as though I were watching myself in a mirror, and it made me feel sick. I couldn't go back to being that person, could I? Could I really close myself off like that after everything that had happened?

"Now, for the results you've all been waiting for!" Pia shouted as the screaming got louder. I could barely hear myself think over the noise. Sabrina and Charisse paraded off the stage, leaving Amy and me alone beneath the spotlight. I turned to look at Amy and saw tears slide over her cheeks. If they named me the winner, Amy would get nothing. There weren't prizes for the runner-up. No ambassadorship, no modeling contract, no new home, no TV appearances.

Pia lifted the white microphone closer to her mouth and said, "To announce the winner of *The Pretty App Live*, I'd like to introduce Public CEO Alec Pierce!"

The crowd applauded as Alec Pierce emerged from the stage-right curtains carrying a beautiful, sparkling gold crown with tiny, multicolored stones embedded around the edges. I hadn't seen Alec since I was younger, but I would've recognized him anywhere: My father's friend . . . The man in charge of Public . . . The one who'd sent Leo to trick me . . . The one responsible for threatening to expose my sister . . . The one who conspired with my father to get me here in the first place.

Rage filled me as I watched Alec stride across the stage. His dark hair was shaved close to his head, and a thick beard covered the bottom half of his face like charcoal. He was inches over six feet and carried himself like he was the president of Public, the United States, and possibly the Universe.

He took the microphone from Pia and said, "Good evening, America. On behalf of Public Corporation and SBC Network, I'm honored to announce the winner of the first annual *The Pretty App Live* competition."

I'd never seen eyes as dark as Alec's, and when he stared at Amy and me I shivered. I wanted to hurl accusations at him, to tell the world what he'd done to me, to Leo, to Amy, to everyone else in the contest who didn't know how rigged the entire thing was. I wanted to do something—*anything*—that would wipe the smirk from his face. But instead I just stood there frozen like an ice queen ready to accept my fate.

"Amy Samuels and Blake Dawkins exemplify everything the youth of our fine country have to offer," Alec said. "Beauty, poise, charm. That's exactly what we created the Pretty App to discover."

What happened to kindness, wisdom, and grace? Amy had those, at least.

"But only one can accept the title of Prettiest, a title that bestows upon her one year of ambassadorship on behalf of this nation's youth." Alec's black eyes narrowed on me for just an instant before he said, "This title can change her life for the better, if she chooses to accept it."

My heart beat faster. Desire sparked within me as he said the words. I wanted so badly to travel the world as an ambassador and do something different with my life, to have people see me as someone special—someone good. It was all so close . . . right within my reach . . .

Alec motioned to someone offstage, and a skinny Trog-looking guy with black-framed glasses emerged. He wheeled a large white computer with the orange Public logo across the stage to Alec. The screen lowered again, but this time there was no video montage or contestant testimonials. Two vertical bars shot up, one captioned *BLAKE*, the other *AMY*. Numbers scrolled, skyrocketing into the thousands above each bar.

Alec grinned like his digital chart was a masterpiece. "Surprise, Amy and Blake! The voting continues!" He turned to the audience. "The race between our top two contestants has been neck and neck, and Public technology enables us to see the final sixty seconds of votes pouring in."

Amy looked like she was about to throw up, and I suddenly didn't feel so good, either. I squinted at the two bars on the screen. They jumped up and down, with each bar taking its turn at the highest spot. The audience murmured, and I could feel them eating out of Alec's hand, like this little surprise was the most exciting thing to ever hit reality TV. I stared at the screen, and I couldn't help it—I felt myself join in the anticipation, especially when my numbers started steadily climbing past Amy's. I could feel it happening . . .

I was going to win.

Everything I thought I'd feel in that moment—the thrill, fear, excitement, pride, confusion, exhilaration— multiplied until I could barely stay standing. A part of me wanted it so badly. I wanted to be Prettiest. I wanted to hold on to everything that being at the top had always meant to me. I wanted to fill the part of me that felt empty, the part that needed to feel special and loved and beautiful.

The theater erupted with sounds from cheers to boos to screams to laughter. Blood whirled in my ears. Alec Pierce was smiling and the judges were standing—all except Leo. He was staring down at his phone, typing furiously. What was going on?

The vertical *AMY* and *BLAKE* bars raced higher up the screen. The space between them lengthened as mine grew stronger, and no matter how conflicted I felt, the sparkling gold crown in Alec's hands was like a magnet, pulling me closer and closer until I could barely stand still. It all suddenly felt like instinct, like the moment was made for me.

Alec was grinning at me like a piranha now, acting impressed and surprised even though he'd rigged the entire thing. I looked into the audience and saw Leo make a phone call. He was saying something that looked like: *Do it now.*

"Twenty seconds to go!" Pia cried out.

My bar stopped moving.

I stared at the screen, and then at Alec. The look on his face told me he had no idea what was happening.

"Ten, nine, eight!" Pia cheered, motioning for the audience to join her.

Alec recovered and started smiling again. He started typing on the keyboard and my bar crawled higher again. It crept toward Amy's and a sick feeling came over me: Alec was cheating on live television in front of the entire country, smiling fakely while he tricked millions of people. It struck me right then that the term *mean girl* didn't only apply to high school girls. *Mean* was a way of being and thinking and existing in the world. It was taking instead of giving. It was bringing others down instead of up.

Could I really be a part of that?

"Seven, six, five . . ." the audience chanted.

I turned to Amy, hoping the sight of her would steady me, save me from the anxiety of this moment. I thought back to what she'd said in our bedroom: *How can everything this girl says about you be true when you're the only person here who's shown me kindness? Maybe that girl was writing about an old version of you, but the past is past.*

And this was now.

I had to believe in *now*. If I was going to change, I had to have faith in the new me. And the new me started today.

I turned to Leo. I didn't care that the cameras were on me. I didn't care what they would see me say. I imagined America watching me, counting on me. I imagined Amy's family at home, watching this all unfold. When Leo's eyes caught mine, I said, "Stop him."

Leo's gaze dropped to his phone and confirmed exactly what I suspected: He was already trying to.

The bar with *BLAKE* emblazoned on it stopped again.

"Three, two . . ."

Amy's shot higher. Alec Pierce was typing wildly now, his thick fingers flying across the keys.

"One . . ."

But Leo was better—the best, maybe. Just like Audrey had told me that night in the Grotto.

"Zero!" Pia screamed.

My bar stayed frozen as Amy's moved higher. I bit my bottom lip as the audience climbed to their feet, most of them on their phones, presumably voting as they called out our names.

"Zero!" Pia screamed as Amy's bar shot up off the screen.

"Amy Samuels, congratulations!" Pia shouted over the fray. "You're the winner of *The Pretty App Live!*"

My heart felt like it might burst. I felt everything rush through me all at once—everything I'd lost, everything I'd given up, everything that had happened to me over the past few weeks. I could barely breathe as I turned to Amy. My entire body shook with everything the moment meant.

Amy's face went into her hands. Trumpets blared and confetti swam through the sky, landing on Amy's shoulders and bare arms as the crowd went wild. Screams and cheers came from every corner until I was sure the theater would burst at its seams. They loved her.

Amy stood still in her floor-length magenta gown. She lifted her head slowly from her hands. She looked so beautiful standing there—truly beautiful, inside and out. Tears fell over her cheeks, and when she smiled at me, I realized I was crying, too. Amy turned to face the audience and wave, free and wild, like I'd never seen anyone wave before. The cameras swarmed us, and the judges moved up the side stairs of the stage to congratulate her.

I turned to see Alec Pierce, and when his eyes met mine, I didn't blink.

"Are you okay, Blake?" I heard a woman's voice say.

I turned to see the camerawoman. She filmed me head-on as I faced the millions of people who could see me—the *real* me—through their television screens. "I'm so happy for Amy," I said into the camera, my voice shaking with emotion. "She deserves this title." I took another breath, feeling myself come alive as I gave myself to them completely. "And I'm really proud of who I was in this contest." My body relaxed, my lungs filled, and I realized in that split second how much more I had to give than my prettiness. I had vulnerability and openness. I had authenticity. I had the truth.

I shrugged a little, feeling sheepish, but strong, too. I caught Leo's glance, and his gray eyes were bright.

"This is the new me," I said, smiling.

chapter thirty-nine

It was Audrey who'd done it.

At five the next morning, we were in the bathroom of the JetBlue waiting area in LAX. Our flight wasn't scheduled for a few more hours, but we'd been at the airport all night because neither one of us wanted to be on Public property in case they figured out what she and Leo had done.

Leo had come to find me early the previous morning at Audrey's guesthouse, and when I wasn't there, Audrey took a chance and confessed everything we'd tried to do to stop Public. Then they went to work like some kind of Trog double-team on what Audrey had called an SQL injection attack.

"I feel bad that I didn't warn you," Audrey said as she passed me a bar of lemon-scented soap. "But I was too paranoid that Public could monitor our phones."

I gave her a small smile. "You have nothing to be sorry for," I said. I looked down at my hands holding the soap. "You saved me. And not for the first time."

I glanced up and saw Audrey grinning. But then her face turned serious. "Are you sure you want to do this?" she asked.

"I'm sure," I said, turning on the faucet.

A cleaning woman made clanking noises in one of the bathroom stalls as she replaced the toilet paper. She sprayed Lysol and made the air smell like chemical flowers.

I brought the soap over my cheeks and forehead, down the strip of my nose, across my chin. I watched my makeup smear and slowly disappear. I passed the soap back to Audrey and cupped my hands beneath the faucet. The cold water pooled in my palms and I splashed it onto my face over and over again until my skin was naked.

Clean. Fresh. New.

I looked in the mirror and stared at the girl gazing back. It was me, but I saw more to me than I usually did when I looked in the mirror to examine my skin, or my hair, or my makeup. I saw strength. I hadn't seen it before, but now I was convinced it had been there all along, just waiting for me to notice.

"You ready?" Audrey asked.

I passed her my phone. "I'm ready."

Audrey snapped a bunch of pictures, most of me staring into the mirror at my makeup-free face. "I think I have the one," Audrey said, showing me a shot. I was wearing her gray hoodie with the black wings on the back, and my

335

hair fell long and loose over my shoulders. My dark eyes weren't as dramatic looking without the eyeliner and mascara I usually wore, but they were peaceful.

"That's the one," I said. "Do it."

Audrey downloaded the Get Real Beauty app onto my phone and created my account. She showed me the screen with my photo and my handle: *@ExBeautyQueen*. I smiled, but Audrey looked kind of stoic. "How does it feel?" she asked.

"New," I said. "Everything feels new. And I feel a little nervous, too, and kind of naked and vulnerable, but in a different way. A good way."

Audrey grinned. "Awesome," she said. "Now let's get out of this disgusting bathroom."

We pushed through the door and Audrey linked her arm through mine. We crossed the shiny airport floor, settling on two chairs near a vending machine.

The loudspeaker crackled with a delay for a six-thirty a.m. flight to JFK, and a crowd of people grumbled, "God, no!" and "Why me?"

Audrey ran a crinkled dollar bill over the side of her Vans. "Want a Snickers?" she asked. I shook my head. "Suit yourself," she said. She hopped up and stuck the dollar and some quarters into the machine.

I tried to relax, but my nerves were still too frayed from last night. We hadn't slept, and I'd been waiting for my dad to call for hours.

Audrey came back with soda and candy as a flight attendant rolled her navy suitcase over the floor. Gold wings were pinned to her collar like an award. She considered us with our bags splayed everywhere and gave us a disapproving look, like we were vagabonds camping out at the airport. Audrey popped the top off her Mountain Dew and the soda fizzed beneath her fingertips. "It's never too early in the day for an MD," she said to both of us, and the woman hustled away. Audrey sat between me and a plant and took a sip. The smell of lemon-lime filled the air. "You okay?" she asked for the hundredth time.

"I'm okay," I said. "Just nervous about my dad."

Audrey pursed her lips. "That's something you can handle," she said. "I mean, think about it: You're *usually* nervous about your dad at any given moment."

"That's true," I said, not sure whether to think her logic was funny or profoundly sad. "Do you think I should call him?"

Audrey nodded. "I do," she said. "I think you should take the first step."

I leaned back against the window and pulled my knees to my chest. I thought about how Audrey would probably give anything to be able to call her dad just one more time. No matter what my father had done, Audrey was right: He was the only dad I had. And unlike Audrey's father, he was *here*, in my life, and there was time for us to make amends, or at least try.

The glass was warm on my back. "I promise I'm going to try with him," I said, and Audrey smiled.

I had so much further to go with my parents before we had anything resembling a healthy relationship. But look how far Nic and I had come, and look how good it made me feel. It was worth trying with my parents, too. That I knew.

Audrey's bony elbow jabbed my side. "Let's get back to the emails, shall we?"

I opened my inbox and Audrey and I scrolled through the emails from New York, LA, and Chicago film and TV agents, all of them asking to have a meeting with me to talk about *future television possibilities*. Audrey and I had searched their names, but we needed Nic. She was the one who would know which agents were the real deal. I couldn't wait to obsess over this with her. I felt the spark of possibility, like I could see all the good stuff in front of me. I took a breath as I reread the emails I'd already practically memorized. I'd have to hold on tight to the person I wanted to be. In a few years, when I went back to Hollywood, I'd hold on even tighter. I'd lost myself during my climb to become Harrison High's queen bee. I wouldn't lose myself on my climb to become the next Pia Alvarez. (A kinder, more genuine version, that is. With bigger boobs.) I smiled just thinking about it. It was going to happen: I could feel it deep in my bones.

"Oh boy," Audrey said. I thought she was talking about the email from the head of the hosting department at Abrams Artists in New York, but then I realized she was pointing down the long hallway past the kiosks and magazine stands. I followed her gaze and saw Leo coming our way with a backpack slung over his shoulders. His eyes were on me, and the way he was purposefully walking made me sure this wasn't a coincidence. He was here to talk, or maybe just say good-bye. Nerves shot through my body, followed by the heat I felt every time Leo was near. I watched him slow his steps as he got closer. He gave both Audrey and me a small wave, and then he set his bag down by ours. He extended his hands and we each took one. He pulled us to a stand, never taking his eyes off me.

"How did you know I was here?" I asked him.

Leo shrugged with one shoulder. "Public usually flies people on this airline," he said. "Plus they have good snacks and extra leg room." He smiled at me, and this time I didn't try to stop myself from melting.

Audrey cleared her throat. "I'm going to take a walk and get some coffee," she said. "Catch you later, Leo?"

"Yeah," he said. "Catch you later, Audrey."

They didn't hug or anything, but they did some kind of handshake that struck me as Trog-like. When they smiled at each other, it was like they got each other, like they understood what made the other one tick, and like maybe what Leo had done to help us had set things right between them.

Audrey took off down the hall, and Leo and I were left standing alone. His blond hair was a mess, but his gray eyes were bright. He was wearing the same dark green thermal shirt that he'd worn the night I met him at Joanna and Jolene's party. So much had happened since then, and there was so much I wanted to say, but I didn't know where to start.

Leo stepped closer, and then I did, too, until we were inches apart. I put my hands on his chest. I didn't want to hold back anymore. Whatever this was between us was unlike anything I'd ever felt before. No matter how short-lived it might be, and no matter how scared I was of getting hurt, I didn't want to waste any more time hiding how I felt.

"I'm sorry for accusing you of releasing that video about my sister," I said. "I know you'd never do that."

Leo shook his head. "I gave you every reason to distrust me. I'm sorry for that." When he dropped his hands to my waist, his touch was careful, like he wasn't sure if it was okay. "And I'm sorry that I didn't realize until last night how much more important it was to care about myself and someone else rather than some company I owed."

I smiled, and we were quiet for a minute. "There's a lot more to you I don't know," I finally said. "And a lot of things I wish I had the time to find out."

Leo pulled me closer until there was no space between us. I could feel his confidence in us grow as we talked. I wanted to stand on my tiptoes and kiss him, but there was more I needed to tell him. "No one's ever done anything like that for me before," I said, emotion filling my voice. "What you and Audrey did last night was . . ."

I couldn't finish my sentence. I didn't have the right words.

Leo shrugged. "It was no big deal," he said.

"It was everything to me," I said. I squeezed his shoulders and narrowed my eyes on him. "How much trouble are you in?"

A devilish grin spread across Leo's face, making me smile, too. "Not too much, actually," he said. "Public can't exactly sue me for using their own strategy against them. And I told them it was all me, to keep Audrey out of trouble. They made me sign a nondisclosure agreement in exchange for everything they have on me to be kept private. A fair trade, I guess. Plus, it gets me out of working for them anymore. Now I'm free."

"So what *did* you do to get yourself in so much trouble?" I asked.

Leo's cheeks flushed. "No more secrets between us," he said, nodding his head like it was important.

"No more secrets," I said.

Leo ran a hand through his hair. He looked conflicted. And then he blurted, "I hacked into a prime minister's cell phone."

My hands covered my mouth. "The prime minister of a *country*?" I asked through my fingers. *"Why?"*

"Because I could," Leo said, and I started laughing.

"It's not funny!" Leo protested.

But the way he'd said it was so funny, and it just seemed so ridiculous, and I hadn't laughed like that in so long that it felt too good to stop. Leo finally laughed, too, and then he leaned down and kissed my forehead. He glanced away from me for a moment before he said, "Maybe there's time for you to get to know me better, like you said, because there's this tech firm in Chicago that's been trying to recruit me for a while now. And this morning I told them I'd like to sign on and start working for them. I know you'll be busy finishing up Harrison, and then at Notre Dame you'll be meeting tons of new people and everything, but I still thought we could see each other on the weekends some-times. It's just two hours away," he said shyly. "I mean, only if you wanted to." He looked away again like he was worried I'd say no.

But I wasn't going to say no. I wasn't going to say any-thing at all. I leaned forward and kissed him—letting all the emotions I'd been trying to hold back flood through me.

"Blake," he said. And then he lifted me up off my feet and into his arms. I pressed my lips against his, feeling just how much he'd wished for this moment, too. When I finally pulled away, I teased, "Are you sure you don't only like me because I'm a beauty queen?"

"I like you in spite of the fact that you're a beauty queen," he said, smiling.

"*Ex*–beauty queen," I corrected him. "And an ex–queen bee, too."

"A queen bee in recovery," he said. "I think it makes me like you more."

"Funny," I said, leaning in for another kiss. "I like me more, too."

acknowledgments

A big thank-you to the best team in publishing: Alessandra Balzer, Brenda Bowen, and Dan Mandel. I am so very lucky to work with all three of you.

Alessandra, your kindness, hilarity, dedication to your work, and all-around smarts continue to amaze me and push me to write a better book. I count my blessings to be one of your authors.

Brenda, your gentle spirit and your ability to plot, support, and encourage all in one phone call make novel writing even more fun. This book (and my writing career) would not be what they are without you.

Dan, you go above and beyond any definition of a literary agent, guiding me every step of the way with sound advice, compassion, and friendship. Your belief in me as a writer makes me want to live up to everything you think I can do. Thank you.

The team at HarperCollins/Balzer + Bray is unbeatable. They are also loads of fun. Thank you to Donna Bray for supporting this series and for sitting next to me at the holiday party when I was too pregnant to stand in my nonsensible footwear choice. Thank you to Susan Katz and Kate Jackson for cheering me on with such warmth and positivity. Thank you to Sara Sargent, Kelsey Murphy, Diane Naughton, Sandee Roston, Caroline Sun, Emilie Polster, Patty Rosati, Molly Motch, Andrea Pappenheimer, Kerry Moynagh, Kathy Faber, Jessica Abel, Deborah Murphy, Fran Olson, Heather Doss, Jenny Sheridan, Susan

Yeager, Alison Klapthor, Jenna Lisanti, Maya Packard, and Kathryn Silsand.

Thank you to all the librarians and booksellers who have welcomed me into their aisles since I was old enough to realize libraries and bookstores were the best places in the world.

Thank you to all the bloggers who supported *The Boyfriend App* and rallied to get to the word out.

Thank you to all of my teachers, especially Linda Harrison from Shaker High School, and Siiri Scott, Mark Pilkinton, and Shannon Doyne from the University of Notre Dame. Thank you to the junior high and high school teachers who encouraged my writing, namely Mr. Bedell, Mrs. Orr, Mrs. Betro, Mrs. Kuthy, and Dr. Danaher.

Thank you to authors and friends who make this writing community an awesome place to be: Kieran Scott, Jen Calonita, Elizabeth Eulberg, Melissa Walker, Micol Ostow, Anna Carey, Alecia Whitaker, Kimberly Rae Miller, and Noelle Hancock.

Thank you to editors who have taught me so much: Jennifer Kasius at Perseus/Running Press and Lanie Davis and Sara Shandler at Alloy Entertainment.

Thank you to TV agents Tracy Weiss, Samantha Paladini, and Mark Turner. Thanks especially to Tracy for being the first reader on this book and setting me straight on reality television. Thank you to early readers Anna Carey, Wendy Levey, and Debra Devi for sound advice.

Thank you to Jason Scalia for answering all of my computer programming questions. I'd be lost without you.

Thank you to friends Erika Grevelding, Claire Noble, Caroline Moore, Jamie Greenberg, Maria Manger, Kate Brochu, Jen Singer, Yana Yelina, Megan Mazza, Jessica Bailey, Tricia DeFosse, Kim Hoggatt, Erin Murphy, J.J. Area, Justin Rancourt, Brinn Hamilton, Molly Cesarz, Jen O'Toole, Liz Auerbach, Stacy Craft, Carol Look, Maureen Sullivan, Cara Compani, Allison Yarrow, Corey Binns, Stacia Canon, Jenna Yankun, Dani Super, Poppy King, Nancy Conescu, Christa Bourg, Kate Gregory, and Tory Donohue.

Thank you to Katelyn Butch for all kinds of things— but especially for friendship and lots of patient, loving, positive energy. I will never be able to thank you enough for everything you did for me this year.

Thank you most of all to my family. To my sisters-in-law Christine Hawes and Ali Sise for being incredible friends and loyal cheerleaders. To the Great Roby Bhattacharrya for his kindness, and for going way beyond the duties of a brother-in-law. To Tait, Walker, and Josey Hawes for being all-around awesome guys. To my parents-in-law Ray and Carole Sweeney, for being the most open-minded and supportive people. Thank you to Bob and Linda Harrison and all of my extended family. Thank you to my aunt Posie and my aunt Joan for setting up book events and spreading the word about their first niece. Thank you to my uncle Bill for reading my books and being such a wonderful god-father—twice! Thank you to my brother, Jack, for being my pal and understanding me. Thank you to my sister and my best friend, Meghan, who means more to me than any words at the back of a book could ever describe, or even a twenty-minute maid-of-honor speech.

Thank you to my parents. To my mom for loving and supporting me in every way imaginable. To my dad for reading every first draft I write and helping me to make each book better. Your involvement in my life continues to strengthen me as much (if not more) than when I was a teenager and living under your roof.

Thank you, thank you, thank you to my sons, Luke and William, and to my husband, Brian, for loving me. You three are my heart.

Don't miss this Cinderella story with a tech twist

Katie Sise

The

BOYFRIEND

App

Get the app. Get the guy.